MW01600361

Bear Runners

David G. Ferguson

Published by
North Channel Novels

Copyright © 2017 by David G. Ferguson

Published in Canada by North Channel Novels
705-849-8238
Toxicwaters001@gmail.com

ISBN: 978-0-9939522-1-0

All rights reserved. No part of this publication may be reproduced or transmitted in any form or by any means, electronic or mechanical, including photocopying, recording or any information storage and retrieval system, without written permission from the publisher.

This book is entirely a work of fiction. Names, characters and incidents are either the product of the author's imagination or are used fictitiously. Any resemblance to actual events or persons, living or dead is entirely coincidental. While most of the places named in this story do exist, the Moosonee winter road is a product of the author's imagination. The idea for the fictional road was borrowed from the enterprising efforts of the Moose Cree First Nation, whose Wetum Winter Road takes a parallel route from Otter Rapids to Moose Factory, Ontario. This story uses a mixture of metric and imperial units of measure — that's just the way it is here in Canada.

Cover by the author.

To Carolyn and Jennifer:

Two little girls who chose environmentally centred careers, both in traditionally male dominated fields. Two apples that fell close to the tree.

Early Reviews for BEAR RUNNERS

"What a story! … The tension throughout the story between Rob & Sam & between Morgan & the good people, kept me going back for more.
"An entertaining story worth my time, with characters I'd like to spend more time with in their next adventure."

Carol Piper Curtiss, a Great Lakes Sailor and retired Psychotherapist.

"Exciting read following the young game warden who is put to the test as he pursues an evil poacher, against the backdrop of the harsh winter in northern Ontario.
"I loved how the action was complemented with a tender, heartwarming love story with a feisty, strong-willed bush pilot who proves to become an equal heroine. Wonderfully written with sincerity and authentic details, which made for a rich and captivating story."

J.E. Schwartz, P.Eng (Environmental) San Diego, California

Acknowledgements

Thanks to Gary Thomson, retired Ontario Ministry of Natural Resources pilot who took me under his wing so very many years ago and occasionally allowed me to take control of the de Havilland Otters he flew. And more recently, for his refresher on Otter and Turbo Beaver operations; Todd Fleet, John Lalonde and George Mersereau at the Canadian Bush Plane Heritage Centre in Sault Ste. Marie, Ontario for updates on aircraft survival kits, radial engines and a nostalgic sit-down in the cockpit of their Otter, C-FODU; Rick Riopelle of the Ontario Provincial Police, for his refresher on aspects of law-enforcement policy regarding proceeds of crime and critical incident counselling; Alli Pfaff and Carolyn Perry for consulting on accepted modern descriptors and terms of endearment used for women — a touchy topic if a male author gets it wrong; Kirk Howard and Marc Blanchette at Algoma Chrysler in Spragge, Ontario for some air bag technology; Peter Noone, the musician, for permission to use a line from the song "I'm Into Something Good" by Herman's Hermits; Gord Ross, Conservation Officer (Ret'd), for his brief on winter road travel; Leslie Anthony, biologist and author, for allowing me to quote bits of his article, Biodiversity Apocalypse, (published in Canadian Geographic, September/October 2017); Norm Brown for his helpful critique.

And to Marnie Ferguson, Principal at Note Editorial and Publishing Services, for her evaluation, editing and helpful encouragement, as she steered me from raw manuscript to finished story.

News item, April 2011:

Demand for polar bear hides soars: auction house

One of Canada's largest fur auction houses says it cannot meet the soaring demand for polar bear hides....

"Supply does not even come close to meeting the demand," the auction house's chief executive officer, told CBC News.

"There's a lot of interest for really top-quality specimens for the Russian market"

CBC News Posted: Apr 11, 2011 10:04 AM CT

Excerpts from:
http://www.cbc.ca/news/canada/north/demand-for-polar-bear-hides-soars-auction-house-1.1110213

Biodiversity Apocalypse

An estimated annual $175-billion business (and growing), the illegal trade in wildlife is the world's fourth-largest criminal enterprise. It stands to radically alter the animal kingdom.

From article by Leslie Anthony, biologist and author, published in Canadian Geographic, September/October 2017

CHAPTER 1

Saturday, January 21 — Cape Henrietta Maria

The man who called himself Eagle Feather bent down and used the crusted snow at his feet to wipe the blood off his knife. The vapour of his breath was torn away by the bitter wind. He had just finished skinning the fifth polar bear he'd taken in the past ten days. Although the local Cree people had once told him that most of the big males would be hunting seals on the ice farther offshore by January, he had found the hunting along the northern edge of Polar Bear Provincial Park to be most rewarding.

The bears were still hunting along the shore because the seals they preyed on had not yet moved offshore onto Hudson Bay. And that was because climate change was affecting the normal distribution of species in the food chain from the tiniest plankton up to the fish species sought by the seals. In addition, the ice cover along the coast was still poorly formed with plenty of open leads allowing the bears and the seals easy access to their respective prey.

Eagle Feather was pleased with his harvest. As with his first hunt of the winter, this trip had been a simple matter of following the coast and finding where the seals were hanging out. If the bears weren't already there, they usually came along within hours. It was almost too easy.

At the same time, he felt he was being cheated by the men who were buying his products. Unlike the hunters and trappers of three hundred years ago or even as recently as thirty years back, Eagle Feather did not live in isolation without news from the outside world.

At his cabin, just a day-and-a-half snowmobile ride from this remote corner of Ontario's Arctic coast, he had a satellite connection to the Internet and there he could track the fur auction sales online. Top grade specimens of the big white bears were selling for anywhere between ten and twenty thousand dollars apiece. It had become all the rage in Russia and Asia for the rich to decorate their homes and offices with Arctic wildlife furs and taxidermy mounts.

All the combined bear quotas in the Arctic nations that still allowed a hunt couldn't begin to keep up with the demand. The black market, already flourishing, got a further boost when the American government declared the bears endangered and shut down the legal importation of polar bear parts into the United States. Prohibitions had a long history of boosting underworld enterprise.

After repeated complaints to his buyers, they had grudgingly agreed to increase his share by thirty percent, but he was still convinced he was getting shortchanged. He figured that if they'd been willing to bump his share by that much, there must be an even greater payoff that should be coming to him. With that in mind, he'd already decided it was time to make some changes. This winter he had come up with a scheme to bypass the middlemen.

Eagle Feather kept his real name a secret because of his checkered past and the interest its revelation would generate amongst a number of North American law enforcement agencies. In fact it was the intense interest of the police that had caused him to leave his previous occupation — stealing and exporting high-end cars and SUVs to offshore clients.

With the law finally closing in on him, he had needed to disappear. He had used the proceeds from his final auto shipments to relocate and assume this new identity.

With his dirty-blond hair dyed black, the half of his genetic line with north Asian ancestry gave the man a facial resemblance and skin tone close enough to some North American Indigenous people to pass off as one of them — or so he felt. He wasn't worried about the blue eyes inherited from his Scandinavian ancestors. He knew there were plenty of genetic anomalies amongst the aboriginal populations after five hundred years of close association with European settlers.

He had drawn his assumed name from his childhood. As a boy he had created an imaginary friend he named Eagle Feather. Of course, as is the fate of so many imaginary friends, he blamed the little Indian boy for any and all mischief he was accused of. Since the young version of Eagle Feather never got caught, it seemed fitting that he should assume the name and identity of his make-believe childhood friend.

He also had a strange affinity for the story of the Englishman, Archie Belaney, who in the early 1900s passed himself off as an Indian trapper and conservationist by the name of Grey Owl. Eagle Feather had hoped the James Bay Cree might somehow transpose that benevolent imposter's values onto his own reincarnation.

The allure of big money in the trade of polar bear and other Arctic wildlife furs led him to choose the seclusion of the northeastern corner of Ontario where he would start his new life. He set up camp on Sutton Lake in a remote and sparsely populated area, but by chartered bush plane within easy reach of Moosonee and Timmins. And there were trees there unlike the barren Arctic coastlines of Canada's three northern territories. He knew he could easily survive in a wilderness with trees.

Thirty-five kilometres long and less than a kilometre wide, Sutton Lake was a pristine body of water located in the only high country of the Hudson and James Bay Lowlands. It stretched from north to south, draining at its north end through the spectacular Sutton Gorge into Hawley Lake, another narrow lake, twenty kilometres long. Both lakes were known for their fly-in summer trout fishing, but there was little human activity there during the long winter months. It was just such isolation that Eagle Feather sought for conducting his nefarious new trade.

Having grown up in the interior of British Columbia, Eagle Feather had used his expertise in bush craft to fashion himself a log cabin near the north end of the lake. He had accomplished this feat within weeks of his unannounced arrival by float plane. A brief but intense career in a military Special Forces unit had further honed his wilderness survival skills to a level that he considered to be even greater than the original inhabitants of the land.

Now, standing over the stripped carcass of his latest kill, the six-foot-two poacher rolled up the heavy ten-foot bear hide and loaded it onto the sleigh hitched to his snowmobile. He did it with the ease of a man used to heavy work.

His snowmobile was the latest Yamaha long-track trapper's model. He had bought it because of its ability to tow a heavily loaded sleigh at good speeds for long distances over deep snow in this vast area.

Eagle Feather had killed this bear on the sea ice just yards offshore from Cape Henrietta Maria, the northeastern-most tip of Ontario where James Bay meets Hudson Bay. The water and islands beyond the coast lie in the Canadian territory of Nunavut. There in the summertime, walrus bask on the gravel beaches sunning themselves between dives for food. Inland is tundra — the treeline lies another thirty kilometres to the south. All that is visible in that direction is a vast wetland, devoid of trees any taller than the low alder and willow bushes that grow along the banks of numerous nearby streams.

During the winter, the same landscape becomes a snow-covered territory extending as far as the eye can see. The land appears featureless to all but those who are accustomed to navigating such terrain; Eagle Feather, however, managed just fine using a handheld GPS unit. He also carried a spare — just in case.

At the moment, that technology wasn't necessary. With his cheeks beginning to tingle — the stage just before frostbite sets in — his immediate destination was an old abandoned Hudson Bay Company building where he was staying. Just a cabin really, it was visible on a low beach ridge overlooking the barren landscape almost three kilometres south of the dead bear.

After supper that evening, he finished cleaning up the bear hide he had field skinned at the kill site. A propane radiant heater, part of the gear he carried with him on these cold winter expeditions, kept him warm while working in the rudimentary shelter of the old Bay building. The heavy odour of the bear fat he scraped from the big hide smelled of money to Eagle Feather.

Although he was an experienced hunter from his

youth, his first efforts at skinning bears for the resale market had turned out to be abysmal failures. The buyers he'd promised to supply with his illegal bear skins were enraged by his pitiful attempts and they threw the two ruined, worthless hides into the bush. Climbing back into their ski plane they told him that they'd wasted more than enough time and money coming to see him and they wouldn't be back.

Pissed off, but not defeated, the poacher resolved to properly learn the trade. But the local Cree people would have nothing to do with him. While they hadn't yet run him out of their territory, they were not about to assist someone who planned on competing for their natural resources.

Determined to carry on, he headed south that winter. South to the rest of northern Ontario where he attended every trapping convention and skinning demonstration he could get to. Quick to learn the proper techniques, he tracked down the buyers who had previously rejected his products.

With a small bear cub skin he had prepared, Eagle Feather convinced them of the vastly improved quality of his work. They were impressed by the turnaround and promised to return to Sutton Lake the following winter to buy as many as he could provide.

CHAPTER 2

Monday, January 23 — Moosonee

Conservation Officer Robert McNabb was chuckling as he walked into the Ministry of Natural Resources district office. Litterbugs and the spoils of their selfish behaviour could be really disgusting. That was certainly not the source of his amusement. And while litterers came from all segments of society, they were all equals when it came to their absolute lack of class as far as the young game warden was concerned.

Still, dealing with the idiots provided some lighter moments, and today had given him its share of those. After hanging up his parka, he laid his ticket book and field notes on his desk.

McNabb was still trying to get a feel for working and living in a community endowed with an early twentieth century frontier atmosphere, a hundred years after the fact.

Many of the inhabitants seemed to exhibit a genuinely cavalier attitude toward life. Who would be the first to snowmobile across the newly frozen river ice in early December was a 'game' that just didn't fit with his upbringing. Sure, he'd dared fate in risky adventures during his own youth, but never anything that dangerous. He just wasn't sure that he was going to be able to fit in here.

Six feet tall and a wiry one hundred and seventy-five pounds, the rookie officer was busting to get out to do the job he'd been hired for. Short, sandy brown hair and a neatly trimmed moustache contributed to his clean-cut appearance. While he wasn't dashingly handsome, he bore a slight resemblance to the actor, Harrison Ford, in his younger days.

Southern Ontario born and raised, McNabb had held contract positions as a wildlife technician and intern CO over the past four years in a variety of districts across the province. Now aged twenty-six, he had recently moved to this, his first full-time posting back in November.

He had been told at his job interview that this district was unlike any other in the province. In other districts, COs could just hop into a truck and drive to an occurrence, whereas Moosonee officers needed to use aircraft to access most of the two hundred and fifteen thousand square kilometres of the Hudson and James Bay Lowlands under their protection.

Planes and helicopters cost many hundreds of dollars per hour to rent, whether from commercial carriers or the government's own air service. As a result, Moosonee enforcement budgets were frequently used up in very short order and the district coffers were almost always drained before the winter was out. That was the case again this year.

With no new operating funds available until the beginning of April, McNabb's first two months had dragged by pretty slowly, and when he wasn't out dealing with local enforcement problems in and around Moosonee, he occupied himself poring over maps and reading archived enforcement and wildlife management reports to get a feel for the vast district that made up his patrol area. It was going to be a long slow winter — April was still over two months away.

Making things even worse, budget constraints had also cancelled the competition for a second officer's position. McNabb was the only field CO in the district at the moment; he had no partner officer.

"What's got ya laughing Robbie?" his supervisor asked as he looked up from his computer. Their two desks were pushed together, facing each other in the centre of the office, a room that could easily fit four. Filing cabinets and loaded book shelves were arranged around the walls. Framed photographs of landscapes and wildlife of the region filled the few vacant spaces above them.

The rookie hated it when his family or friends called him Robbie, but somehow it worked when the boss did — it provided him with a measure of acceptance he felt he needed. McNabb normally preferred to be called Rob.

"Litterbugs, James. They're a bunch of ignorant jerks. All of them," McNabb started. "But still, some of their excuses make me laugh."

"Yeah? Like what?"

Bird, a stocky five-foot-ten-inch, fifty-year-old man was born and raised in Winisk, formerly a Cree community set along the river of the same name. It had been located just inland from the southern shore of Hudson Bay. Following the disastrous flood of 1986, the residents moved upstream and established a new village named Peawanuck. By then, James was already living down south; he had finished college and was starting a career in natural resources law enforcement.

After years as a front line CO, he had taken that one step up the ladder to become the MNR enforcement supervisor in Moosonee, pretty much on the doorstep of his home turf. Contrary to the belief held by some folks, his positions had not been handed to him. He was not a token Indigenous body put there just to make the government of the day look progressive.

But in the early years, he had had to prove himself to just about everyone he worked with — one conversion at a time. Once converted though, every one of his fellow officers knew he was the real deal. And as his good reputation spread, he became one of those individuals that everyone in the profession wanted to have as a partner at some point in their career.

"James, just like the littering complaints I got when I worked down south, this one led to a real jackpot of domestic trash and abandoned appliances — and no, there isn't any humour in that. As usual it was totally disgusting.

"And while the caller mentioned just one heap of garbage, I found two others within half a kilometre farther up river. Of course, the part I always hate is digging through the used Pampers and all the other crap to find some indentifying information. At least the juicy things are frozen solid at this time of year, not like it was when I worked down south during the heat wave last August.

"So armed with pay stubs, phone bills and bank statements found amidst the grunge, I came back into town and started knocking on doors. And you know, there must be a rampant garbage theft crime wave sweeping across the province, because the first guy told me someone stole his garbage. That was the single most common excuse I got down south too. I mean, do they really expect us to swallow that line?

"The second most common excuse I got was...."

"My buddy borrowed my truck and must have dumped the stuff out along the way," James offered. A big grin spread across his face as he leaned forward, resting his elbows on the desk.

"How did you know?"

"Ah, you have to remember, most of my field career was in districts down south too."

"Oh yeah, I was forgetting about that. Anyhow, that was the next guy's excuse, except today it was his snowmobile sleigh that got borrowed," Rob continued. "But I always chuckle when they can never seem to remember which good buddy they loaned it to.

"Each of those guys got charged today and they both have until noon tomorrow to get their stuff moved to the dump … or face a second ticket for the continuing offence. I'm sure not going to move it for the classless bums.

"The third guy surprised the hell out of me. He actually admitted to being frustrated that the dump was closed and just ran the stuff down over the bank behind his Ski-Doo and left it out on the ice. For being honest enough to be the first person *I've* ever had own up to littering, I gave him a warning. But he's got twenty-four hours to get the stuff picked up and delivered to the dump … or else."

"I like your style Robbie. Especially the way you dealt with the last one. A lot of guys would have charged him too, justifiably enough. But in a small, close-knit community like this, word will soon get around that the river isn't a garbage dump. And just as importantly, the word will also go out that you will give folks a fair deal if they're straight up with you. You'll be surprised how quickly that will pay dividends."

"I sure hope so. I won't be disappointed if I never have to sort through another bag of used diapers for evidence, frozen or not." He returned to entering his enforcement reports.

After lunch, with his morning's charges recorded and

court documents sent off, he was back at his desk filling time once again, reading more of the old reports. There seemed to be an endless supply of them. And at the moment he was having a hard time keeping his mind from wandering.

His thoughts kept drifting to somewhere else — anywhere else — just to relieve the monotony of being office-bound for so long. What was worse, it was 2:15 in the afternoon and it felt as if half an hour had gone by since 2:10. For McNabb, it was that part of the day when, if he wasn't physically active, his digesting lunch or some other physical phenomenon began to slow his metabolism and make the time drag by.

He perked up a moment later however, when his attention was drawn to a new email notification on the screen in front of him.

CHAPTER 3

"This doesn't look good," McNabb said, more to himself than to the boss, and then he followed with, "Hey, James, check this out. We've got an intel report from the Department of Natural Resources in Michigan, passed along by the big smoke. It'll be in your inbox."

He had no problem distracting his supervisor. An urgent message from head office would have that effect on anyone, and Bird was also a victim of the monotony. He was reluctantly labouring through the coming year's budget proposals. It was that time of the year again — ask for more funding and settle for less.

"What ya got Robbie?" the senior officer asked, as he switched screens to open his email.

"Check out the email from head office re: polar bear seizures."

James Bird clicked on the message and was already reading it before McNabb finished speaking. A deep frown distorted Bird's normally cheerful face,

"That's six illegal bear hides that have shown up in different parts of the States in the past year. I wonder how many of those bears are from our Ontario population."

"How about testing for DNA? I mean, according to

these old reports I've been reading, they used to do live capture surveys up here … tranquilized the bears from helicopters, then landed and took weights, measurements and tissue samples. Those samples must still be around somewhere. If they are, we could get comparisons done with the hides showing up down south."

"Alright, can you see if you can track down those old samples? When you find them, get in touch with Michigan DNR and see if between us and them we can find a lab to do the work."

"One of my college biology professors got recruited by Trent University a couple of years ago. I think they were working on setting up a global wildlife DNA data bank. He might be able to steer us in the right direction … maybe even do the testing."

"Good thinking Robbie. Find those samples, then make the call."

McNabb picked up the phone and spent the next half hour trying to track down the archived bear samples. After contacting a couple of senior biologists and leaving voicemail messages on half a dozen other unanswered phones, he decided to spend a few minutes online, researching polar bear marketing — in both the legal and the black markets.

The young CO knew the biology of the beasts from his college years, but he wanted to know who was buying polar bear pelts, especially from the black market. It was something he'd never really thought about before — didn't realize it was much of a problem until the Michigan report arrived.

Most websites he checked pointed to the nouveau riche in Russia and Asia but several sites still indicated a hunger for them in the US and Canada.

After a while, he found he was surfing in fruitless

circles, just going from one website link to another. It was too wide a field for one lone CO to narrow down without a whole lot more information.

Frustrated at not being able to learn more, he donned his winter gear and headed out of town on a ministry Ski-Doo to measure the snow that had accumulated in the bush. It was a mundane weekly duty he enjoyed, simply because it got him out of the office for almost an hour.

In the black spruce and tamarack forest just out of town, a series of ten posts was set up through a cross-section of the wooded area. Measuring the snow depth near each post provided an average depth that would give some senior biologist an idea of how the provincial cervid populations — deer, moose, elk and caribou — were struggling through the winter. With the amount of snow he was measuring, it was going to be a tough winter on those species living in the lowlands.

On his way back into town, McNabb snowmobiled down First Street. The wide main street ran from the railway station down to the riverfront. With several classic, false-front clapboard buildings facing the street, the nearly flat lowland terrain reminded him of a prairie community. He figured that was part of what gave the place its frontier feeling.

Moosonee had its share of modern structures as well. It was a growing transportation hub for supplies bound for communities farther up the James Bay and Hudson Bay coasts. The late twentieth century saw new schools, businesses, government offices and a community centre spring up to support the influx of people into the region. Food, fuel, building supplies and heavy equipment brought north by rail were all forwarded to the remote coastal communities by tug-powered barges in the summer, tractor trains on winter roads when the land was frozen, and by air, all year round.

Turning left through traffic, comprised as much of snowmobiles as cars, McNabb headed east on Ferguson Road passing his government rental house on the way back to the office.

His house was a comfortable thirteen-hundred-square-foot, doublewide bungalow. It was large for one person, but being a bachelor wasn't a lifelong ambition of his, and he'd seen a number of eligible women around town.

Most notable was Kathleen Burke, the sweet-faced, blond elementary school teacher living right across the street from him. Katie was an idealistic young woman from southern Ontario and this was her first year of teaching. Sudden immersion was teaching Katie about life in the north and she had admitted to Rob on one brief meeting at the post office that she wasn't sure if she would stay after June. He only had a few months left to win her attentions.

The problem was, he wasn't a guy always ready with a quick pickup line, and she hadn't really seemed to notice him, other than to politely return his greetings each time they met in passing. Well, if she didn't fall head over heels in love with him as the winter went on, he'd just have to broaden his search.

CHAPTER 4

Tuesday, January 24

A day after the intelligence report from Michigan DNR arrived in Moosonee, McNabb received a satellite phone call from Gabriel Whitegoose, a guide, resort owner and trapper from Hawley Lake, four hundred and fifty kilometres northwest of Moosonee. The caller was also a part-time warden at Polar Bear Provincial Park — a position he held by virtue of the fact that the park lay within his vast trapline area. He and Rob had not yet met. When he took the call, the rookie officer soon realized that the conversation was going way over his head.

"James, it's a fellow who calls himself Gabby," McNabb explained, cupping his hand over the handset as he transferred the call to his boss. "He says he's in the park and there's dead Wabusk — that's polar bears, isn't it — all along the coast at the mouths of some creeks and rivers up there."

"Hey Gabby, what's up?" Bird asked, taking over the call. And for the next ten minutes, James Bird and Gabby Whitegoose carried on their conversation in a mixture of Cree and English. Both men had gone through the infamous residential school system and like many of the James Bay

Cree they were fluent in both languages.

"You might want to hear this too Robbie. Have any questions, just ask. He's our go-to man up in those parts," Bird said, inviting him to pick up and listen in. "So where do the snowmobile tracks lead Gabby, or are they all blown in by now?"

"Right here at the Cape they seem to go everywhere and the most recent ones are no more than two days old," Whitegoose came back after the satellite-delayed pause. The cape he spoke of was Cape Henrietta Maria.

"But that's going to be a problem. Before I sort out which trail they took to leave here, every one of them could be buried under windblown snow. It's starting to pick up here this afternoon. The freshest tracks I've seen were at the skinned carcass I found this morning on the ice up here, and they led to the old Hudson Bay Company building. Whoever it is has been staying there, some of the time anyhow."

"Mr. Whitegoose, its Rob McNabb on the line again, did you say how many snowmobiles there might be?"

"Ah, young game warden; you want to learn the ways of the wild from the old Indian guide do you? When we meet I will teach you about tracking. Until then, my answer is: I don't know for sure. There was too much coming and going. But there is only one narrow cot in the Hudson Bay building, so I will guess that there was likely just one poacher here. Or two very friendly ones at most."

"So Gabby," Bird asked, smiling at the last comment, "is there any chance that this guy on Sutton Lake might be tied in with this?"

"Yes, unless someone is flying up to the park loaded with snow machines and sleighs and hunting and camping gear, I'd bet my winter's catch of marten that this business has *everything* to do with the Sutton Lake poacher. I haven't trusted him since he first set up camp there."

"Gabriel, is there any chance you could take a small sample of muscle tissue from at least one of the bears?" McNabb asked. "I'm having a hard time tracking down the samples they took during the bear surveys back in the 1980s and '90s but I was hoping we could do some DNA testing on the dead bears to compare with bear parts that are showing up in other places."

"I can do that for you. I will take samples from all five bears on my way back home and keep them safe until you have a chance to come and pick them up."

"Thanks Gabriel. That could be very helpful if we start finding where these bears have gone."

"The Sutton Lake poacher. I am certain you will find them there, young game warden. But be *very* careful. I think he could be a dangerous man."

"Thanks Gabriel."

"Alright Gabby, thanks for the call," Bird said, starting to wrap up the conversation. "And you be real careful out there too, eh? I'd rather you were headed back home now with something as serious as this going on up there. With the price of bearskins going through the roof, guys like that aren't going to be too happy to have an old Indian trapper snooping around the area. There's a lot of money riding on it for them."

"Don't worry about me. I'm headed home in the morning. My gas caches out here are getting low anyways. I'll call you when I get back."

"And call if anything comes up in the meantime too, okay?" Bird urged as he signed off.

"So, it appears that this Eagle Feather guy is poaching polar bears in a big way right in our backyard, Robbie," Bird said, as he relayed the rest of the conversation he'd had with Whitegoose. "One skinned carcass just south of the Cape on the James Bay coast, one on the ice at the tip of the Cape and three more along the Hudson Bay coast to the west. All males of course, 'cause the sows have denned up inland for the winter to drop their cubs. And Gabby also found skinned Arctic fox carcasses at the kill sites, probably caught out feeding off the bear parts … or catching the voles that are feeding off them. Some were trapped, others shot. Timid as they are, they'd be easy picking for a patient poacher.

"Despite all the activity in the States, I have a sinking feeling that a lot of this fur is going to the new millionaires and billionaires in Russia and China just like you were finding online yesterday. Maybe not so much the Russians, now with oil prices tanked, but then I guess those rich oil barons won't be hurting as much as the average Sergei on the street. It sure would be nice to know if the American seizures are connected with the offshore trade."

The two men sat silent for a few moments, trying to absorb the enormity of the problem.

"It would be tempting to fly up and search this Eagle Feather's camp and catch him red-handed," McNabb said, breaking the brief silence. "But that would only deal with one small part of the problem. There's bound to be other poachers who would fill the demand even if we put him out of business. It would be even better if we could follow his furs when he moves them out and grab whoever's organizing this business."

"That's the way I think we should be approaching it too," Bird said. He was encouraged that his rookie wasn't just looking to go after the low-hanging fruit, but had designs on cutting down the whole tree.

"With the district budget flat broke since you arrived,

we've had no wiggle room to do any northern patrols. Of course, you already know that's why I've had you sharpening pencils and reading old case files. But I think the covering message that came with the Michigan Intel report shows they're finally getting pretty worried down in the big city. So I hope that by the time I've finished telling them what we've learned today, they might just get worried enough to shake some dollars out of a secret contingency fund they probably don't want us to know about.

"If that happens, Robbie, you're going to get thrown into this business at the deep end. You'll be learning real quick how to plan and implement a major enforcement project, because I don't think it will be long before things start hopping up here." He picked up the phone and punched in the number for the enforcement director at head office.

CHAPTER 5

Sutton Lake

Eagle Feather made it back to his Sutton Lake camp late in the afternoon, a day after leaving Cape Henrietta Maria. The trip home had been a simple matter of heading southwest across the treeless tundra for twenty-five kilometres until he came to the Black Duck River. From there, he followed the faint traces of his old tracks upstream to the short portage over to the Brant River where he camped for the night. All of the rivers in the region, even in places where rapids run during the open water season, were frozen solid. Despite the abnormally slow freeze-up patterns farther north on Hudson Bay, it had been an old-fashioned winter in this area so far.

Of course, the trip had not been without its obstacles and setbacks. His difficulties had come in the form of three episodes of getting stuck in deep snow. While returning along his outbound trail, there were places that required alternating between travelling down in the stream beds, and running up on the top edges of the riverbanks. In a few of those locations the wind had created deep drifts that extended out over the actual stream, but looked like an extension of the natural bank.

Twice, while transiting such drifts, the snow had let go, sliding the five to ten feet down and out onto the ice surface in a mini-avalanche. In both instances, his machine had suddenly dropped into the deep gap where the snow used to be. The only escape involved half an hour of digging out the machine and sleigh and then packing a fresh trail with his snowshoes through the remnants of the drift, back to a firmer surface.

The third event happened during a brief squall while he was driving in total whiteout conditions. He disappeared, with his machine, straight into the base of an unseen deep drift, like a knife into soft butter.

He was totally on his own. Extrication involved hot sweaty work for more than an hour in bitterly cold temperatures. He had to alternate between working with his parka wide open and resting with it fully zipped up to avoid having his sweats turn into dangerous chills.

From the headwaters of the Brant and Lakitusaki Rivers, it was a fairly direct forty-kilometre run across a series of nondescript, unnamed pothole lakes, west to Sutton Lake. Finally, the big Yamaha cruised easily up the remaining twelve-kilometre home stretch, northward, back to his camp.

He was towing a big load. It included the five polar bear pelts, seventeen Arctic fox and four wolves. They were all good specimens, suitable for use as taxidermy mounts or for rugs and fur garments. He also had a small sack of willow ptarmigan he'd shot, frozen whole to fill some enthusiastic taxidermist's order.

Following a marathon fleshing and stretching session the last items from eight weeks' harvest of skinned furs were either stretched and drying, or already dried, stored and ready for pick-up. An email sent out after his return had brought the reply he was waiting for. The plane would arrive in four to six days, weather permitting. He was ready. No longer would the tail be wagging the dog. He'd be back in command, the way he had been in his auto smuggling days.

CHAPTER 6

Thursday, January 26 — Moosonee

James Bird was at a meeting at the Moose Cree First Nation band office in Moose Factory, across the river. His phone began warbling, so Rob McNabb reached across his desk and picked up.

"Enforcement, McNabb speaking."

"This here's Agent Tommy Sturgis of the U.S. Fish and Wildlife Service calling. Is Agent Bird there?" The accent a strong southern U.S. drawl — Mississippi or Alabama, Rob thought.

"I'm sorry sir but Officer Bird is out of the office and I'm the only conservation officer in the building right now. Can I take a message or have him call you back?"

"Well, I was hoping to parlay with him directly. Him and me did some goose hunting up Kapiskau Goose Camp a few years back. He showed me a real good time an' I was looking forward to chewing the fat with him again. But anyhow, you'll probably do. How long you been a game warden up there anyways?"

"Well, don't let me frighten you off sir, but it's my

first full-time position and I just started here in November. I did do four years of contract work around the province before then, if that helps."

"Well, don't sweat it young feller. Once upon a time, I only had two months on the job. And most all the other fellas my age did too, come to think it. You'll be surprised how quick you'll be looking across the desk 'n' thinking about how some young feller, or even a gal, looks too young to be setting there.

"Anyways, this ain't just a social call. I've got some information to pass along about all these here polar bears y'all keep losing down this way.

"Y'all are going to have to hustle to be ready for it though, see? The word is, sometime in the next four days, a plane … no description … will be flying up there … no location, other than the Ontario side of James Bay … to pick up a bunch o' bearskins. They said sixteen, but that sounds like an awful lot to us.

"Can't tell you how we got this info or I'd have to come up there an' kill you, see?" he chuckled. "Gotta protect our sources don't you know. But it did come from a reliable source … one that's proven over ninety percent success rate for us here.

"Now, y'all be real careful, you hear? Them scoundrels can be *real* dangerous. Got a lot o' greenbacks riding on the success of their venture. Remember McNabb, this here's real serious shit.

"Oh, and have old James call me when he gets the chance will you?"

"Yes sir, I will. Thanks for calling."

"Bye now."

'Weird call,' McNabb thought as he transcribed his hurried scribblings into an electronic occurrence report.

Still puzzled by the accent that seemed too strong to be true, he didn't immediately press the 'Submit' command, but first Googled a reverse phone number lookup on the phone this guy Sturgis called from.

"Hmm. U.S. Fish and Wildlife Service, St. Louis, Missouri. That seems to check out," he spoke to the empty office. "Well, if he's who he says he is, and they hunted together, James would certainly remember a character like that." He clicked on 'Submit' and the occurrence report was sent. In addition to the copy going to James, several 'need to know' higher-ups, including the provincial director, also received copies. Rob McNabb crossed his fingers, desperately hoping that he hadn't been the butt of someone's prank.

When James Bird returned to the office twenty minutes later, McNabb outlined what had transpired. At the same time he expressed his concerns about the caller. Bird's face broke out in a big smile.

"Tommy's always been like that, Robbie. And that southern accent, well, there is a real one buried in there with it, but he sure paints it on thick when he wants to. He may sound like a hillbilly hick, but he's got a PhD in criminology and Masters in biology. He's no dummy and...." he paused while visually scanning a new email message flagged 'Urgent.'

"You did the right thing submitting the occurrence immediately. Director says to us, and she's copied the air service, 'Pull out all the stops. P. Bear situation untenable. Will figure out funding later. Keep me informed.'"

As of that moment, Robert McNabb's apprenticeship in pencil sharpening came to a grinding stop. James Bird immediately had him on the phone to the Ontario Provincial Air Service requisitioning aircraft that the Timmins facility supervisor claimed he couldn't produce overnight.

Furthermore, the man explained that most of the pilots were either burning off accrued summer overtime on warm sunny beaches, or away on specialized training courses.

"Yes sir, I understand, and I know I may be a very junior cog in the wheel," McNabb replied as diplomatically as he could, "but I think if you check your email, you will see that there is a directive from 'on high' that requires us to take whatever measures are required … or words to that effect." There was a long pause on the other end of the line. The air service boss obviously didn't read as quickly as James could.

"Well, okay then." There was another brief pause before he continued. "I've got one Turbo Beaver pilot available to start with. Then there's a retired pilot who keeps hinting that he'd like to come back for an occasional job. I'll see if he's available. But to come up with the third driver I'm going to have to cancel one pilot's weekend off. Won't be a happy camper there I'll tell you.

"As for the planes, I can supply two of the three birds without too much hassle, but I'll have to see what I can do for a third one. Everything else we have is either down for regular winter maintenance or lying about in pieces, getting a major overhaul. I'll have to get back to you McNabb. Don't worry, we'll shake something out for you."

"Thanks sir. I sure appreciate that." McNabb was relieved by the change in attitude when the 'memo' was quoted. He had half-expected the air service guy's heels to dig in even harder when he mentioned it, but the man seemed genuinely willing to help.

CHAPTER 7

Sunday, January 29 — Sudbury

"You dumb piece o' shit! Why in hell didn't you listen to what I told you, bonehead? What you got between your ears? I gave you the name of the one taxidermist I know we can trust down there, but you go and take your bear hide to a guy who does it as a hobby so you can save a few bucks. Only it just so happens, his day job is a friggin' game warden. In all the years I've been in this game, you gotta be the *stupidest* A-hole I ever done business with."

An exasperated Billy Joe Boyd, cell phone stuck to his ear, looked longingly at the can of beer sitting on the tailplane of his Cessna 185. The upset caller whined on about what the wardens were going to do to him next and wondered how he was going to replace his illegally imported polar bear pelt.

"Well *I'm* not gettin' you another bear! Jesus H. Christ, you ain't even goin' to *need* one when they finish with you, 'cause they supply all the warm fuzzy bedding you'll ever need in the crowbar hotel. It's because of a bunch of morons like you I'm goin' to quit supplyin' the 'merican market. We're done here, g'bye!" The burner phone dropped to the asphalt of Sudbury airport's parking apron and Billy Joe's boot crushed any traceable signs of life out of it. Of course, the American black market in polar bear parts was thriving so there was no way he was actually going to quit.

"Dumb shit. You were right, Cy. Everything we sell to the Chinese and the Russians goes real smooth. Not one hiccup come back to bite us. But our own dumb-ass, red blooded 'mericans just keep trippin' over themselves to get tangled up with the law. How many's that now? No, don't tell me, my blood pressure's already up an' those pills jus' don't agree with this Canuck beer."

Cyril Smith, Boyd's pilot and right-hand man, kicked the fragments of the expired cell phone into the deep snow behind the plane. "We've only got three of those left, BJ. We can't get any more 'til we get back over the border."

"Yeah, I know, and the law may be watchin' us when we do finally go home. All them stupid idiots donatin' their bear hides to the warden service is bound to give us problems one day. Jeezus that pisses me off! I mean, yeah, we've still got their cash, but one of 'em's bound to talk. Sure's shit it'll come back to bite us.

"Aw, fuck it anyhow. That's a problem for another day." He paused long enough to chug down the rest of the beer, then crumpled the aluminum can in one hand and tossed it after the dead cell phone. "What's the word Cy, you got the plane ready to go again?"

"Sure thing, BJ. Just waiting for you to give the word," he said as the boss started helping him pull the wing covers off the aircraft.

The 185 was set up with wheels and skis. Equipped with the best short takeoff and landing features available, it was a very capable six-seat bush plane. With the back seats removed, as they were on Boyd's plane, you could almost stuff the contents of a small minivan into the passenger area, making it a decent machine for small-cargo transport too.

Cyril Smith was not entirely a willing partner in this business, but he had been offered the position right after losing his job as a pilot for a regional airline in the American Midwest.

His dismissal there had occurred after the portside landing gear collapsed when he landed the company's newest short-haul jetliner. That unintended letdown had caused major damage to the plane. Both Smith and his co-pilot swore up and down that they had three green lights on the gear indicators both before and after the one leg had collapsed. But when the transportation safety inspectors powered up the system multiple times during their investigation, all they could get were red readings for the portside gear.

With mortgage payments due, the ex-wife to support and a kid going off to college, Boyd's offer couldn't have come at a better time. It had all looked to be above board, complete with a stack of what were purported to be fur buyer's licences covering every northern jurisdiction from Alaska to Labrador. And of course, Boyd, the plane's owner, shouldered all the overhead; Smith simply had to drive the thing.

It didn't take long, however, before he realized he'd been suckered. Perhaps it was hints like the throw-away cell phones the guy went through like cigarettes, or maybe the news of the seizures of so many of the polar bear hides they'd carefully 'imported' into the States from all across the Arctic the previous year.

While his big redneck boss had an explosive personality and just wasn't the sort of person Smith liked to be around, he did pay top dollar. And by now, Smith had already been involved in the commission of numerous offences against state, provincial and federal wildlife import and export laws in both countries. So he'd gotten himself thoroughly wedged between the well-known rock and the hard place — he didn't want to go on, but he couldn't quit either. Extricating himself from this situation was not going to be easy — in fact he didn't have the foggiest idea how to do it.

Well, as BJ so often said, 'That's a problem for another day.'

The Cessna, loaded with a supply of empty gasoline jugs, climbed quickly out of Sudbury airport and turned north, levelling out at a couple thousand feet. The gas jugs would be filled at the last municipal airport before stepping off the edge of civilization and heading into the wilderness. And on this flight, that last place was Kapuskasing. There were no significant communities between there and Sutton Lake.

An hour after arriving in Kap, they took off once more. With full tanks and a maximum load in their portable gas jugs, the 185 made a more laborious climb to cruising altitude. The three-hundred-nautical-mile trip was interrupted three times to land and replenish three previous fuel caches on the way to Sutton Lake. On the return flight south they'd be short-hopping between refuelling stops with a minimum fuel load in the Cessna's tanks on each leg of the trip. This meant that the plane could carry an even bigger load of goods. And Eagle Feather had promised a maximum payload to haul back south.

On the monotonous flight north, Boyd kept up a running commentary on his hunting exploits, his fishing exploits, his womanizing exploits — there didn't seem to be any facet of American life to which he didn't claim to have made some contribution. For the most part, Smith just tuned him out.

The sun was getting low in the sky when Sutton Lake came into view. Smith set the plane down on the snow-covered ice at the north end of the lake and taxied up to Eagle Feather's cabin.

Smith had met the poacher a few times before and the man had always been a tough-looking customer with a mean attitude. He was always haranguing Boyd for more money — he wanted a bigger cut. Boyd was always throwing back in his face his excuses about the exorbitant cost of doing business in the north and how hard it was to keep drumming up new customers. Some of it was the truth, and some of it outright lies. But on this trip, the poacher appeared strangely at ease, as if he'd finally come to accept his lot, willing to do business on Boyd's terms.

He invited them up to his camp and provided them with a wild game dinner like they'd not had in a long time. The crowded camp was not the best, but the grub was top notch. Boyd accepted endless rounds of Canadian Club rye whisky while Smith stuck with coffee. Even that was good.

There was something different about the poacher that the pilot couldn't put his finger on, but it didn't bother him at all — it was just a pleasant change to have this host treating them like guests, not opponents.

They would overnight at Sutton Lake and then load up and head south in the morning.

CHAPTER 8

Monday, January 30 — Sutton Lake

It was late morning and the temperature had climbed to almost -25° Celsius; a little on the mild side, though pretty close to normal for January in those parts. The wind chill was something else, but real men didn't put much stock into wind chill readings, they just dressed for the elements.

Rob McNabb sat in a camouflaged, pop-up hunting blind on an uncomfortably small camp stool. In addition to wearing his down-filled parka and snow pants, he was wrapped in his Woods 5-Star sleeping bag, cocooned against the cold in a thick insulating layer of goose down.

He'd arrived there an hour before dawn. And he had been at the same place for most of the previous day too. Peering through a spotting scope, he was watching an unexpected situation develop down on the snow-covered surface of Sutton Lake. When he had first arrived in the morning, the bush plane he was watching had been parked in front of Eagle Feather's camp. It hadn't moved since he departed from his hiding spot after dark the previous evening. But shortly after ten this morning, the engine had started and McNabb figured that the loading must have taken place during the night. It seemed as if the show was about to begin.

Thoughts of immediate action were quickly dispelled, when instead of leaving, the plane taxied behind a man who was hurrying ahead on snowshoes. It stopped about half a kilometre southwest of the poacher's camp, near the opposite shore of the narrow lake. Unfortunately it now sat almost a full kilometre from his present position and keeping track of the loading activities was very difficult from this new angle.

'Why couldn't these guys stick with the program?' he mused to himself. He had chosen his spot on top of the cliff, thirty metres above the lake surface, because of the good view it gave him of the poacher's camp. But the unexpected change in the plane's position put him at a bit of a disadvantage despite the high-quality optics of his scope. Nonetheless, he knew that whatever was being loaded into the Cessna was most certainly the object of the investigation. He could see white commercial fur bags being carried to the plane. Now he just had to wait until the aircraft made its departure so he could put in the call that would initiate an intercept.

Sitting in the blind watching the action down the lake, McNabb felt pleased that he'd been put in charge of planning such a major investigation. He was glad that he'd had project-planning experience in several of his previous contract positions, so setting up this special operation wasn't totally beyond his abilities. It was just the speed of developments that had tested his organizational skills.

McNabb had spent two days in the office organizing and requisitioning everything he'd need. He had asked Bird to review his preparations before putting the plan into action. The supervisor found no loose ends.

The following day started with an early morning flight up here, and now he'd spent the better part of two days sitting in the blind waiting for something to happen.

When the Cessna arrived at Sutton just before sunset yesterday afternoon, he knew this was the real deal. It was only the fall of darkness and the bitter cold finally penetrating his goose down defences that let him leave his post for the night. He was confident that he would be safe leaving the plane unwatched until he returned before dawn the next morning. Only then did he snowshoe back over the hill and start the snowmobile for the run down to the government camp near the north end of Hawley Lake.

Now, just after 11:00 a.m., it appeared that the loading activity was winding down. McNabb observed two of the three figures he'd been watching, start to snowshoe back across the lake toward the poacher's cabin.

It was an illegally established camp, situated on a small west-facing bay near the north end of the lake. According to Gabriel Whitegoose, the poacher was a non-native man from parts unknown. He had tried to convince everyone that he was just like Grey Owl, but Eagle Feather had not fooled any of the local Cree people. They certainly weren't buying into his conservationist claims. Everyone knew that he had been hunting and trapping on First Nations lands without approval from any of the area band offices, and he certainly had no such licences issued by the province. However, no one had suspected him of being anything other than a minor nuisance until Whitegoose had found evidence of several dead bears the previous winter. Even then, making a connection to Eagle Feather had just been speculation.

The ministry enforcement staff had decided to leave the Eagle Feather camp alone, at least for the time being.

Chasing him out now would just mean that he would go to ground and move to another location — whereabouts unknown — until someone stumbled onto him again. And in this vast region, a man could stay hidden in plain view for a very long time.

McNabb's butt was getting sore. He chastised himself for the umpteenth time for not bringing a cushion for the tiny three legged stool. A regular folding camp chair would have made even more sense, he figured.

As he began to shift to a kneeling position to alleviate the discomfort, he observed the two men on snowshoes leave the lake and approach the illegal camp. The remaining man at the Cessna was doing a pre-flight walk-around. Rob knew that was what he was doing because he had recently completed his first eighteen hours of flight training for his private pilot's licence.

He watched the pilot climb into the plane, and after a pause, the engine began to crank. Not heard over the wind, but seen from his hideout, the plane's propeller stirred up a cloud of soft snow, then began to taxi across the lake, back toward Eagle Feather's camp. Coasting to a stop out front of the camp, the pilot throttled the engine down to an idle, but kept it running. Now the plane was close enough, and angled better to finally get a look at the registration.

'Hmm, C-GFKU — a Canadian plane. That's weird. This was supposed to be an American operation,' he thought. He had kicked himself the previous evening after realizing that in the excitement of watching the plane arrive, he had completely forgotten to record the registration. It was a truly amateurish error that could have ruined the entire project. And when the sun had risen this morning, its glare off the smooth wing surface, made it impossible to read the registration letters.

Just as McNabb finished scribbling this critical information in his notebook, he heard the distinctive crack of a rifle shot. A loud, sharp echo rolled off the hills down the narrow lake's shoreline.

In the next instant, one of the men came running out of the camp, lunging hard through the snow toward the plane. The runner hopped onto a ski and began to pull himself into the plane as the engine revved. The aircraft spun around and immediately throttled up to taxi southward, bouncing heavily on snowdrifts that had formed away from the shore.

—

Cy Smith was sitting in the idling Cessna, updating his flight log, when he heard the rifle shot. His guts tightened instantly. He had not signed up for this. He was tempted to leave Billy Joe right there, fly back to civilization and turn himself in, but knowing his boss's explosive temper, the man would just as likely put a couple of rounds into him before he was able to taxi a few yards. So he waited, his knuckles white from the death grip he had on the controls.

Seconds later, Eagle Feather, not Boyd, came bounding empty-handed down the beach toward the plane. Knowing that something had gone dreadfully wrong, Smith immediately took the Cessna up to full throttle. He wanted nothing to do with this crazy man. But an airplane doesn't instantly leap forward on command like a car or a pickup can and that initial sluggish acceleration gave the poacher just enough time to jump on a ski strut and grab the door handle. Swinging himself into the passenger seat he drew a Colt .45 pistol from his parka pocket.

"If you want to live past the end of today, fly us outta

here. I'll tell you where; but for now, just go south. I can fly this thing myself if you're not interested in the job."

"Look here …" Smith began to object. But he knew enough not to ask about Boyd. "I've only got enough avgas onboard to make it to the next fuel cache, so wherever you want to go, we have to follow our line of caches."

"I know that, dumbass. Why do you think I told Boyd to plan on short hops? I knew we'd have a maximum load. But seein' as how he refused to see things my way, I've decided to go into business for myself. You can come along for the ride or...." Pausing, he looked meaningfully at the .45 in his hand. ".... or be retired. Now get this fuckin' thing in the air."

CHAPTER 9

'Shit, something's gone wrong,' McNabb thought as he pulled the satellite phone from his warm inner pocket. 'First the gunshot and now they're in an awful rush to get going.'

The high-tech phone he had brought with him was fully charged when he had flown up to the government camp on Hawley Lake the previous day. He had kept it warm and turned it off to save the battery. But now, when he pushed the power button to turn the unit on, nothing happened. Rapping it hard on his other palm — a hold-over response from his father's era — did nothing to help either. Taking the battery out then reinstalling it was no more rewarding. The phone was dead. Worse still, he had no spare.

"Shit!" He watched helplessly as the Cessna, now easily a couple of kilometres away, turned into the wind and began its takeoff run. Despite having three hundred horses 'under the hood' the 185 appeared reluctant to leave the surface of the lake. The plane, now audibly straining, finally left the snow beneath its skis. It was heading straight for the base of the cliff below McNabb's blind and was still just a few feet above the ice as it laboured to build up airspeed. McNabb was certain that the plane was going to slam into the rock face beneath him and now it was boxed into the narrow north end of the lake, leaving no room for it to turn either left or right. Grabbing his camera, he got ready to record the coming crash.

At the last possible moment the pilot banked slightly to starboard, aiming for the narrow gorge between Sutton and Hawley Lakes. The Cessna was only halfway up the height of the rock walls of the gorge as McNabb watched it pass beneath him, its wingtips just yards away from the cliff face on either side. With an echoing roar, the plane charged through the gorge and disappeared from view. He looked at the screen on his camera. Although the picture wouldn't make the front cover of Time Magazine, he had captured the Cessna's wing top registration in the image.

—

"You *stupid shit*," Eagle Feather yelled over the bellowing engine. "What the fuck do you think you're doing? You could have gotten us both killed!"

"Sorry, I didn't think we were that heavy," Smith lied. In fact, knowing that he was facing a limited future, he had started his takeoff run fully intending to end their flight and their lives on the face of that cliff.

But when he realized he was looking at a hunting blind above the very spot he was aiming for, it confirmed his hope that maybe something was in the wind. A few minutes earlier, while he was waiting for Boyd to come out of the camp, he thought he'd caught the briefest twinkle of light reflected off something up there. It might have been a scope, or a pair of binoculars — but he had dismissed it then as improbable. And up until that moment, being under surveillance would have been bad news. But considering his sudden change in fortune, catching sight of the blind was enough to give him hope. Someone was watching. And as much as he'd broken a whole bunch of laws since joining up with Boyd, he would rather take his chances with the authorities than with the crazy man sitting beside him. Although his change in plans almost came too late, his long years of commercial flying allowed him to squeeze the plane through the gorge with little room to spare.

—

Thinking that the men in the plane would probably be looking for some clean underwear about now, McNabb stuffed the sleeping bag into his backpack, collapsed the blind and strapped on his snowshoes. As he hurried through the sparse trees on his way back to his Ski-Doo, he saw the Cessna off to the west, now safely above the rugged landscape. And it was flying southward. South toward an unknown destination.

Originally, he was supposed to phone James Bird the instant the plane left. The home team would set up a net to intercept the southbound bad guys and Rob would make his way back to the government camp and fly back to Moosonee. But circumstances had changed — he wouldn't be able to call in until he was airborne. Worse still, the rifle shot he'd heard suggested that the whole investigation might have just become a lot more complex.

On returning to his hidden snowmobile he quickly loaded his gear onto the sleigh but disconnected it from the Ski-Doo so he could make a quick run to check out Eagle Feather's camp. He just hoped to hell that it wasn't a sucker move planned by the bad guys to flush out anyone who'd been watching them. The boss would be extremely disappointed if he burned the investigation by showing up at the poacher's camp to find the guy drinking coffee and wearing a shitfaced grin because he'd just radioed some code word to the Cessna, warning them that the heat was on.

But by virtue of being a conservation officer, McNabb was also a peace officer and was obligated to check into a possible violent crime — even at the expense of his major wildlife poaching investigation. He really wished he didn't have to do that.

The Ski-Doo he was driving was a 1980s single-cylinder Tundra. It was nowhere near to being fast by modern standards, but it ran well enough, and the strong low-end torque made the machine ideal for work in the bush. It was a surplus asset that the outfit kept for northern patrols, along with a similar one in a shed at the Hawley Lake camp.

After bulling the snowmobile through deep powder snow over the portage trail and down onto the lake, McNabb quickly buzzed over to the poacher's camp, stopping just short of the footprints and ski-plane tracks left out front. If this turned out to be a crime scene, he didn't want to contaminate the evidence any more than was absolutely necessary.

Pushing a fresh path through the deep snow, he trudged up the beach, this time without snowshoes. Keeping parallel to the poacher's footpath, he cautiously approached the cabin in combat stance — his pistol drawn, held in both hands and arms extended at chest height. The door was wide open. Was that to give a shooter waiting inside a clear sight path to anyone approaching?

He slowly approached the cabin. His heart was pounding and sweat was gathering between his shoulder blades despite the cold.

Shaking now, McNabb inched his way forward. This

was the first time in his brief career that the young officer had drawn his pistol other than at a shooting range. On top of the stress of confronting the unknown, he knew that the clock was ticking on the Cessna's southbound flight. Every minute that passed meant it had gone more than two miles toward its destination. If he wasted too much time here there'd be no way the guys at home could try for an intercept.

As he finally got within the last twenty metres of the cabin, he observed two things. First: protruding from the snow beside the poacher's path was the butt of a long-gun. Judging from the marks in the snow, it had been dropped in haste by someone moving quickly away from the building. Second: he could see through the doorway what appeared to be a booted leg lying on the rough cabin floor and as he moved closer, he could see that the top end of the leg was attached to a man — who appeared to be quite dead.

On entering the cabin it was pretty obvious to him that a shot to the abdomen, probably made by a high-powered hunting round, had painted the back wall of the room with more blood and gore than he thought a human body could possibly contain. It made a ghastly mess. He took a quick look around to verify that the one-room cabin was otherwise unoccupied, and without having time to holster his pistol, McNabb raced back outside to lose his breakfast in the snow. After regaining his composure, he realized he had several decisions to make — fast.

Not sure what to do about the gun lying by the path, he took his camera from inside his parka and snapped pictures of the gun butt where it lay protruding from the snow. He also got shots of its position relative to both the footpath and the camp. Only then did he pick up the firearm and examine it.

"Winchester .30-30. That's almost too light for serious big game hunting in these parts. And why would they want to knock off their supplier anyhow?" He received no answer from the northern wilderness.

The rifle was not cocked, and on slowly opening the lever action, he discovered one spent shell casing in the breech, probably the shell that fired the fatal bullet. That was critical evidence in a murder investigation. Looking down into the rifle's receiver mechanism below the spent casing, he could see that there was at least one live round. He didn't want to mess up any evidence for the police, so he closed the action and gently lowered the cocked hammer again leaving the firearm's contents as they were when he found it.

Now Rob was faced with a double dilemma. He knew that there wouldn't be a recognizable fingerprint left anywhere on the rifle if he brought it out with him — he had no carrying case for it. But if he left it here, he was leaving the evidence of a murder unsecured. Worse still, it was a loaded firearm, likewise unsecured.

The only option open to him was to take it into the camp. There he snapped his handcuffs through the lever handle and around the stock so that the action couldn't be opened to chamber the live round. Satisfied that the weapon had been made as safe as he could make it, he hid it at the back of the topmost kitchen shelf. From floor level it was not visible from anywhere in the room. Against the advice of his churning stomach, he took one last picture, this one of the victim in the camp. Then he exited the building, closing the door behind him so the foxes and wolves wouldn't move in to dine on the body. Bent over outside the front door, McNabb retched some more, but nothing came up. They didn't exactly teach about human gunshot victims at game warden school.

By this time he was in a sweat because he'd lost way too much time at the cabin. Twenty-five minutes had elapsed since the Cessna had turned south. With the tailwind, it could be making one-hundred-and-fifty knots ground speed, and at that rate it would get down around Hearst or Kap in less than an hour and a half. He quickly returned to the Ski-Doo and began the twenty-kilometre sled ride back to the government camp.

CHAPTER 10

Rob McNabb stopped on the portage trail from Sutton to Hawley and re-hitched the sleigh, then headed north down the lake. If he could coax the Tundra to maintain a steady 60 km/h, he could be back at camp in twenty minutes. Gord Clark, the retired pilot brought back to fly the old ministry Otter on this mission had promised that they would be able to leave any time after McNabb's return.

The de Havilland Otter was an odd machine for the air service to be flying in the twenty-first century. Built in the 1950s, it was an exceptionally good, heavy-haul bush plane, but the province had sold off most of its remaining Otters in favour of maintaining its newer fleet of gas turbine-powered Turbo Beavers and Twin Otters. However, some commercial air services had started refitting the radial engine Otters with gas turbine engines, so provincial air service had decided to hang on to three of its old birds and mothballed them until they could come up with the time and money to make the conversions.

When the air service manager had only been able to come up with two Turbo Beavers, he got back to McNabb later that day and said they would re-activate the best of the three warehoused Otters and send it north.

The plan was that the Otter, not known for its speed, would be used to fly McNabb to Hawley Lake. And when his call came in, two Turbo Beavers would lift off from Moosonee and Hearst. They would do overlapping east-west patrol circuits at around nine thousand feet altitude, watching for the wanted southbound aircraft to pass beneath them.

Whoever saw the plane first would verify its identity and then follow it from a distance, hopefully to its destination. The second Beaver would refuel ASAP and be ready to take over when the first one had to break for fuel.

It was assumed that the Cessna would be making at least one refuelling stop on the way to wherever it was going. At that point, a ground assault would be mounted to take the guys down. COs in every district south of Moosonee were on standby in case the action should take place in their area.

McNabb pointed the Ski-Doo out toward the centre of the lake where the soft snow had been blown clear. There the machine was riding on either hard crust or patches of nearly glare ice allowing it to run unimpeded by anything other than the headwind and the slight drag of the sleigh. He gradually worked the Tundra up to 75 km/h.

With a wide, sweeping s-bend in the lake, McNabb wouldn't be able to see the Otter or the government camp until he was about three kilometres away and he was beginning to wish he'd brought walkie-talkies to communicate with the pilot. If the sat-phone had worked, the next phase of the operation would have already been set in motion. He just hoped that Gord would see him coming when he rounded the final corner and start peeling the engine tent off of the yellow bird.

When he did round that last bend in the lake and the Otter and camp came into view, the Tundra was really moving. He knew that even after they got the plane airborne, they would still be way out of range for any VHF radio transmission to Moosonee, but they could buzz Gabriel Whitegoose's place and ask him to use his sat-phone to call James Bird. Gabriel lived at the north end of the lake, three kilometres beyond the government camp. Still, even if they could get the word out within the next twenty or twenty-five minutes, the Moosonee Turbo Beaver would be hard pressed to play catch-up, but the one out of Hearst could be on patrol in time.

Two kilometres to go. With the throttle wide open, the Tundra's Rotax engine was really singing and to his surprise, still gradually building up speed. McNabb was beginning to feel optimistic about his chances of pulling this off. Not much more than a kilometre now.

BANG... flappety... flappety... flap... flap... flap. The Ski-Doo coasted to a stop. He thumbed the throttle on the still idling engine. It revved up, freewheeling, but there was no sign of the machine moving any farther. Ignition off. Silence.

"Aw, shit no … not now!" When McNabb lifted the engine cowling, he was greeted by a scene of utter chaos. Shredded rubber chunks and reams of drive belt wire were strewn around under the hood. The belt had chosen that very instant to self-destruct. There was a spare belt lying on the running board under the cowling, but after taking a quick look toward the camp, he told himself he could run the distance faster than he could ever change the belt — the old one a tangled, gnarled mess and the new one cold and stiff. Leaving everything sitting where it died, he began a fast jog toward the camp and the Otter. He would have to ask Whitegoose to come out and tow the machine back to the shed for them.

As he approached the big yellow bird, McNabb could

hear the portable generator running where it sat beside the nose of the aircraft. It was providing power for two electric heaters under the engine tent and one back in the battery compartment. But there was no sign of Gord yet. Probably in the camp, he thought. The generator would have easily covered the noise of the approaching snowmobile — before it had stopped approaching.

"Gord!" he shouted as he finally reached the plane. No response. He called again in the direction of the camp, "Hey Gord, we've got to get airborne right away." No response.

Though he was in pretty good shape, McNabb was sweating hard and starting to wear down, but he turned and ran the final sixty metres up to the camp. Flinging open the door, he stepped inside.

CHAPTER 11

Hawley Lake

"Oh shit! *Gord!*" McNabb knelt down to look at the pilot lying on the cabin floor. Considering the events of the day so far, he could be forgiven his first impression — that the poor man had been murdered too. But there were no gaping holes, no blood and he was still warm. In fact, once his first aid training kicked in, a quick assessment revealed that old Mr. Clark was still living — sort of. Heart: beating. Breathing: a bit laboured. And during this preliminary look-see, the patient tried to speak.

McNabb rocked back on his heels where he squatted, pondering, only briefly. His mother, an emergency room nurse for many years, had often enough described what he was now seeing. 'Poor guy's had a stroke,' he reasoned. What boggled his mind was the question: 'How do I deal with a stroke patient way out here in the frozen north?'

Mentally working through his options he realized that he would have to gas up the other Ski-Doo, drag it out of the shed, race over to Gabby's camp, phone for an air ambulance chopper … "Oh Christ, it'll take the rest of the day just to get up here. That is, if there is even one immediately available. Shit!"

He looked around the small camp, as if something there might trigger an inspiration; nothing clicked right away. But he did notice that when he went down, Clark had toppled a small shelving unit to the floor, wrecking the government's forty-year-old Westclox tin alarm clock in the process. It *had* been working when he left camp early in the morning. Picking up the battered timepiece and then checking his own watch, he realized that the clock's demise had marked the time of Clark's stroke! It had only happened about fifteen minutes earlier. The golden hour was ticking by fast. That revelation made up his mind for him.

"Okay, here's the scoop Gord. The government brass hats are probably going to skin my sorry ass for this, but I'm going to steal Her Majesty's Otter and fly you back to Moose." Clark had let McNabb take the controls of the plane for a while during their flight north. It was a true delight to fly — so much more stable and forgiving than the tiny Cessna 152 trainers back at the Brampton Flying Club.

In fact, Gord's comment on the topic went something like, 'these Otters will pretty much fly themselves. You just have to start them up, show them which way to go and tell them when to stop.' So, aside from the likelihood of an unsteady takeoff and a landing even less polished, he had the confidence that he could do it.

"So, ready or not, let's get this show on the road."

"Machnaav...." Clark's slurred mumble caught McNabb's attention. Then with his non-paralyzed hand, the man gave him a slow thumbs-up.

Grabbing the sleeping bag and foam mattress off of the pilot's bed, McNabb told Clark, "I'll be right back." He dashed out the door and down to the plane, boarding through the aft cargo door. Stripping seatbelt assemblies from several of the stowed seats, he rigged what he hoped would be a secure bed for the pilot's trip south.

Back in the camp, he turned off the propane heater and knelt down to pick up his patient. If the man weighed more than a hundred and fifty pounds, McNabb didn't notice — his adrenalin was pumping. Within a few minutes he had the pilot strapped in place on the floor of the Otter's cabin.

Out on the ice, McNabb turned off the generator and pulled the heaters out of the engine tent while removing the cover. He threw the loose gear into the plane, but the generator was still hot, so he left it where it was. His mind kept spinning through all the things he had to do in order to pull this off.

Finally, he made a quick pre-flight walk-around to check the outside working parts of the Otter. Before re-boarding the aircraft he remembered to open the low-point fuel bleed briefly, to make sure there was no water — or ice — in the fuel system. He knew that Gord had checked the oil and other essential items yesterday.

Strapped into the pilot's seat, Rob McNabb scanned the impressive array of instruments and dials. It was a little intimidating compared to the simple instrument panel on the Cessna trainer he was used to. Fortunately, on the way north the other day, Clark had briefed him on the various instruments' functions.

"Okay," he breathed deeply, speaking out loud as if his flight instructor was quizzing him from the next seat. One by one he went through the start-up procedures, just as he would in a little Cessna, adding the steps required on the Otter as he remembered them from Clark's briefing. And when the big nine-cylinder radial engine came barking to life as it was supposed to, he let out a fist-pumping "Yes!"

And it immediately died of fuel starvation because he hadn't been ready with another gradual plunge on the fuel primer handle. But he caught it on the second start and after some loud snorting and farting, the six-hundred-horsepower Pratt & Whitney engine gradually smoothed out to a steady throaty rumble.

While waiting for the engine oil temperature to start to register on the gauge, he got the aviation and government radios turned on and made sure that they were tuned to the appropriate frequencies.

"Gabriel Whitegoose, Gabriel Whitegoose, Gabriel Whitegoose, this is government Otter CF-ODL, Charlie Foxtrot Oscar Delta Lima, over." No reply.

With some temperature now beginning to register on the gauges, McNabb smoothly advanced the throttle a little to get the plane moving over the snow. However, he wasn't aware that water had crept up into the snow by capillary action over the last day and a half and had frozen the skis to the ice surface.

Even with the big engine turning at a medium-high idle, the skis stayed frozen in place. He tried pumping the foot pedals vigorously back and forth, hoping that the Otter's giant rudder, standing vertically in the propeller's slipstream, would wiggle the bird free. Still nothing.

'What do you do now, smartass?' he asked himself. Looking out the side window he remembered that the skis were extended because they'd landed and taxied in on snow. On an aircraft rigged with wheel-skis, the wheels remain fixed to the suspension struts, and the skis are raised and lowered the few inches required to transition from one mode to the other. McNabb moved the lever controlling the skis, and gradually the cold hydraulics began to try raising the skis from the frozen surface. As the tires began taking more of the weight of the aircraft, the hydraulic pump ground to a halt. No good.

He recycled the system again, hoping that the thick oil would pump more freely a second time around. But the skis still didn't budge.

Frustrated, McNabb carefully raised the engine speed to 1500 rpm. Once more he pumped hard, back and forth on the rudder pedals. Suddenly with a loud 'chunk-kachunk' the ice let go and the plane leapt forward.

"*No*! Not up on the beach!" Hard right rudder, his toe squeezed down on the pedal to apply the right wheel brake, the big plane began to swing — now coming around smartly — now headed for the recently abandoned generator. Another hurried steering correction cleared that obstacle, and after thinking to idle the engine back down to 1000 rpm he began to feel more in control of the situation.

One last issue he needed to deal with was cabin heat. There's not much of that to be had on a cold winter's day in a radial engine bush plane, but he verified that the vents were open and a token amount of warmth — nothing he could call 'heat' yet — was flowing into the aircraft's interior. Back in the passenger compartment, lashed to the cold floor in his 5-Star sleeping bag, the pilot could end up a hypothermia victim before the stroke did him in.

McNabb taxied back up the lake to his abandoned Ski-Doo and braked to a stop beside it. Setting the parking brakes, he climbed quickly down to the sleigh. He threw his sleeping bag, hunting blind and snowshoes into the back of the plane and then re-boarded. He wrapped the extra bag over Clark's 'bed' and returned to the cockpit.

CHAPTER 12

Sitting at the controls of the Otter, McNabb started through the pre-takeoff checks and engine run-up.

"Okay, this is your final exam," he told himself. "1500 rpm and propeller speed control all the way to feathered position." It took a moment for warmer oil to work its way into the propeller pitch mechanism. But gradually the big blades changed their angle, biting into more and more air until the engine rpm fell way off.

He returned the control to fine pitch, cycled it once more and then worked his way through the checklist, testing the carburetor heat and magnetos as he went. Finally the skis were lowered again and the flaps set in the take-off position.

Throttling up, he began his takeoff roll. At 2200 rpm the big engine took the nearly empty aircraft from standing still to airborne in such a short run that McNabb wondered briefly if he'd done something wrong. But no, just as Gord Clark had said, 'these big old birds will pretty much fly themselves.' And so it was.

Now he just had to stay ahead of the curve and manage the flaps, propeller speed and throttle setting, first for climbing, and then in a few minutes, for level flight. He didn't want the ailing pilot to suffer from oxygen deprivation, so he figured on a cruising altitude of no more than a thousand feet. And before climbing any higher than the five hundred feet he was at now, he needed to go and buzz the Whitegoose place — which he was already over top of.

—

Five hundred feet below in their simple bungalow, nestled amidst five guest cabins on the northern shore of Hawley Lake, Gabriel and Edna Whitegoose were finishing their lunch tea at the kitchen table. Edna was grumbling to her husband about running low on potatoes and onions, when they heard the distinctive throbbing of the de Havilland Otter overhead. Gabby reached over to the VHF set where it sat on one end of the kitchen counter and turned it on.

".... Whitegoose this is ODL, that's Oscar Delta Lima, over." The last part of Rob McNabb's nervous radio call came through just as the unit came to life.

"Old Dirty Laundry, this is Gabby here," he called back, using one of the affectionate phonetic names the air service pilots used to give their Otters. "I thought you guys got rid of all those old birds a few years back."

"Gabriel, this is Rob McNabb, the new amisk hookimaw in Moosonee, and I'm up here on the project I think you are aware of, but we've run into a double emergency and I need to get in touch with James Bird immediately. Is your sat-phone working? Over."

"ODL, I just pressed the speed dial now and I'll put it on speaker phone so you can talk to him directly. Standby one." The Cree title 'amisk hookimaw' had been bestowed by his people on the province's game wardens for many generations. The English translation was 'beaver boss.'

The satellite phone made its connection and Whitegoose pressed the VHF transmit button to call to the Otter at the same time he began to speak to James Bird in Moosonee.

"James, its Gabby here. I've got your young game warden on the radio, and he says it's urgent. Over to you ODL."

"Roger, thanks Gabriel. James, everything's falling apart up here," he began. His voice clearly showed the strain.

"The package departed at 11:30 this morning, but only after the supplier was murdered by his clients. My sat-phone wouldn't turn on so I couldn't call you from there. Can we still scramble the chase planes now or not? The police are going to want to find them in a big way too.

"Looking for a big guy with shoulder-length, black hair from what I could see. It's a white Cessna 185 with blue trim, registration C-GFKU, that's Charlie Gulf Foxtrot Kilo Uniform that you're looking for, and up here he had a ten or twelve knot tailwind in his favour.

"Worse still, Gord Clark has had what I'm pretty sure is a stroke. All indications are it just happened, so I'm flying the Otter to get him back to Moose ASAP. Uh … over."

There was a long pause while James Bird absorbed McNabb's message. He gave a few quick instructions to those around him while rapidly scribbling some notes for himself.

"ODL, Moosonee. Okay, I've just scrambled the Turbos and we've got the police on the other line. Are you okay? Are you airborne now? Over."

"Roger James. I'm a little shaky still but I'm okay. I'm about halfway down Hawley Lake right now. I just levelled out at a thousand feet and she's settling at about a hundred-and-seventeen knots air speed. The GPS says I'm two-forty nautical miles from home, so I figure I should get there in about two and a half hours.

"One request though," he continued. "This *is* my first solo flight, so when I get down to Moose, if the wind direction is anything but straight down a runway, I'd really prefer to land on the river, then I can taxi to meet the ambulance on the winter road out there. Over."

"All roger Robbie. We'll take it one step at a time. We're bound to ruffle some feathers at the air service, but you're doing the right thing. And just remember, those Otters will pretty much fly themselves. Over."

"Thanks James. I think I've heard that somewhere before. Anyways, I'll radio in when I get south of Fort Albany. There's a few things I need to ask Gabriel to look after for us before I sign off, over."

"Later, then. Have a good flight. Moosonee, out."

Hearing James taking everything in his stride, Rob was beginning to feel his confidence return. And when he heard the boss say, 'we,' when it came to ruffling the air service feathers, he knew the man had his back.

"Gabriel, ODL, over."

"My friends call me Gabby. You can too, if I can call you Robbie, over."

"Sure thing Gabby. And thanks for the radio relay, you're a real lifesaver. Anyhow, there's a few things down at the camp that need putting away." Rob outlined the loose ends that needed attention.

And Gabby cheerfully came back with, "Don't worry young hookimaw, consider it done, over."

"All roger then. Old Dirty Laundry out," he signed off. Despite the urgency of the situation, a relieved smile crept over his face. He knew now that fitting in wasn't going to be as hard as he had feared during those first couple of months — assuming he survived his first solo flight.

Working steadily at 1800 rpm, the radial engine slowly pulled the big bush plane toward its destination. McNabb chuckled to himself when he remembered Gord saying that the Otters were so slow, the pilots used a calendar as an air speed indicator. Looking back into the passenger compartment he saw the sleeping bag stirring. His patient was shifting his good hand under the covers. So far, so good.

—

Down in the Whitegoose residence, Gabby turned to Edna with a cheeky grin and said in Cree, "There, he says we are to take the potatoes, onions, carrots and other produce. I don't know why you always worry about running out of food, old woman."

"Well, go and do your chores for that boy right now, because I need those vegetables for tonight's supper … old man."

CHAPTER 13

Near Pledger Lake

Cyril Smith had landed the Cessna on a small lake just north of the Attawapiskat River. It was the location of the first fuel cache. There he had poured in the three, twenty-litre jugs of avgas that he and Boyd had left just the day before. He never felt comfortable starting a flight with only a quarter tank of fuel on board, but he knew that with what was still left in the plane's tanks it would be more than enough gas to get to the next cache. His main concern right now was, if Eagle Feather actually could fly, as he claimed, the man probably planned to 'retire' him as soon as they were fuelled up there. At that next cache, there was enough gas to get the plane to Hearst or Kapuskasing.

With that in mind, part way into the next leg he began watching for a lake with a hunting camp or trapper's cabin on it. It had to be somewhere he could land, claiming it was the next fuel cache. And after a while, a lake appeared that he felt would suit his needs. He began his descent and the murderous poacher didn't clue in to his ruse.

Coming in low on one side of a long narrow peninsula, he brought the Cessna down and taxied it close to shore before shutting it down. Pulling on his parka he asked the poacher if he'd give him a hand carrying the gas jugs. The man refused.

"Asshole," he muttered as he strapped on the snowshoes once more.

"You lugged them in there, so you can lug them back out."

He'd been pretty confident that that was the response he'd get and he desperately hoped that the guy wouldn't actually agree to help; he certainly hadn't at their first stop. He just needed Eagle Feather to believe this really was another fuel cache.

Smith walked toward the shore pretending to be in a huff, but was thrilled that there was distance building between them with each step he took. And when he got to the bush line, he struck off across the peninsula, in the general direction of a trapper's cabin he'd seen on the other side.

Keeping the view of that potential shelter on his side of the plane as he lined up for his landing had apparently paid off; Eagle Feather had obviously missed it.

Heading farther into the bush, he decided not to go directly to the cabin yet, just in case the poacher caught on to his plan and came around to the other side of the point looking for him. He resolved to stay hidden until he heard the 185 leave.

—

Back in the Cessna, five minutes after the pilot walked into the bush, it suddenly dawned on Eagle Feather that unlike at the last gas cache, something was missing here. At the last cache, there were snowshoe tracks left the previous day by

Smith and Boyd, but here the snow had been untouched until the pilot walked away from the plane. The poacher had been too busy thinking of his own next move to pay much attention to what Smith was up to.

"Aw Jeezuz … Shit!" Royally pissed off for missing such a simple sign, he cursed himself and got out of the plane to trail after the pilot. This was going to be the location of the man's retirement.

The snow, over the thirty metres between the Cessna and the beach, ranged from ankle to mid-calf deep — not bad for walking. But as soon as he entered the bush line along the shore, he was immediately fighting his way through crotch-deep powder. After twenty metres of laborious progress, Eagle Feather stopped. Why was he worrying about catching this guy anyhow? There was no way he could get from such a remote location back to civilization on his own.

Satisfied that Smith couldn't cause any future problems for him, the poacher turned back toward the Cessna. Within ten minutes he was back in the air, enjoying taking the controls of a plane again after so many years of letting others do the flying.

It was only after getting airborne that he saw the cabin down on the other side of the point. "You crafty bastard. I oughta go back down there and finish you off, asshole." But he knew that the plane was flying on what military pilots called 'bingo fuel.' He only had just enough gas to get to his destination. So he continued on.

—

For Cy Smith, walking that distance, even on snowshoes, had been tough. His knees were weak from the effort, and inside his parka, his shirt soaked with sweat. He stopped to sit on a fallen tree he found in the midst of a black spruce stand three or four hundred metres from the aircraft. He unzipped the parka briefly to cool off as he waited. He wondered if the poacher would bother struggling this far to find him — if he'd even bother to leave the plane. Next question was, whether the guy would try to wait him out, or just leave.

He had barely finished that thought, when he heard the Continental engine revving up. Minutes later, through the treetops, he caught sight of the blue and white plane flying off to the east. Smith wondered why the man would choose to fly east; but then with fuel low, he'd probably head straight for Moosonee. Well, no matter. The 185 was likely down to less than a hundred miles of avgas and Eagle Feather might not even get that far. The miserable bastard might get to spend the night in the bush too.

Thinking about the coming frigid night spurred the pilot into action. He stood up and began making his way through the spruce trees, heading in the general direction of the trapper's cabin. Fifteen minutes later he arrived at the bay the cabin was on — or so he thought. But there was no sign of it. He was seized by panic. Lost out here with nothing but the coat on his back, he was a dead man.

"No, I've just gone too far, that's all." Hearing his own voice eased his fears somewhat and he walked a few metres out onto the ice, keeping an eye to his left. Soon he was rewarded with a view of the camp, tucked in the bushes, a couple hundred metres back toward the point. He had, in fact, gone too far. Now he just prayed that he would find more than a snow-filled shell of an abandoned building when he got there.

The twelve by sixteen-foot log cabin stood in a small clearing, just twenty metres from the lakeshore. It wasn't in great shape, but at least it had a roof and was still standing.

There was just one opening — the doorway, and the door was not locked. It was cold as a grave inside. Colder actually. And it was dark, so he left the door open until his eyes adjusted enough to see a kerosene lantern sitting on a crude table on the left side of the room. Lighting the lamp was not an issue — Smith had learned to travel with a supply of waterproof matches when he first took up bush flying with Boyd. Relieved to hear the sloshing sound of a healthy supply of oil in the lamp, the camp was soon bathed in its soft yellow glow.

There was an ample supply of dry spruce and tamarack firewood outside, stacked high across the front and end walls of the cabin and he found dry kindling and scrap newsprint in a box behind the homemade wood stove.

As soon as he had a fire going, he began a quest for the trapper's emergency food supply. But he found nothing other than a jar of tea bags. No salt, no flour, no sugar — none of the basic staples — just the tea. That was a concern, but not yet alarming, because on the back wall was a gun rack, occupied by a lone shotgun.

It took him a few more minutes to find ammunition for the old gun. And then there were just three shells — number 2 shot — goose shot. Well, he'd have to make them count — if he could find anything to shoot at.

—

Near Onakawana

Eagle Feather's stolen ride was on its last legs. The fuel gauges on the Cessna both showed empty although the needles bobbed a bit whenever the movement of the aircraft sloshed the last gas in the tanks around the fuel sensors. But he wasn't worried. He had found the spot he was looking for and was making his final approach to a small lake that petered out into the black spruce forest just a few kilometres from the Ontario Northland Railroad.

Expecting to land in deep snow that could possibly flip the plane as the speed dropped, he gave it some additional throttle just as the skis kissed the snow. As a result, the aircraft did not begin to settle to the ice beneath until he was close to the tree-lined shore. Only then did he cut the power.

Like a floatplane landing on water, the skis continued planing briefly over the snowy surface, and then settled, the plane coming to a sudden stop against a spruce tree just inside the treeline. It wrecked the propeller and damaged the leading edge of one wing, but it did not flip. Not that the damage bothered him any — he wouldn't need it again as an aircraft. He would charter someone else to take him back to Sutton for his last bear skins at a time of his own choosing.

Before he had started his final approach, he disabled the Emergency Position Indicator Radio Beacon. With the EPIRB shut down, no alarms would go off. No one would come looking for the missing Cessna. And once he took care of a few details, no one would be able to spot it from the air.

CHAPTER 14

One thousand feet above the James Bay Lowlands

The southeastward flight of ODL progressed without incident. When he was about halfway home, Rob McNabb trimmed the Otter to fly on its own. There were no autopilot controls on the old bush plane, but as he had learned, with the elevators properly trimmed, it did pretty much fly itself. When he was satisfied that his flight was straight and level, he slipped out of his seat and went back to check on the pilot. The plane began a very gentle climb when his weight shifted back those couple of metres, but it wasn't significant, so he resumed checking on the patient.

Gord appeared to be asleep, but he was definitely still breathing and his heart still beating. Just as Rob was about to leave him, the pilot gave his hand a light, reassuring squeeze, and the hint of a nod with his head.

"I should have done this before, Gord," he yelled in the man's ear over the bellowing engine — there are no quiet corners in an Otter during flight. "Do you want a headset to cut down the noise? Squeeze once for yes, twice for no." One light squeeze brought results, and as he rigged the headset over the pilot's ears, he was caught by an inspiration.

He fitted the headset's remote intercom button into Clark's good hand just before returning to his place in the pilot's seat.

"Gord, we're about an hour out of Moose," he announced on the intercom. "When we get there, can you give me one and two click answers on the intercom if I describe my approach actions and control settings to you? Or do you feel up to it?"

Click.

"Thanks. If I don't hear from you, I'll assume you've drifted off to sleep and I'll carry on by myself. Don't worry, I won't circle endlessly, waiting for an answer."

Click.

Forty-five minutes later, McNabb radioed his location to Moosonee airport on the general aviation radio, indicating that he was approaching Moosonee airspace with a medical emergency aboard. The radio operator assured him that there was no conflicting air traffic. Then he called his office on the ministry VHF and got an immediate reply.

"ODL, Moosonee," James Bird's reassuring voice came back.

"Moose, ODL, where am I landing James, over?"

"Well, the wind's gone calm here Robbie, so a crosswind landing isn't an issue, but to shorten the ambulance ride, they've asked us to put you down on the winter road, out front of town. Approach from the northeast, heading upriver. The police will close off the road for you and you can taxi up close to the ambulance. They'll manage things from there.

"Oh, the Turbo Beaver pilot is here and advises that you remember to raise your skis. If you land on skis on the ice road, the idling engine alone has enough power to keep you sliding forward until you run into something. You'll need to use your wheel brakes … lightly. Over."

"All roger, James. I can see the flashing lights on the river from here. ODL, out." And to Gord Clark on the intercom he asked, "You still with me Gord?"

He was answered by silence. Then came the 'Click'.

Down on the river in front of Moosonee he could see a two kilometre straight stretch of ice road blocked off by the police. Describing each new setting he made to the throttle, propeller speed and flaps, McNabb continued to receive reassuring single click confirmations from Gord Clark. The student pilot's approach in the calm afternoon air was as smooth as silk.

However, just as he passed over the police car at the near end of his temporary runway, the replies from Clark stopped.

"Oh, shit, don't die on me now Gord," he mumbled. And after only a brief moment of hesitation, he resumed easing back the control column ever so lightly, continuing to slow his descent rate and airspeed.

He took a deep breath and said to himself, "Alright, you can do this. The plane will fly itself. Just tell it when to stop. It's just like a Cessna trainer, only not as twitchy."

With those reassuring words, he put his full attention to getting the big bird down safely. He used only small corrections on the controls, mentally urging the plane down toward the frozen road surface — he'd used up almost half his runway already and the big bird just wanted to keep on flying. The cluster of emergency vehicles ahead was getting closer by the second.

Suddenly, the Otter stopped flying. It dropped to the ice, those last few inches. He'd just made the best landing ever in his short flying career. Flushed with relief and grinning ear to ear, he raised the flaps and lightly touched the brakes to get the feel for their effect on the ice surface.

Gradually bleeding off speed by just coasting, Rob didn't use the brakes again for any serious action most of the way to the end of the emergency runway. As he taxied to within the last hundred metres of the waiting ambulance, two things happened. The first was a final 'click' from Gord. The second was a rather abrupt instruction, given over the radio.

"Don't shut it down. Set the parking brakes if you know how, and *I'll* take it to the airport." He knew that he wasn't going to be able to keep the lovely old Otter to call his own, but it was more than a bit deflating to have a woman's voice treating him like an uninvited interloper.

However, he did as the voice instructed and as he turned to watch the paramedics prepare Gord Clark for transport, a little redhead pushed past the sick pilot and stood expectantly at the entrance to the cockpit.

"I've got it," she snapped.

Dumbstruck, McNabb shuffled out of the way. The sharp-tongued redhead took possession of the pilot's seat and started checking over everything in the cockpit as if she was counting all the things he had broken. He turned his attention to the stretcher while the attendants strapped Clark in place.

"How's he doing?" he asked the paramedics.

"Well, you got him here alive, and in these parts your three-hour delivery is about as close to the 'golden hour' as anyone could ever hope for," one of them replied. "And hey, I'm no pilot, but that looked like one real smooth landing you made. Nice job."

"Thanks," he smiled. "I'm not a pilot yet either. The plane did all the hard work." The ambulance driver's compliment took at least some of the sting out of the Beaver pilot's cold attitude. He followed the stretcher-bearers out onto the ice road.

His knees felt weak and he was upset by the redhead's gruff manner, but he was still proud of what he'd just accomplished.

CHAPTER 15

Moosonee

As soon as he saw Clark safely loaded into the waiting ambulance, McNabb turned to face a crowd of cheering onlookers standing on the other side of the snowplowed bank. It seemed as though most of the three thousand citizens of Moosonee had turned out to watch. His boss was standing with the provincial police staff sergeant. He started over to meet them, looking back briefly as the Otter throttled up and pivoted on one wheel to face the direction it had just come from. After taking a moment for pre-takeoff checks, the plane thundered off downriver to make the two-minute flight to the airport.

"Hey Robbie," Bird greeted him with a reassuring pat on his shoulder. "That was a great landing. Half the town's got aviation radio monitors, and after you called in, the word sure spread fast. You've really impressed everyone today … well, almost everyone," he said, looking at the departing Otter. "I'll explain about her later, but first, Staff Sergeant Ballard wants a full debriefing on what happened up at Sutton Lake."

When he first arrived in Moosonee, McNabb had

been introduced to George Ballard. Six-foot-three and built like a football linebacker, the undisputed leader of the Moosonee detachment had in turn introduced the young CO to all of his staff and assured him that if he ever needed a police presence at any time, all he had to do was ask. As big as he was, Ballard spoke with a quiet voice.

Since that first meeting, they'd already had a couple of brief working sessions to set up joint snowmobile patrols with his people. At least there had been a little money left in the CO's budget for local patrols. A good working relationship with the police force was already well established.

"I've got some takeout pizza coming to the detachment," Ballard said. "If you guys want to follow me over, we can do the debriefing in the quiet of our conference room."

—

Ten minutes later, after downloading the day's pictures off McNabb's camera, they gathered in the comfort of the detachment office around a fully loaded, deluxe pizza. After taking a few eager bites, McNabb began to describe, in detail, the events of his long, challenging day. Referring to his notes, he went through everything from the time he arrived at the site of his observation blind, forty minutes before dawn, until the Cessna 185 took off.

As Rob detailed what he had done with the rifle at the scene of the murder, the staff sergeant nodded, clearly pleased with the young officer's practical solution to his dilemma.

Then, he went on to describe his race back to the Hawley Lake camp, and his hurried departure for home.

"Well, here's where it stands to this moment as far as the search for the Cessna goes," James Bird said, after McNabb was done.

"We put both Turbo Beavers up as soon as you called in. The Hearst plane immediately began a wide east-west sweep. The Beaver from here raced south and began an overlapping circuit between Cochrane and Kapuskasing. Each plane had two ministry observers aboard, along with the pilot — all seasoned wildlife survey observers, used to spotting hard-to-see objects from Turbo Beavers.

"They saw nothing while they were up. They were joined by the police Beaver out of Timmins. The Moosonee plane spelled off the Hearst bird long enough for it to refuel and continue patrolling until dark. They just got in twenty minutes ahead of you.

"Of course, not seeing the bear runners' plane doesn't necessarily mean they are gone. True, they could have slipped out the side of our search area, but it's more likely that they've landed at a private cache of fuel, or a camp somewhere along their route; good chance they're still in our area. So to cover that possibility, we're resuming flights with all three Beavers before daybreak. This time, we'll have one of our observers and a member of the police in each plane. Your turn George."

"From a police perspective, Rob, it's really important that we find these guys," the staff sergeant began. "While solving the murder is our primary concern, they may be up to more shenanigans than just wildlife offences; drugs being the most likely sideline. Anyone going to the expense of doing unlawful business with an aircraft will often pick up jobs wherever they can, anything to improve their profit margin.

"Anyhow, we checked the federal database and could

find no Canadian aircraft with the registration C-GFKU. A quick call to the Feds confirmed that nothing by those letters has been recently added. What they get, automatically goes into the online registry in real time. What we see is what they've got. But seeing this picture you took, there's no doubt that you read it correctly. Whoever they are, they are obviously well-organized, although as you pointed out, it does seem odd that they would kill off their local supplier.

"As soon as your report came in, we sent out word to get police units to every airport and landing strip from here down to Sudbury, but no plane matching your description has shown up. And considering the thousands of lakes they could land on, we may never find them."

"I wonder," McNabb broke in, "if they might have printed a false registration on white plastic protective film. You know, it's the stuff they put on new vehicles to protect the paint finish while they are being transported. As I think back, the top of the wing near the registration was a slightly different shade of white than the rest of the plane.

"Look, it's even different here in the picture. It didn't mean anything to me at the time, but if there is no such registration, maybe they plan to peel the film off and continue on under another identity."

"That's a feasible explanation," the staff sergeant agreed. "Good thinking Rob. I've got one of my detectives trying to track their movements through fuel purchases. I'll have her look into hangar rentals at the same time. I think they'd need a warm environment to put that stuff on, and I'd bet they waited until they got the plane into the country before applying the stuff."

Finally, as their discussion came to a close, the staff sergeant looked carefully at McNabb. "Are you going to be alright? Not everyone gets to see a murder victim so early in his career, let alone respond to a medical emergency. I've got a critical incident support team leader right here in the detachment you can have a chat with if you'd like."

"Actually, I've already got one of our counsellors coming up from region to meet with him tomorrow," James Bird interceded. "He doesn't get any choice in the matter, but thanks for the offer, George."

As James Bird and Rob McNabb left the detachment together, Bird asked, "Robbie, are you still planning to go curling tonight, or would you rather take a pass it on this week?"

"All I want right now James, is a brisk walk home, a hot shower, a cold rum and a warm bed, all in that order. The team will have to get along without me tonight. And I will keep it to one rum … well … maybe a second one won't hurt. See you in the morning."

Bird paused, watching his young CO start off down the street. As he climbed into the ministry Suburban for the drive home, he wondered if any long-term effects would come back to bother the young man.

CHAPTER 16

Near Onakawana

It was dark by the time Eagle Feather had finished the next phase of his plan. Within minutes of landing he had spread a large, white plastic tarpaulin over the Cessna. It was tied off to the spruce trees around it. Additional ropes, all white, were tied over top of the tarp to prevent it from flapping in the wind and beating itself to shreds. The camouflaged aircraft would serve nicely as a storage unit for the time being. And the first decent breeze to come along would cover the 185's ski tracks with drifting snow, keeping its location a secret from prying eyes above.

After finishing up at the plane, he snowshoed about halfway to the ONR railroad tracks which passed three kilometres east of where he'd landed. When he found a good spot, he set up a six-by-ten foot white canvas tent in a tiny clearing he cut in the midst of a thick stand of black spruce. He had made the tent himself back at camp the year before and had camped in it during his polar bear hunts up in the park. Sewing was not his forté, but even its stovepipe thimble, stitched into the back wall, looked like a professional modification.

When he returned from town with his pre-ordered lightweight airtight stove in a few days, this would be a perfectly comfortable temporary home, until spring if need be. But he wasn't planning on being here nearly that long.

All of the supplies for this new venture had been hidden in the commercial fur shipping bags that he'd loaded into the Cessna that morning. Everything had been carefully wrapped inside the bear hides. The bags containing items that were difficult to conceal due to their weight, he had carried and loaded himself. That was why the load had been so heavy. And while they were loading, he had also asked Boyd to take one of his hunting rifles on the plane and deliver it to a gunsmith for repair. The rifle was now lying beside him in the tent. It was in perfectly good condition — had been all along.

When they were loading the plane, Boyd had been so impressed with the size of some of the bags that his greed had overcome his caution. His most intense scrutiny of Eagle Feather's catch was reserved for the five remaining bears, still drying in the shed — bears he was told he'd be picking up in another five or six weeks. All he had been able to think of was the financial return he would get on such large bears. They would be a real boost to his bottom line — and he never thought to doubt the honesty of his supplier. After all, last winter, Eagle Feather had taken great care to deliver, as promised, all of his hides in excellent condition. There had been no reason for Boyd to suspect a change in the routine, even with their running disagreement over what he was paying him. After all, most of his suppliers were on his case about not being paid enough.

After eating a quick meal of freeze-dried stroganoff heated over a tiny portable stove, Eagle Feather rolled out his down-filled sleeping bag on the tent floor and climbed in for the night. His day had gone pretty much to plan.

Admittedly, the pilot had almost screwed things up for him when the dispatch of B.J. Boyd had gone badly. He was originally going to quietly knife the buyer, commando style, and drag him behind the cabin for the wolves, ravens and other critters to dine on. Unfortunately, Boyd had suddenly become suspicious at the very moment of the payoff and had grabbed Eagle Feather's camp rifle. The struggle had ended as only it could — Boyd, despite his equal size and strength, was no match for the ex-soldier's Special Forces training. But the rifle shot that had redecorated the cabin, had spooked the pilot, and it was only Eagle Feather's speed down the snowy path that allowed him to get to the plane before Smith got away.

He could have stopped the pilot right then and there — not harmfully of course, because he had still needed the man to locate the fuel caches. But on the spur of the moment he had decided to take advantage of the momentum of the situation to get the show under way. Not necessarily the best decision he'd ever made, but hindsight was, as they say, 20-20. Anyhow, he was now rid of both men, and for the second one, he didn't even have to do the deed himself — not that it would have bothered him to do so.

What pissed him off most about his hasty departure was having left without his computer. Although everything stored on it was password protected and backed up on the 'cloud,' he was uncomfortable with the fact that one day someone would probably find it. And in the hands of the experts, his secrets could eventually be discovered.

Of lesser concern were the five bear skins and some foxes and wolves still drying in his shed. He was disappointed that he'd not been able to bring them all along, but the 185 had been overloaded as it was. But with his drying shed intentionally located across the lake from the camp, he was confident it would remain undiscovered until his return.

So, tomorrow was the first day of his newly minted fur export business. It would just take a trip out to civilization — already in the works — and there, with a replacement laptop, he'd be able to contact his clients and set up the final details. Then he could start moving his merchandise. Thanks to his Internet connection back at the camp, he already had customers in Asia eagerly waiting — and now there was no middleman to bleed off his profits. But for tonight he would sleep soundly. There wasn't even a need to rise early. The next southbound train wouldn't be going through until early the next evening.

CHAPTER 17

Tuesday, January 31 — Moosonee

It was another snappy cold morning. Although it was nowhere near record breaking, the temperature was hovering at -35°C and the snow squeaked under McNabb's boots as he walked to the office. He'd brought his pickup truck in on the winter road to Moosonee the first weekend after the road had opened for the season, but it was pointless to start it in such cold temperatures just for the one-minute drive to work. In fact, he almost always walked around town when he was on his own time.

It wasn't quite eight o'clock yet and District Manager Archie Foulton and a few other staff members were leaning on the front counter, finishing up their coffee before the office opened for business. All avid hockey fans, they were in the midst of discussing the latest Toronto Maple Leafs' loss when McNabb entered the foyer. Suddenly he became the centre of attention, leaving the poor old Leafs to lick their wounds on their own.

"Aye, that was a great landing you made there yesterday Rab," exclaimed the DM in a Scottish accent that was as thick as the day he'd left the old country over forty years ago. The rest of the gathered staff added their compliments to his. "We closed the office a wee bit early so we could go down to watch your arrival." Foulton was a rotund man in his early sixties. Though he stood only five-foot seven, no one ever thought of him as being short. His vivacious manner and booming voice more than made up for his shortfall in inches.

"Good morning, Archie … everyone. A spectator sport now, am I?" McNabb asked, not entirely certain whether that was a good thing or not, but he quickly realized that a smile had been plastered on his own face all along. So maybe it was a good thing he'd been the object of the entire community's attention. Maybe it meant his co-workers were accepting the new boy as one of their own.

"Oh, Rob," Marion, the young Cree receptionist got up from her desk waving a pink phone message slip at him. "This was on the main voicemail this morning. The caller wasn't happy the system wouldn't let him leave a message directly in your box." She was a really pretty girl with a perpetually enchanting smile. McNabb would have easily considered vying for her attentions but she was already married.

"Thanks Marion," he returned her smile, taking the slip as he passed.

By the time he'd walked to his office, he had already read the message. His heart sank and he dreaded making the return call. It was from the Weeneebayko General Hospital, just across the river in Moose Factory. 'Poor old Clark mustn't have made it,' he thought, 'or worse, he's paralyzed and bedridden for life.' With a leaden weight in his gut, McNabb punched in the hospital number and asked for the extension.

"Yes?" The voice sounded a little hollow, distracted

even. Probably a sleep-deprived doctor trying to do up his notes before heading off for his first nap in thirty-six hours, he thought.

"Hello, I'm calling about a patient who was brought in yesterday afternoon by ambulance, suffering from a possible stroke. Name of Gordon Clark."

"Oh … him," came back, hesitantly. McNabb prepared himself for the bad news. "Well, let's see now."

At that moment he could hear a chuckle build up to a hearty laugh. "You saved my life Robbie, and I've got to thank you in person. Can you come over to the island this morning? I'm in Room 214. They're not letting me out for another day or two and I'm going up the walls in here. Oh, and bring your flight log with you too, okay?"

Twenty minutes later McNabb entered Room 214 at the hospital. Sitting up in the bed, Clark bore little resemblance to the frail old man he'd carried out to the Otter less than twenty-four hours earlier. In fact, he was looking positively radiant.

"Hey, here's the man of the hour! God am I glad you had the balls to do what you did, getting me out of there yesterday Robbie. The Doc said it wasn't a really bad stroke, but if I'd had to wait for an air ambulance to find me up there and fetch me back, the outcome wouldn't have been nearly so good. Oh, this is my wife, Charlotte. Lottie, meet our hero pilot, Robbie McNabb."

A tall, attractive silver-haired woman in her sixties stepped around the bed and gave McNabb a generous hug. "Thanks for saving my Gord's life, Rob. We've still got way too many things to do on our bucket list for me to lose him now. I just hope they don't give you too much trouble over flying the plane without a licence."

"Oh, don't worry about that," Clark broke in. "There

will be a week-long shit storm over the matter and then they'll move onto something else.

"Anyhow, the outfit actually sent the King Air executive plane from Toronto, just to fly Lottie up here from Timmins during the night. Sometimes the government does manage to show a streak of compassion. But now my flying days are over for good I'm afraid. Events like that don't go unnoticed.

"So I wanted to see your logbook in case we don't happen to meet again. As soon as the docs say I can drive, we're trailering to the Grand Canyon and the rest of that beautiful region of the southwestern States."

And with that, the retired pilot flipped through the first two pages of the young officer's flight log. Those were the only pages that contained any entries so far.

"You might be the first person ever to have done his first solo flight in a de Havilland Otter. And the Feds can try to disagree with me if they want, but I was conscious for enough of that flight, including that sweet landing you made, to know you aced it. So we are entering your flight — you got the times? It'll be a permanent record in your book, and I'm signing off on it, for you."

"Well I sure feel honoured Gord, and aside from the urgency of the flight, I have to admit I just loved the way that old bird flies. What a rush!" McNabb briefly relived the moment of his perfect landing. "That is, until some woman pilot came aboard as soon as we were down and treated me like a kindergartener who'd peed his pants."

"Oh, her," Clark laughed. "Don't worry, she'll get over it. Cute eh?"

"Yeah, like a wicked wildcat." McNabb felt a sudden flash of anger, thinking back on that humiliating moment.

CHAPTER 18

Back at the office, the rest of McNabb's day was taken up with a series of administrative duties, all spawned by his activities of the previous day. It started with a ninety-minute session with one of the ministry's critical incident counsellors. Those were the folks who told you that you had experienced a traumatic event, but you shouldn't worry if it bothers you afterward.

The rest of the day was occupied writing up one report on the flight of the polar bear runners for Enforcement Branch, and another for the air service, explaining why he had flown their airplane with only eighteen hours in his student pilot's logbook. The wildcat wasn't the only one in that branch whose nose was out of joint.

"Don't worry about it Robbie," James Bird reassured him. "Yesterday's events didn't fit their model as to how things are done, so you write a report, and I'll write a covering report, and Clark's doctor will write a page for me to staple to our reports, and the district manager will write another page to attach to them and the regional director will do the same after him.

"By the time it hits the deputy minister's desk, all hell

will have broken loose in another far-flung corner of the province and this will all be forgotten — except by those of us who appreciate working with guys who know when to grab the bull by the horns. You did great yesterday and I'm sure glad we chose to hire the southern rookie that hardly anyone knew."

In fact, when the district had been notified that they could only fill one of their two vacancies, Bird had gone out on a limb when he'd chosen McNabb. Both applicants had done extremely well in their interviews. Their final scores were identical and Jack Colbrook, the officer not chosen, actually had five more years of law enforcement experience than Rob. As a pair, Bird was confident that the two new officers would have bonded and worked well together. And he really did want to hire them both. But allowed to choose only one, a minor mechanical problem that occurred when James had picked them up at the airport that day had led him to lean in favour of the rookie.

It was McNabb's immediate diagnosis when the Suburban wouldn't start that clinched it for him. The apparently dead battery was not dead at all. McNabb had simply lifted the hood and wiggled a corroded battery connector and the SUV started without a problem.

It wasn't a major automotive repair he'd performed, but he had tipped the scales by showing his mechanical aptitude — a real asset for someone working in that remote region. Colbrook, on the other hand, had simply asked if there was a CAA agency in Moosonee.

Archie Foulton had argued strongly in favour of taking the more experienced applicant, but reluctantly deferred to Bird, saying, "Well, he's your employee, James. But I want the other one called up as soon as the budget freeze is lifted." And James had agreed.

—

Just before five, Bird returned from a meeting with the police.

"Here's where things stand at the moment Robbie. Staff Sergeant says their CSI team got up to Sutton Lake late this morning. Gabby skidooed over to help them with logistics — and promptly advised them that the body is not the man he knows as Eagle Feather. And no, you are not being blamed for assuming it was. None of us had a good description of him and given the circumstances, any of us probably would have called it the way you did.

"The police team will be bunking in at our camp on Hawley Lake tonight, and tomorrow they want you to join the search of the poacher's camp for evidence that might help our case — as well as theirs. Today they are doing all the forensics related to the body.

"Since you've been tied up all day, I jumped through hoops for you and got the Justice of the Peace to issue a search warrant for this Eagle Feather's place. It's probably a bit of overkill in the case of an illegal camp, but some judges can be picky about little details like that."

"Thanks boss. I would have had to scramble to get one issued this late in the day."

"So tomorrow morning I need you to drive over to the pilots' staff house and pick up Sam Williams. The two of you are going to go back north to start looking for a ski plane or ski plane tracks on every landable lake between Sutton Lake and Highway 11.

"Take your overnight kit and survival gear and sign out a 30-06 from the gun locker. I want you on your toes out there, but if you catch sight of those guys, you fall back until the police join you. Understand?"

McNabb nodded his agreement before his supervisor continued.

"The police want the Turbo Beavers to expand their search to the south, so you'll be using the Otter. I hope you don't mind. Slow as molasses, but a good stable platform for observation."

"I think I can put up with a few more hours in the old bird before they mothball her again."

"Okay, I've got grub organized for you two for four days, plus Ski-Doo gas and a few extra things Gabby wanted sent up. It's all in the Suburban out in the garage."

—

Near Onakawana

Late in the afternoon Eagle Feather set off on his snowshoes. Using his GPS, he made the one-and-a-half-kilometre hike to Onakawana, a railway section house on the ONR. When he came to the winter road on the way, he took off his snowshoes and wallowed across the cleared right-of-way on foot. He took care to go through the deep snow making a random zigzag path, such as a moose might make. He didn't want to leave an obvious snowshoe trail leading back to his camp. Anyone looking closely at his trail beside the road would know it was man-made, but it was far less likely to attract attention than the distinctive tracks that snowshoes leave.

He arrived at the old section house fifteen minutes before train time, and the train arrived only five minutes later than that. He flagged it down and was soon on his way to Cochrane in a half-empty coach. Not wanting to draw any attention to himself he chose the seat farthest from other passengers and immediately slouched down, pretending to sleep.

It was 10:15 p.m. when the train pulled into Cochrane. Stepping down onto the platform, he made his way directly to the Station Inn. Despite his rough appearance and insistence on paying cash, the desk clerk had him quickly booked in — many of the forestry workers and diamond drill gangs came in looking even tougher than Eagle Feather, so his anonymity remained intact. Next step, complete.

CHAPTER 19

Wednesday, February 1 — Moosonee

It was five minutes before eight o'clock in the morning. The sun was rising over the Moose River and a thin fog of ice crystals hung over the landscape. The air was still and the temperature was -39°C as McNabb wrenched open the stiff garage doors behind the office. The snow squeaked under the Suburban's tires as he backed out into the yard. After slipping into the office to sign out a rifle and ammunition, he returned to the SUV and headed over to the pilots' staff house on Wabun Road.

Without knocking — nobody ever knocked at a staff house door — he entered the front hall of the residence. It was a double-wide bungalow just like McNabb's. But unlike the modern laminated hardwood flooring at his place, this house still had 1970s orange and brown shag carpet throughout that was well past its 'best before' date.

Not wanting to remove his boots, he stood in the front hall and called out for pilot Sam Williams. Rustling sounds of someone carrying a big load down the hallway from the bedrooms culminated with the appearance of the pilot in the common room.

"You ready to go?" she asked.

McNabb stood there, his jaw agape. He was looking at the same red-headed wildcat who had confronted him a day and a half earlier in the Otter.

Samantha Williams knew that the ball was in her court. She had been more than a little rough on the guy when he landed the other afternoon.

"Um, can we maybe … start over again? Hi, I'm Sam Williams, and I shouldn't have brought my own bad day on board the Otter with me and thrown it in your face. I understand you had a truly shitty day of your own to deal with. I'm really sorry I treated you the way I did. And that was a beautiful landing you made with that plane."

"Hi Sam," he finally managed to get his lower jaw winched back up into its proper position. And it was then that he realized that in all the uproar of the last couple of days, no one had thought to introduce him to the lady or even tell him her name. Nor had James ever explained her attitude issues as he had promised he would.

"As you may have guessed, I'm Rob McNabb, though folks around here have taken to calling me Robbie," he started politely. "And yes, that day presented me with more challenges than I ever believed it was possible to face in a single five-hour period. And yes, I'd very much like it if we could start over again.

"I'm learning really quickly that if you're going to be working together with someone in this part of the world, you have to be totally committed to working as a team."

It slowly dawned on him that he was still shaking the hand she'd extended while making her apology. It was the small hand of a small woman, but it maintained its firm grip until he relinquished his own. And with his acceptance of her apology, a heart-stirring smile came to the young woman's face. She wore no makeup, and a light sprinkling of freckles on her cheeks and nose gave her a girlish look. Sparkling green eyes completed the picture.

Under her open parka Williams wore a bright blue flight suit — basically, insulated coveralls with Ontario Provincial Air Service shoulder flashes and lots of pockets. And although the outfit didn't do anything to enhance her modest five-foot-four-inch figure, the curly red hair, cut just above her shoulders, made her look — well to McNabb, she was *really* cute. His sister would lop off his head for calling a woman cute — cute was for little children she would argue — but it was the best description he could come up with.

"Got all your gear? We've got a few long days ahead of us," he said as he reluctantly brought himself back to earth, and the job at hand.

Sam had already shouldered her big backpack and picked up her pilot's flight case, but she nodded at the 5-Star sleeping bag on the floor just behind McNabb and he turned and picked it up as he headed out the door.

CHAPTER 20

"So, I think everyone in town knows about *my* day, the other day," McNabb said as he drove toward the airport. "Care to enlighten me on how yours got such a failing grade?"

"Well, I'm afraid if I tell you, you'll be really pissed off at what, in reality, was pretty trivial compared to what you had to deal with," Sam replied, looking cautiously in his direction. She most particularly didn't want to get into telling him how she had been disappointed that they'd picked him for the CO position over Jack Colbrook. She'd met Jack late last summer at a moose survey training seminar in North Bay. They'd struck up a casual relationship and when she learned he had applied to work in Moosonee, she'd been privately rooting for him. Now the guy was still down in Cornwall, patrolling the far eastern corner of the province. They'd kept in touch, but it was kind of tough nurturing a relationship at that distance.

McNabb shrugged his shoulders. "Well, maybe … maybe not. But if there's something I did that got you riled up, I'd sure like to try to put things right."

"Well, it's got several parts to it I guess," she began. "It wasn't just one day's worth, and no, none of it was your fault. The first part that set my day off on the wrong foot …

actually got a whole weekend screwed up … was that I had to cancel a trip to Montreal to my best friend's wedding because of this sudden polar bear flap. I had purposely asked her not to include me in her wedding party because things like this *can* happen, but nothing like it was on the horizon and I was really looking forward to going.

"So then the airline says I can't get my money back because I cancelled less than twenty-four hours before my flight and it wasn't a medical or family emergency. The fact that I was a government pilot recalled on an urgent work-related crisis cut no ice with them at all.

"That *really* pissed me off. They've always got people on standby because of all the flights they overbook, so what's the big deal refunding one overpriced ticket when there's probably a whole lineup of anxious people just waiting to buy my seat?"

"I think the outfit will cover your lost airfare for something like that, Sam," McNabb suggested.

"My supervisor said that too, thanks. And he's already started a paper storm over it with the accounts people.

"So anyhow, I flew the Turbo Beaver up here and went into 'hurry up and wait' mode along with everyone else. The weekend went by with nothing happening — when I could have been at Sheila's wedding. Then, when things finally did start to happen, we took off and did our patrol and saw no sign of the plane we were supposed to find and follow.

"And then there's also an ancient history part to this sob story. See, I started working on my commercial licence right after high school. Worked a bunch of crappy retail jobs, often two at a time, just to buy the flying hours I needed for my ticket; then I busted my butt doing short-term gigs with a bunch of cheap-assed, seat-of-the-pants fly-in outfitters, and eventually pulled some longer contracts with the air service. But it took six years to finally get a full-time position. I started this job the same month you came up here.

"And finally, no offence, but it just hit me wrong that a guy with less than twenty hours total flying time would be doing his first solo flight in a plane I had been dreaming to fly my whole adult life and just got qualified on last year."

They were approaching the parked Otter at the Moosonee airport just as McNabb began his response. "Hey, I can see how that would cheese you off, especially the part about the lout without any flying experience," he said, an easy grin spreading over his face. "I mean, *I* felt upset by the fact that someone would just come aboard and take over what had been *my* plane for the last three hours — even though I had absolutely no right to be flying it." He summed up the discussion with the grand proclamation: "So let's load up *OUR* old Otter and go hunting for bad guys!"

"Let's do that," she returned the grin as she exited the Suburban. 'The kid isn't bad — likeable even,' she thought to herself. 'His self-deprecating manner is so disarming.' She would have to stow her disappointment over who they chose for the job. 'Looks like he could be fun to work with,' she told herself. It wasn't the end of the world. After all, she'd be seeing Jack when he came up to Timmins at the end of May. They had a pair of tickets to see Shania Twain perform at the McIntyre Arena that weekend.

It took twenty minutes to load the plane to Samantha's satisfaction. As fast as McNabb could heave the heavy gasoline jugs and boxes of groceries up through the door, Sam had them stowed and tied down. Her strength and endurance were obviously not limited by her small stature.

Fifteen minutes more saw the engine tent and heaters removed, the pre-flight walk-around completed and the engine fired up and running.

"Moosonee radio its Oscar Delta Lima, ready for departure for Hawley Lake. Please advise any traffic, over," Sam Williams spoke confidently into her headset boom mic as she taxied the big bush plane across the airport parking apron.

"ODL, Moose, no traffic to report, wind calm, altimeter three zero point one two inches and Air Creebec advises other than this local ice fog, conditions are CAVU all the way north. Use runway three-two and you are clear to take off when ready, over."

Small northern airports with relatively few arriving and departing aircraft don't necessarily have a full time radio operator. In fact, it was the clerk at the commercial airline's ticket counter who replied to Sam's call. But he gave her the information she needed, including the ceiling and visibility being unlimited all the way north. That would make for easy eyeball navigation on their first day out.

The plan was to fly to Hawley Lake where they would offload supplies for the camp and for Gabby's wife. From there, Sam would fly to Peawanuck to take on a maximum load of avgas while McNabb headed up the lake to join the police at Eagle Feather's camp on Sutton Lake. Later, they'd meet back at the ministry camp and determine if there was sufficient time to begin their search or not.

—

Cochrane

Eagle Feather took his time over a hearty breakfast at the Station Inn Restaurant — it was a real treat to have food cooked by someone else for a change. Afterward, he checked out and headed on foot to an address on 5th Avenue. He'd already replied to the guy's used truck ad online and they had tentatively agreed on a cash deal price, assuming the truck was in the condition that the owner claimed it was. When he arrived at the house, the truck, a late 1990s extended cab Chevy, was sitting in the driveway buried under a month's worth of snow. The owner was at work at the plywood mill but his wife was home and she let Eagle Feather have the keys so he could start it up.

After clearing off the worst of the snow, he popped the hood. Things looked clean — or as clean as they could look in a truck of that age. More importantly, there was no sign of fluid leakage from any of the major components. The oil was clean, the engine started right away and it sounded really good.

Without rolling any more than a few feet down the driveway he could feel the transmission firmly engage both forward and reverse. At the same time, the brakes held the truck in place and the brake pedal remained firm and didn't sag. In fact for a Chevy of that age he was pretty impressed by its overall condition, so he handed the woman twelve hundred dollars in cash and she came out to move her van to let him onto the street.

He was rolling down the road toward Timmins before eleven. The owner had not thought to remove his licence plates from the truck and that suited the poacher just fine. He'd change plates later on — but only if it became necessary.

CHAPTER 21

One thousand feet above the James Bay Lowlands

The flight north to Hawley Lake could have been boring, had it not been for the lively conversation between the pilot and the conservation officer. As they kept scanning the landscape below them for any sign of the missing Cessna, they learned among other things that they'd been born just three days apart — she being the elder — in neighbouring towns. Samantha came from Georgetown where her dad was a senior constable with the police department and her mom was a high school teacher. They were divorced, but in that post-marital state they got along far better than they had during the last five years of their rocky marriage.

In Brampton, less than ten kilometres away, Rob's mother was now the director of nursing at the hospital and his dad ran a busy small-engine repair shop in their backyard. Sam and Rob each had a sister. Sam's was younger by three years and Rob's two years older, and each sister had a child — both boys. And as they talked, the similarities in their lives just kept piling up.

"So what got you interested in flying, Rob?"

"Well, I probably shouldn't tell this to a government

pilot, but back when I was in grade nine my dad rebuilt the engine for an old farmer friend's little Taylorcraft. I don't know when the last time was that the plane had a valid Certificate of Airworthiness, but the guy took really good care of that little cloth moth and my dad said the engine in it was just like an air-cooled VW engine … in that it was a cinch to rebuild."

"So, stretching the limits of the Aeronautics Act runs in your family then, does it?"

"Jeez Sam, please don't remind me. I don't think the air service will ever forgive me for flying this old bird.

"So anyhow, where was I? Oh yeah, Dad had me come along to help reinstall the engine, the uncertified engine that is, and the farmer took the plane up for a test flight. When the guy lands he taxies up to where we are standing and asks Dad if he wants to go up for a ride. Dad says no, he even gets airsick on a Ferris wheel but he says I can go if I want.

"Well, I wanted and I went. What a cool experience. I just loved it and would have gone off and started taking lessons that afternoon but my summer jobs didn't pay well enough and saving for college took all my income. So I didn't get my start until after my last contract expired. How about you Sam?"

"The lady next door to my grandparents' cottage on Georgian Bay was a bank bigwig in Toronto, and to get past the weekend traffic she bought a Cessna 185 on amphibious floats. Unless the weather was going to be bad, she commuted from the city up to the cottage by plane on weekends.

"One day when I was fourteen, she had just landed at her dock and was about to tie up, when a sudden gust of wind caught the plane. It snatched the dock lines right out of her hands and began to drift away. She was left watching the plane heading for the rocks by Grandpa's dock, so I jumped into the water and held it off. Fortunately it was just a short-lived gust, because even then it was all I could do to keep it off the rocks until she jumped in to help me.

"Instead of tying it up after we got it back to the dock, she offered to take me up, with both of us still soaked to the skin. Grandpa, who had just arrived to help said he thought that would be okay as long as I didn't catch pneumonia, so up we went. I was hooked. It was she who later encouraged me to go beyond my private licence. And the rest is history as they say."

So many commonalities made for an easy back and forth conversation between them as the Otter slowly thundered its way northwest. In fact, McNabb was quite relieved at how easily he could carry his end of the conversation. As a child he had played easily enough with his sister and the other girls on his street, but then puberty struck and ruined everything.

From the time his hormones began their teenaged rampage, he always found himself tongue-tied the moment he tried to talk to a girl he felt attracted to. His awkwardness with girls had followed him all the way through his high school years and into adult life. So it was an immense relief to finally find a woman he could converse with and not freeze up, or trip over his tongue at every turn of the conversation. Especially considering how strongly attracted he was already becoming to Sam.

Still, there were some gaps in his newfound comfort level, the most significant being his lack of understanding of some of the finer points of this particular woman's sense of humour — even though he had grown up in the shadow of an older sister who'd teased him ruthlessly.

As a result, he learned through firsthand experience that Samantha Williams was quick with a play on words and was having fun repeatedly pulling his leg. At one stage, when she'd just finished a radio call to the Moosonee office reporting their position over Attawapiskat, she was watching the instrument panel and adjusting the gyrocompass setting. At the same time, she pointed in the general direction of his lap. Over the intercom came her question, "So if we have some spare time at the camp, are you going to show me how to use that thing Robbie?"

His mouth moved wordlessly, and he flushed pink to the ears.

"Y'know, my dad showed my mom how to use his when *they* were dating," she added, straight-faced.

Now McNabb was totally tongue-tied and his face turned beet red. As delighted as he was with the suggestive nature of her comments, he was feeling awkward about things developing so rapidly.

"He's got a Glock 9 millimetre. What's yours?" she asked.

"Aw Sam," he realized he'd just had his leg pulled again, but managed to fire off a quick comeback this time. "I'm sorry but I don't show anyone my Heckler & Koch .40 on a first date." They both laughed and then the pilot finished the topic on a more serious note.

"I really would like to shoot your sidearm sometime, but more importantly, I need you to show me how to use the rifle you brought. It isn't something they teach in flight school, but seeing as you keep bumping into these serious conflicts with Murphy's Law, I think it's something I should become familiar with."

"Yeah, I agree, and if there is still some daylight left after we get all our other stuff done today, then maybe we'll set up some kind of target near the camp," McNabb said.

They both fell silent for a time. The thundering of the big radial engine comfortably filled the gap in the conversation.

The plane's throaty roar slid to the back of McNabb's mind and he began to wonder if Sam's request to 'show me how to use that thing' might have meant that she was interested in other more personal things. And then he immediately chastised himself for letting his imagination get so far ahead of the situation. 'She's just ribbing me,' he scolded. 'After all, we've only just met.'

Furthermore, even though Sam might get to fly in his patrol area on occasion, they were each headquartered hundreds of kilometres apart. It was too much to expect to be able to carry on a long-distance relationship like that with anyone. And with this goddess, he realized he'd probably never stand a chance. Guys in Timmins were likely lined up ten deep waiting to get a date with her if she wasn't already spoken for.

CHAPTER 22

Sam Williams busied herself with the intricacies of running the big bush plane. Like McNabb, she found it a real pleasure to fly despite its slow progress across the sky. She was strongly committed to her hard-won career in a field traditionally dominated by men and she found herself alternately running between hot and cold on the idea of romantic relationships.

As much as she was proud of her gift of good looks, she often felt that the gift was a liability to her independence, especially considering some of the lecherous men she attracted. And, reflecting on her own history, it seemed as if she kept choosing the wrong guys to go with.

Her first experience — a boy in her grade eleven class back in high school — had turned out badly. She had mistakenly thought he was one of the 'nice' boys — the sort who, if she dated him, wouldn't send her parents into a screaming rage. That part was true enough, but things hadn't worked out well at all.

The first time they'd gone parking, she had wanted to kiss and do a bit of cuddling. But he wanted to go all the way — right now! And when she explained that she wanted to take things slowly, he didn't just stop — he dumped her —

right there on the spot. She had to walk home from the far side of town on a cold rainy autumn night. At least she hadn't been raped, but being unceremoniously dumped like that had been humiliating just the same.

And then when she was nineteen she was drawn into a relationship with her instrument flying instructor. It wasn't like a teacher-student relationship in high school — she was an adult, and he was only three years older. But after a couple of fun dates and her first time in bed with a guy, things had taken an unexpected and disgusting turn. On their next flight lesson, he instructed her to climb to 5,500 feet. As soon as she had climbed the plane to an altitude above one mile, her so-called boyfriend had undone his seat belt and whipped down his pants.

"It's time you joined the mile-high club Sammie," he had said, demanding that they have sex right there, cooped up in the cramped cockpit of a Cessna 180. Sam was not impressed.

Not only was the space limited, but she almost gagged when she caught a strong whiff of womanly odour mixed with his. He'd already been with someone else *that morning* — probably his one other female student pilot. Sam didn't report him — she needed her ticket and he was the only instrument instructor at that school — but she had kept the threat of reporting him hanging over his head, in order to keep him in check.

Then when she was twenty-two, she finally met the man of her dreams. He was a true gentleman during the 'getting to know you' stage and she had enjoyed a few nights with him at his place. But once she was hooked on him, he had become way too possessive and controlling — on the verge of physical abuse. And his 'love' for her was geared only to the gear that lay inside his pants. Since that horrible experience, she'd avoided getting seriously involved with any man. There were a few casual dates along the way, but none of those ended up going anywhere. And that suited her just fine.

When she met Jack Colbrook last summer, he piqued her interest and she quickly warmed to the idea that something might develop between them. He was entirely different than the others. The big huggable man came complete with a wide open 'take me as I am 'cause I ain't changin' for no one' attitude. He had no secrets, and for the few days they shared together — social outings only, no bed-time — she had found that he was just plain fun to be with. And he was the first guy who'd been willing to let her set the pace.

'So now, *just* to screw up my life again, along comes Rob McNabb.'

Multi-tasking, she increased the Otter's throttle setting by just a smidgen, pushing the manifold pressure back up to 28 psi, where it belonged.

'Don't make it any more complicated than it is,' she told herself. 'Deal with them one at a time. I met Jack first. I'll stick with him. I've already invested emotional capital in Jack and that's that. McNabb will quietly fade from the picture with no effort at all.'

But even with his apparent inexperience with women, the guy did make for a refreshing change from most of the others. 'So what?' she asked herself. 'Jack is obviously not at all like the others either. And he's a big, strong, good-looking, intelligent, worldly guy — way more worldly than McNabb.'

She willed Colbrook's image to come back into the centre of her mind. And it worked. It worked that is, until just seconds later. During her routine visual scan, watching the sky around her for other air traffic, she ended up with a peripheral view of McNabb sitting there beside her. It was obvious from his distracted gaze, that the CO was deep in thought.

'This is really dumb. Jack, I know. Jack, I like. Jack, I've already spent time with. So why do I even *think* of McNabb that way? After all, we did just meet today — well, meet properly.'

She really wanted to forget that unfortunate encounter the day before yesterday. She was still embarrassed by her own performance then and after hearing from Gord Clark about McNabb's life-saving flight, she realized that the guy was a strong cut above the rest. He didn't panic or fall apart. He just did what had to be done.

'Maybe it's a guilt thing,' she thought. 'Maybe some cranky angel is sitting on my shoulder, paying me back for being such a bitch that day.'

She involuntarily glanced his way again. He was really likeable and they had discovered the amazing coincidences of their ages and hometowns and all those other things. And he could talk without drooling over her, even though it was obvious to her that he was already smitten.

She just loved how she could catch him off guard each time she pulled his leg. 'Shit, I really have to cool it on that front,' she rebuked herself. 'Jibes like "learning how to use that thing." I'm really leading the guy on. But *why* does he keep popping back into my mind like that?'

"So, what kind of music do you like Robbie?" she asked in an effort to find at least one area where their interests clashed. She knew she'd finally get him on this one. She pictured him a strong disciple of alternative or heavy metal rock — definitely twenty-first century genres.

"Bit of this and a bit of that. But my absolute

favourite era is the '60s and '70s. You know, good old rock and roll. And next to that, I like newer country, from the 1980s onward."

"That's just plain weird, Robbie."

"Well … I'm sorry." The colour drained from his cheeks. He didn't want to put up any barriers between them, but he still had to defend his musical tastes. "That's the music I grew up with … it's what my dad always had playing on the radio in his shop. I spent a lot of time out there helping...."

"No, I mean weird because that pretty much covers my musical taste too … that is, as long as you don't include disco." Disappointed that her ploy hadn't forced a gap between them, Sam was at the same time strangely okay with the idea. She didn't know why. But while she still hoped to find a wedge to drive between them, she appeared to be running out of options. The intercom became silent again for a spell.

When Hawley Lake finally came into view and conversation between them resumed, they firmed up their scheduling and general logistics for the rest of the day. Both agreed that a late-day patrol would be out of the question. They would carry out their individual duties and then rendezvous back at the camp and plan for their search flights to begin tomorrow.

Upon landing, Sam taxied up to the government camp where they were met by Gabby and Edna Whitegoose. Knowing that fresh supplies were coming, the couple wanted to be on hand to meet the plane and to finally meet the new amisk hookimaw. Samantha, they already knew from her time doing contract work with the air service. Sam, they already liked.

The Otter was quickly off-loaded and Williams took

off immediately, bound for re-fuelling in Peawanuck. And although he was expected to show up at Eagle Feather's cabin by noon to join the police search, McNabb took a few minutes to become acquainted with Gabby and Edna.

Gabby was a tall, large-framed man in his late fifties. Despite a thin scattering of black whiskers on a broad, weathered face, he was a handsome man by anyone's standards. Edna was a short, full-bodied woman of indeterminate years. Though prematurely aged by a lifetime of hard work in the wilderness alongside her husband, her deeply creased brown face wore a perpetual smile.

Gabby handed McNabb a small Styrofoam cooler taped shut and labelled 'Polar Bear Samples.' "Here are the samples you wanted for DNA testing Robbie. I've marked on each sample bag, the date and location of the bear I took it from and signed my name." The park ranger in the man wanted the amisk hookimaw to know that he knew about evidence gathering. "They taught us that on a park warden course I attended. You will not find any stray DNA on those samples."

"Thank you Gabby. And maybe this afternoon I'll find samples down at the poacher's camp which when tested, will match them. I'll take these with me, and see if the CSI unit will deliver them down south for secure storage."

They spent a few more minutes getting to know each other. Gabby and Edna both impressed on Rob that they enjoyed a good relationship with the ministry 'family' and were always ready to help in any way they could. Furthermore, their door was always open and even if they were not at home, he was to make his way there any time he was in need of emergency supplies or access to the radio or telephone. To press home his point, Gabby promised to stow the government supplies in the camp so Rob could shake a leg and not keep the CSI team waiting any longer than necessary. He said that the police hoped to wrap up their work on Sutton before the end of the day.

CHAPTER 23

Sutton Lake

McNabb arrived by Ski-Doo at Eagle Feather's camp just as the police were loading the body bag containing the deceased gunshot victim aboard their Twin Otter. He introduced himself to the Crime Scene Investigation team leader. Detective Inspector April Jones, a no-nonsense investigator in her late forties welcomed him to the team. She was also the unit's primary pilot.

Despite fighting a continuous battle with middle-aged spread, the five-foot-eight-inch grey-haired unit leader cut a commanding image in her uniform parka and fur cap.

"And by 'team' I mean the team of all law enforcement folks in this unique region. You'll find that our paths will cross much more regularly here than in more densely populated parts of the province, Rob. And I have it on good authority you are the go-to guy for outside-the-box thinking in your outfit. Gord Clark is going home today and has been spreading the word at every opportunity."

"I'm not sure that the air service administration shares his enthusiasm, Inspector. I just spent most of yesterday afternoon writing a report for them that covered my life history, the theory of flight, Newton's law of gravity and admitting that if conservation officers had been meant to fly, God would have given us wings."

"Oh, we can work with you young man. You've *absolutely* caught the essence of government work in the north. The bad guys we can deal with. It's the administration that always gets in our way," she laughed.

Getting down to business, Inspector Jones introduced him to her two team members. Detective Constable Lloyd Macdonald was a tall thin fellow in his forties. His uniform fur cap hid his silvering crewcut. He had worked with Jones for six years and was also a pilot.

Ranjit Singh, a stocky man in his early thirties and no taller than the inspector, was also a detective constable and had been with the unit for only a year. However, like the inspector, his education included a spell at the FBI's training facility at Quantico, Virginia.

When the introductions were finished, Jones asked McNabb to take them through his activities while he was at the camp two days earlier. He detailed his actions and answered their questions as they walked the path he'd made to avoid disturbing any evidence. The police members had obviously used the same path for the same reason, and now it was a heavily packed trail.

"You know, I was in such a hurry to get going that day, I never even thought to check out what was in his shed," McNabb confessed. "And I never did get across the bay to see where they were loading the plane from."

"That's okay — there are no human remains in either place," Jones replied. "But there is a snowmobile here, and a lot of trapping equipment, as well as scraps of animal skins, flesh and fat.

"We took a quick peek in the other building across the lake on our way here. It's bigger by half than this one, and there are some skinned bear hides stretched in there, drying I suppose. We didn't notice anything else in our hurry to get over here and get started. By the way, do you have a search warrant? It's an illegal camp on crown land so you probably don't need one, but some judges get picky about these things, especially when egged on by whining defence lawyers."

"Yes I do. James Bird got one issued for the same reason.

"I see he had a solar electric system and satellite dish set up here," he commented, eyeballing the camp from the front yard. "Was there by any chance a computer in there?"

"Good deduction Officer McNabb," replied the youngest police officer. "Yes there was, and we have already seized it. I assume you'll want access to any documents or emails related to his poaching activities, so we will have the IT guy make you a copy of what's saved on it. Is that alright?"

"Yes, thanks, Detective Singh. Is there a treasure trove of paper records lying around too by any chance?"

"No," the inspector replied. "He has outdone the government bureaucracy and appears to have gone entirely paperless — if only we could be so green. I don't want you to minimize the intensity of your search just because we've already been through the place, but my guess is that the most productive area for your purposes will be out in those sheds."

"Okay, then if you don't mind I'd like to do a quick tour of his cabin, more to get a feel for the guy than to search what's already been gone over. And after that we can tackle the sheds in detail."

It took no more than ten minutes looking through the twelve-by-sixteen log building to satisfy McNabb that the CSI folks hadn't missed anything of use to him.

When they walked toward the shed the police officers admitted to McNabb that the wildlife stuff was more in his domain than theirs.

"Hey, blood and guts is blood and guts, regardless of the species of origin, and you guys are the experts in that field. I'm just the rookie," he countered.

"Most of my experience in searches is based on simulations completed during my training. During the three real-life searches I participated in while I was doing contract work down south, I was relegated to the security detail — you know, use the big guy to keep the occupant under control — don't let anyone in or out," he admitted.

"That may be the case Rob, but sometimes it's the fresh set of eyes that sees things more clearly," Jones encouraged him.

"Excuse me while I take this," she added as her sat-phone began to deedle. Everyone hesitated when they heard the inspector's end of the conversation. Three minutes later she briefed them on what she had just learned.

"Interesting. We transmitted the dead man's prints and others from the camp last night by satellite connection, Rob, and that call has given us the first set of results. The dead guy was a known American poacher, turned wildlife black-marketeer, named William Joseph Boyd … went by Billy Joe. Originally from Louisiana, but he bounced all over the United States in the last few years. A U.S. Fish and Wildlife Service agent named Tommy Sturgis is a little upset that the poor man has expired. I gather he had a few things he wanted to discuss with our Wallpaper Man."

"Wallpaper Man?" McNabb asked, looking puzzled.

"Sorry Rob. Someone on our team gave him the nickname after we saw the mess he left on the camp walls. We in the trade tend to develop a rather morbid sense of humour. It's supposed to help us keep our sanity, but considering you found him while the mess was still fresh, I should have been more sensitive."

"Don't worry Inspector, I'm getting over it … I think. My mom was always bringing gory stories home from the ER when I was growing up. And she always seemed to wait until we were eating supper before telling them.

"By the way, I talked to Agent Sturgis just last week. Quite a character, but I *cannot* tell you it was he who called to give us the heads-up on the bear runners, or he said he'd have to come up here and kill me to protect his source," McNabb said with a grin.

"I *know* the boy will fit in," Jones reiterated to her constables, smiling as she opened Eagle Feather's shed door.

Working in two teams, the four of them began a detailed search of the poacher's shed behind the camp. McNabb, worked with DC Macdonald and they quickly gravitated to the Yamaha snowmobile and the sleigh it towed. The inspector and DC Singh started processing the area around the workbench and the skinning table.

The building measured ten feet by sixteen, and like Eagle Feather's main cabin, it had LED electric lights powered by his roof-top solar array. The shed had a drive-through arrangement with doors at each end so the poacher didn't even need to disconnect the sleigh when he returned to camp.

Immediately noticeable were patches of blood with coarse white hairs stuck to the sleigh and the carrier rack on the back of the snowmobile. And frozen to one side of the Yamaha's running boards were two ptarmigan. On the other side lay a marten carcass, still wearing its fur coat. In the sleigh, under several layers of tarpaulin they found numerous padded leg-hold traps the poacher used for the foxes, and two giant leg-hold bear traps, complete with serrated tooth jaws. These brutally inhumane devices had been illegal for anyone to even possess, let alone use, for years.

"Boy, those ugly things would sure screw up the value of a polar bear hide, not to mention the leg of anyone, or anything, unfortunate enough to step in them," said McNabb. "But they are so rusty I don't think they've been used in a long time. I don't see any blood or hair on the teeth anyhow."

Dragging the snowmobile to one side, McNabb used the toe of his boot to poke around on the ground it had been sitting on. Then he began tapping the dirt floor with an ice chisel that was leaning against the wall. His efforts pretty quickly revealed a small wooden hatch that covered a shallow earthen dugout, less than half a metre in diameter. A plastic, one-kilo coffee container was carefully lifted from the bottom — only after Detective Singh stopped what he was doing and came over to check it for booby traps.

"I supposed we should have checked for that even before lifting the hatch, Ranjit," McNabb sheepishly offered.

"Yes, and hindsight is 20-20," Singh replied. "He seems to be learning faster than us, eh, Mother?"

McNabb was puzzled by the name 'Mother'. It was obviously in reference to Inspector Jones. An inside joke he guessed.

"Aha! Impressive. It appears to be his savings account," Macdonald offered.

"Swiss bank's more like it," the CO suggested, amazed at the size of the two fat rolls of cash it held. "So, how do we figure out if this is 'proceeds of crime,' or just his hard-earned life savings?"

"*We* don't, at least not yet," replied the inspector. "In fact, there is a reverse onus on people found in possession of large stashes of cash. They have to prove that large sums of money found during an investigation were lawfully come by.

"The source of the funds may be revealed after a forensic auditor looks at his computer records, or if we ever get to interview him, or after the banknotes themselves have been examined for any documentary connection to other crimes, or maybe never. For now, it is simply evidence found during the investigation."

"Pretty good nest egg," Macdonald said after they had counted just over twelve thousand dollars.

"Whose seizure is it, then?" asked the rookie. "And no, I'm not looking to move to the Cayman Islands. It's just that, well ... how do we do this?"

"There's probably more money to be made in selling polar bear hides than there is murdering one's fur buyer, so it could be attached to the wildlife offences. But since it has to be investigated as part of the whole picture and might even be from some past criminal enterprise, we'll take responsibility for it," the inspector said.

"That's fine with me," McNabb nodded. Maintaining the security and continuity of seized evidence was something he was trained to handle, but a seizure that straddled the jurisdiction of two agencies was beyond his experience.

CHAPTER 24

Eagle Feather's second shed, located on the opposite shore of Sutton Lake, was well concealed inside a dense stand of spruce. The police wouldn't have known it was there if it hadn't been for the tracks left by the poacher and Boyd and his Cessna. The path from the shoreline to the building even had a tight "S" bend in it to mask the narrow opening in the trees.

The shed itself contained five polar bear skins. Each was stretched on a large, rectangular spruce-pole frame and hung from the rafters. There were also a number of arctic fox and several large wolf pelts drying on stretcher boards hanging from the walls. There was a wood stove, cold now, but no workbench or skinning table in this shed, so they all decided that Eagle Feather simply brought his skinned furs over here to dry and wait for shipment.

It was pretty obvious that unless the event of Boyd's murder had drastically changed the poacher's plans, he intended to return at some point in the near future. He still had a lot of inventory to move out.

They were just about finished in the drying shed when McNabb suggested that the earthen floor had a slightly different sound in one area each time one of them walked over it. Digging several inches down in the sandy material, they found another wooden hatch. It was even better concealed than the other one had been. McNabb deferred to Singh to do his bomb sweep before touching this one. There were no booby traps and another plastic coffee container was waiting for them. Another nine thousand dollars in cash was counted out.

"For his picking up on those secret compartments you two missed, I'm tempted to offer McNabb a job," the inspector ribbed her two constables.

"I believe I saw you walking over that same spot several times yourself, Inspector," McNabb threw in. "But no thanks, I just couldn't accept the position. I've seen all those CSI shows on TV, and I probably wouldn't be able to keep my eyes focussed on my work with all the female agents there wearing their tight pants and low-cut tops."

"You're lookin' at her," the inspector said. McNabb blushed and the constables were in stitches.

Still laughing, they began cutting the bear hides down from the stretchers and rolling them up for transport; they were dry enough to be stored like that for the trip south. The fox and wolf pelts were piled with them and everything was recorded on seizure receipts. McNabb dutifully left the 'client's' copy in the shed, along with his business card.

At the end of the search, the CO and his CSI colleagues' list of seizures included the laptop and cash, all of the bear pelts and other furs, the leg-hold traps, a small cooler full of biological samples and skinning tools to be sent for DNA testing, and of course the poacher's snowmobile and sleigh.

"Thanks for showing me the ropes, Inspector and Detectives. Despite all the training I've had, I would have found it mind-boggling dealing with it all, especially the buried treasure. Where are you headed next?"

"Our first stop will be in Moosonee," Jones told him. "Staff Sergeant Ballard needs to be briefed on what we've found up here and he has a new detective constable there who is a computer whiz. We'll leave this laptop with him to unlock any secrets pertinent to either investigation. We'll overnight there and then return to district HQ in the morning."

"Could you take the snowmobile in your Twin Otter? If you have room, that is. We could probably squeeze it through the double cargo doors on our bird, but Sam Williams and I are going to be pounding the sky between here and Moose for the next few days, and every extra kilogram on board is going to eat into our flying range." He paused, feeling a pleasant rush at the mention of Samantha's name.

"Sure, we can do that for you," Jones replied, and seeing the brief vacant look flash across his face, she asked, "Is everything alright?"

"I'm sorry, I was just thinking of … uh …"

"Yes, she's a very nice girl," the inspector's female intuition filled in the blank. "And she's a really good pilot too. She worked hard to get on staff with the air service. So if you have designs on her young man, you just make sure you treat her properly. 'Mother' will be watching!" McNabb gave her a cautious smile in reply.

With more and more of the old guard headed into retirement, April Jones had a soft spot for the new generation of staff beginning to fill the ranks. And she'd taken Samantha Williams under her wing when she had first started contract flying for the government. It was Jones's mentoring nature that led to the 'Mother' moniker.

"Anyhow, I was about to say before we got all

dreamy-eyed, if you want to sign over the furs and your biological seizures and Gabby's samples to me as well, I can turn those over directly to the lab. The evidence chain will be shorter than if you ship them from Moose when you get back home and they'll be there sooner. We'll turn over the rest of your seizures to James tonight."

"Thanks Inspector. I figured I'd have to lock everything up in one of these buildings until we could come back for it all."

"While not an ideal solution, that would have worked too," she said. "It was good to meet you Rob, and a real pleasure working with you. Oh, and if you have any plans to start to calling me 'Mother' behind my back, well you might as well call me that in front of my back too — except not in the company of these two," she nodded mischievously toward her two detective constables. "They're still having a hard time remembering to call me 'sir.' Now let's get your seizures loaded. My stomach is telling me it's time to head for the inn."

It was after 3:30 when the police Twin Otter took off for Moosonee. After watching them leave, Rob McNabb headed back to the Hawley Lake camp.

—

Timmins

Eagle Feather was frustrated. He'd spent several hours trying to find hotel accommodations, but every bed in town had been booked for the big prospectors' convention already in full swing. He hadn't expected that, otherwise he would have reserved ahead. He eventually had to settle for a motel room in South Porcupine, east of the city.

Now he was trying to get to a rental storage facility out in the west end but was sitting in a traffic jam on Algonquin Boulevard. A loaded log truck just ahead of him had slid downhill into the Mountjoy Street intersection on the red light. It hit a city transit bus. It was only a minor collision, but nothing was moving. All he could do was sit and watch the pedestrians scurrying along the snow-packed sidewalks. There were plenty of hardy souls out. Each was bundled up against the biting cold in parkas, scarves and fur hats; each exhaling clouds of vapour after every frozen breath they took.

A traffic cop finally started getting the vehicles behind him turned around and cleared out. After a forty minute standstill he was allowed to pull a U-turn and make a detour around the block. He was finally free to get to his destination where he made arrangements to rent a patch of ground at the storage facility.

He reactivated a false identity he had used during his previous life and went to a bank. Opening a chequing account, he deposited a couple thousand dollars of the cash he'd grabbed from B.J. Boyd at the time of his demise. Some of it was the money he was owed for his furs. The rest was the bonus he figured he deserved. Keeping the deposits small and irregular in size, he would gradually fill the new account to a level suitable for his needs.

After finishing up at the bank, he found an older model Polaris snowmobile sitting in someone's yard with a for sale sign on it. Eagle Feather took it for a spin and decided it would suit his short-term needs just fine. Six hundred dollars was peeled from his cash wad and the machine was his.

His final business of the day was the purchase of a new laptop out at Timmins Square Shopping Centre. All he needed now was to connect to the motel Wi-Fi so he could access all of his files on 'the cloud' and carry on business as if he'd never been out of touch.

He had been contemplating getting his hair cut, but since there was no indication that he was a wanted man yet, maintaining his long hair, at least for the time being, gave him additional disguise options should he have to change his appearance later. He'd been down this road before in his auto smuggling days.

CHAPTER 25

Hawley Lake

When McNabb drove the Ski-Doo up to the government camp he was impressed that the Otter was already parked and the engine covered for the night. The generator was running and the heaters were tucked in place. As he entered the camp, he let out a good natured "Honey, I'm home!" But there was no reply. The camp was deserted.

"Oh, shit, this can't be happening again." Coming home to this same cabin to find his pilot gone after what had happened to Gord Clark just two days earlier was too much to bear. He went back out to see if maybe she was doing something inside the Otter. But she wasn't there, and she wasn't in the outhouse either.

It was only when he dashed, half panicked, back into the cabin that he caught sight of a sheet of paper on the plywood dining table. He read: '*Rob: Gabby and Edna asked us to supper. I'm going over with them now. C U soon. Sam.*'

McNabb was worried that he'd jumped so quickly to the wrong conclusion. But then he remembered the critical incident session yesterday. The counsellor had told him there might be times when some small, normally insignificant event, could trigger just such an emotional reaction. He wasn't to let that worry him.

'Okay, don't worry about it. You've been invited out to dinner, so just get cleaned up and leave.'

—

Gabby met McNabb at the kitchen door. The house was a simple bungalow set on blocks with plywood skirting to keep the worst of the cold from under the floors. Basements didn't work well in that region of semi-discontinuous permafrost. The exterior plywood siding was painted pale blue and the trim done in white, all a bit weathered, but still quite presentable.

"Welcome to our home Amisk Hookimaw."

"Megwich, good neighbour," McNabb thanked his host as he entered. It was toasty warm inside and he quickly closed the door behind him to keep out the frigid, late afternoon air. The interior of the house was also simply done in painted plywood — light brown floors, pale yellow living room walls and a bright yellow kitchen. Floral print curtains framed each of the windows, making the winter afternoon view of the lake appear much brighter and warmer than it actually was.

The two women were sitting at the kitchen table where Edna was showing Sam a pair of caribou skin gauntlet mittens she was making. She was halfway through stitching an intricate pattern of colourful beadwork to the first mitten.

A modern wood-fired space heater at the far end of the living room matched the heat thrown off by an ancient, gleaming Findlay Oval wood-burning range in the kitchen. The whole place was immaculately clean and smelled deliciously of some as yet unidentified meat dish cooking on the Oval.

Curtained off doorways to three bedrooms were spaced along the living room wall opposite the south facing picture window. But what really caught his attention was the abundance of bookshelves around the living room walls. They were loaded with enough contemporary fiction to rival a small town library.

"I've been guiding fishermen and hunters for many years now," Gabby offered by way of explanation for all the books. "Most of them leave books with us when they head home. At first it was just to reduce their baggage for the flight out. But once they realized we enjoyed reading, many of our repeat guests began to bring in extras, just for our collection. Any that we already have, we give to the library in Peawanuck.

"Like me, my father was a hunting and fishing guide, and when I was a boy he taught me some of the ways of the white man. I learned from his guests too. One guest, who returned every year, taught me to read. When I was sent away to residential school in Fort Albany, I could already speak the languages of the priests and the nuns and I learned easily the lessons they taught us. The children who did not have my gift of learning were treated much worse than I was. It was painful to see them mistreated, but I was small then and did not dare to stand up to them."

McNabb could see that the memories of that experience still hurt the man, but he wasn't sure how to respond. He was ashamed and embarrassed that he'd had to learn of that chapter in Canadian history from the TV news, not in school.

Whitegoose made no mention of his two years of college education before returning home to run the guiding business. It was not his style to be boastful, but just listening to him, McNabb suspected that he either had some advanced schooling, or he was very well self-educated.

"Edna and Samantha have been catching up on woman talk, so I'm even more pleased you are able to join us. We don't get many visitors here in the winter, and she has a winter's worth of talking to get in before you leave," he said with a straight face. But the twinkle in his eyes made it clear that the serious topic of his residential school history was now closed. And he too was delighted to have company.

"When I returned to the camp I thought I'd lost another pilot," McNabb said, taking his host's cue for more lighthearted conversation. "I was just about ready to uncover my Otter and fly it back home again, but then I found Sam's note."

"You touch *my* Otter, McNabb, and I'll have your stripes!" came back at him.

"I hope you like caribou, young Robert McNabb," Edna said.

"Well, I really like all animals, Edna, and as a small boy I wanted to become a zookeeper … ouch!" Sam gave him a good-natured kick in the shins under the table.

"Caribou stew Robbie. Do you like to *eat* caribou?" the pilot chided, putting on a stern expression that didn't begin to hide her amused grin.

"Yes, Edna," the young officer grinned back at Sam. He'd finally accomplished a little leg pulling of his own. "Although I've never had caribou before, if that's the delicious smell that's been lingering since I arrived, I do love it. I'm really looking forward to this dinner."

Edna began dishing out the stew with a knowing smile spreading across her face. The boy was in love; but it would be an uphill battle for him to win Sam's heart. Edna knew. She had been that girl many years ago.

Gabby, who'd been silent and looking pensive for a moment, spoke tentatively, "Sometimes our guests leave us gifts of wine. Would you like a glass of wine with your meal? Edna and I don't touch alcohol. But don't let that stop you if you would like to have some."

"Thanks very much for the offer Gabby," McNabb replied, bracing for another kick as he noticed Sam's eyes ready to throw daggers in his direction. Seeing that there were no wine glasses set out on the table, he gave his answer.

"I'd actually prefer tea. And while I don't want my pilot waking up in the morning with a headache, I'll let her speak for herself. Ouch!" Kick received. And that was how the evening progressed, the men poking fun at the women, and the women turning it right back at them.

When they drained a third pot of tea just after seven o'clock, Sam suggested that they should start back for the camp. With the temperature already below -40°C, she wanted to check on the plane and refuel the generator for a long night's run. While she was pulling on her parka and giving Gabby a goodnight hug, Edna spoke quietly to McNabb.

"You take good care of that woman, young Robert McNabb, and always remember to show her respect." With a sly smile creeping over her time-worn face, she added, "And if I hear you haven't, I'm real handy with each one of those things hanging on the wall over there." She nodded at half a dozen hunting rifles and shotguns cradled on a caribou antler gun rack.

"Message received, loud and clear, Edna," he replied with a mischievous grin as he gave her a hug. After a firm handshake with Gabby, he quickly headed out into the cold clear night.

Out in the yard at -43°C, it was so cold that when he inhaled the night air through his nose, he could feel the hairs in his nostrils freeze together. And he knew that by the time they got back to their camp, he'd have icicles growing from his moustache.

Because of the extreme cold, pulling the starter cords on the old Ski-Doos was harder than usual, but the engines started with only a little extra coaxing. However, Rob had to lift the back end of each machine off the ground in succession as Sam revved up its motor to get the stiffened track turning freely.

Minutes later they pulled away from the Whitegoose home bound for the government camp. The white fog of their snowmobile exhaust lingered motionless in the yard for some minutes after their departure.

CHAPTER 26

Sam checked the aircraft and the heaters while Rob refuelled the generator. Then the two of them headed into the camp and turned up the heat. For the next twenty minutes, sitting in their unzipped parkas, they filled out their daily logs — aircraft for Sam and enforcement for Rob. Then they spread maps and aeronautical charts of the region out on the table and Rob brewed a pot of tea.

The cabin soon warmed and for the next couple of hours they planned the search pattern they intended to follow over the coming days, hoping that on one of the lakes in the district, they'd find evidence of the Cessna having landed to refuel or perhaps pick up furs from another source. But since the bad guys had a two-day head start, which would be three days by midday tomorrow, they weren't overly optimistic about their chances. They knew however, that they had to rule out all possibilities. Meanwhile, the police were still using the Turbo Beavers to comb the southern reaches of the district and beyond.

It was after ten o'clock when they finished and with tomorrow promising to be long and tedious, it was time to turn in. As McNabb began to unroll his sleeping bag on the cot nearest to the propane heater, Samantha chuckled.

"You know, young Robert McNabb, once we've turned it off for the night, being close to the stove isn't going to keep you any warmer than if you slept in the far back corner of the camp."

"Turned it off? What do you mean turned it off? It's forty below out there."

"Maybe you and Gord Clark survived okay sleeping in here, but during my short career in the bush I've already heard of enough carbon monoxide deaths to know that none of these things is completely safe, no matter how new it is. But seeing as how they were kind enough to provide us with a high-end model, one of us can keep the remote control under our pillow and turn it back on an hour before we get up in the morning. Don't worry, the cabin is well insulated and the 5-Star bag will keep you warm enough."

"Well, you know all about control," he joked as he hopped across the cold floor, "so I'll leave the remote in your care." But she wasn't smiling when he sneaked a look in her direction. "Um, sorry. I guess that was uncalled for. I uh...." His apology appeared to be falling on deaf ears, so he said no more but reached up to turn off the last of the propane camp lights.

Furious with himself for planting his foot firmly in his mouth, he pulled the sleeping bag up around his ears and tried to go to sleep. But he couldn't. Not with unfinished business hanging over him.

"What a day," he spoke out into the dark room. "I met a person today who turned out to be really fun to work with, even though she kept pulling my leg when I was least expecting it. Then I met a police inspector who suggested that I treat the lady properly, because 'Mother' would be watching. And then I met a fine Cree woman who advised me to be good and show respect to the lady. So now with our first date not even over yet, I've failed to follow their advice and much worse, I've offended my new friend. I'm sorry Sam."

"Oh I can't stay mad at you, McNabb. You're just too much fun. Good night."

"Good night, Sam." Relieved, he soon drifted off to sleep.

—

It took Sam a couple of hours to drop off. She was tormented by her sudden attraction to Robbie McNabb — an unwanted attraction as far as the logical side of her brain was concerned, but it was just something she couldn't seem to turn off. Tossing and turning just made it worse, so she willed herself to lie still — a mental exercise that sometimes worked. Eventually she slept.

Some time after midnight she was dragged from the deep sleep she had just entered. The anguished shouts of a man in the same room brought her fully awake. With her heart pounding, she flicked on her flashlight to reveal McNabb thrashing about in his sleeping bag. He was obviously in the midst of a nightmare.

Reaching over to his cot, she tugged on his sleeping bag. "McNabb, you're dreaming." The guy kept thrashing. She got out of her sleeping bag and leaned over his bed. "Rob, it's okay. You're just having a bad dream." The dream continued.

"Robbie, it's me, Sam," she said as she took a firm grip on his shoulder. Whether it was the reassuring voice or the strong hand pulling him back to the conscious world, Rob McNabb mentally clawed his way back to the safety of the government camp at Hawley Lake. Sam relaxed her grip on his shoulder, just resting her hand there and reassuring him in a quiet voice.

It had been a horrible dream and McNabb was in a sweat. His heart was still hammering in his chest as the terrifying images began to fade away — fade away far too slowly for his liking. He recalled that he'd first been faced with a dreamlike representation of the gunshot victim at Eagle Feather's camp. Bad enough on its own, it was nothing compared to what he'd seen next when the body had morphed into Gord Clark, also a bloody mangled mess, struggling to fly an airplane. And then to his absolute horror, all he could see was Sam's curly red hair — just her hair. That was all that was left of her.

"Sam, I don't think I've ever had a dream like that. Not in my entire life," he managed. Shaking, fighting to catch his breath, he worked to sit up in the bed, but remain cocooned in the warmth and safety of his sleeping bag. "Am I ever glad it's you who woke me. If it had been anyone else, I don't think they'd have been able to convince me that you were still okay. It was horrible." He was obviously badly shaken by the experience.

"Well, I haven't had to do this since my little sister had nightmares, but it always helped her back to sleep. So here goes nothing. But just remember friend, it ain't what it might seem like." With that, she went to the far side of her own cot and pushed it up against his. He watched surprised as she undid the snaps that closed each of their sleeping bags and then started snapping the two together to make one bag, a bag as large as a queen-sized bed.

"It isn't the bridal suite at the Chelsea Hotel, but then we're still on our first date," she said as she climbed in and snuggled up against him. "Now, whatever happened in your dream, didn't happen. I'm right here. I'm safe, and you're safe. And there's two layers of longjohns between us, and that's what I expect to find when I wake up in the morning young Robert McNabb."

He turned to face her and gave her a one-armed hug. Then, not wanting to violate the boundary she had just set, he turned his back to her, snuggled closer and murmured a grateful "Thanks." She, in return, wrapped an arm around his waist and returned the hug before the two of them gradually drifted back to sleep.

It couldn't have been comfortable sleeping on the ridge formed by the meeting of the two iron cot frames — the foam mattresses were thin. But this time it was a peaceful sleep.

CHAPTER 27

Thursday, February 2

Just after six o'clock in the morning, McNabb reached under Sam's pillow and gently pulled out the remote control for the propane heater. Hitting the power button, he listened for the unit to ignite. Then he lay back, enjoying the moment.

The 1960's Herman's Hermits song "I'm Into Something Good" immediately sprang to mind. The first line "Woke up this morning feelin' fine," instantly became an earworm he was sure would replay in his head all day long. And that was okay. He *had* met a new girl yesterday and now he felt that he was in for something good. Of course, nothing had happened between them during the night, but he was entirely happy about the way things were working out. The thought of a long-distance relationship didn't bother him anymore. Lots of people managed such affairs just fine. They'd make it work.

The nightmare he'd had was embarrassing and it bothered him that he could have had such a dream, but somehow he wasn't afraid of a recurrence. Sam's close presence provided him with a strong sense of security.

The camp gradually warmed and soon Sam began to

stir. He was about to lean over and give her a hug, but then thought better of it. He'd leave the next move up to her.

"Good morning dream-boy. You okay this morning, Robbie?"

"Yes, thanks Sam. Having you tucked close beside me was very reassuring."

"My sister's nightmares started around the time Mom and Dad's marriage was approaching its worst. Screaming arguments, meals eaten in stony silence, and then Dad finally moving out. She had a really rough time of it. But climbing into bed with her wasn't just for her benefit either. I guess I needed the comfort of her presence too. It worked for both of us."

"And here, last night? After I probably scared the living crap out of you?"

"Well, last night, yes it was comforting to be close too. But...." she paused, truly upset with herself. "Oh Rob, I'm not being fair to you." And she lay there in the predawn blackness, her mind reeling — tormented by her own ability to get in over her head with a man.

"Rob," she sighed, "I've got to come clean . . . I've got to tell you . . . I'm . . . oh, shit. I'm making a real mess of this." Another sigh escaped, and an emotional shudder came with it. He sensed she was close to tears.

"Take it easy, Sam," he tried to ease her obvious discomfort. He didn't know *exactly* what was coming next, but he had a pretty good idea, and his heart was sinking fast.

"I'm a big boy; just tell me. I can take it," he gently urged her. At the same time his mind was screaming, 'Please don't say it. I don't think I can take this.'

"Rob, there's … another guy . . . sort of."

'I knew it,' flashed through his mind.

"But it's even more complicated than that," she said.

McNabb's heart sank still lower, if that was even possible. "Do you know a CO by the name of Jack Colbrook?"

"Yeah. We flew up from Toronto and back when we were interviewed for the CO positions in Moosonee last fall. So you're going together then?" He tried to put as positive a note to his reply as he could, but she easily detected the disappointment in his voice.

"Well, not really . . . together . . . yet, but we met last summer and saw something of each other during a four-day seminar. I really like him, but I'm not sure and . . . Oh, I'm really making a mess of this, I'm sorry. I don't want to hurt you Rob. We work together so well. You're so easy to like. And all day yesterday, I kept pulling your leg and kidding you about our 'first date' and then climbing into bed with you after your dream . . . I've been leading you on Robbie and I shouldn't have done that. I'm so sorry . . . so confused . . ." He heard her quietly sobbing in the darkness.

McNabb was hurting badly. He was hurting for his own sense of loss and for Sam's obvious torment too. He searched for something helpful to say, and meanwhile, inside the sleeping bag he reached over and took her hand gently in his. She didn't pull away.

"Sam, don't tear yourself up about it," he said. And while he tried desperately to come up with something to follow his opening line, she intertwined her fingers with his. "I think you need time to sort things out," he went on, totally unsure of himself. "I won't push. And in the meantime, I'm hoping we can continue working together," he swallowed, a lump forming in his throat, "just being friends."

Those last three words, spoken with a noticeable catch in his voice, were the hardest words he'd ever had to say.

The only other girl he'd managed to get close to before had said those same words to him. And on that occasion, they had all the comforting effect of having a bucket of icewater poured on him. A guy's hormones aren't adapted to 'just being friends.' Men aren't wired that way.

As he lay there, his morning's opening optimism crushed, he began wondering about several of the phrases she'd used. The meaning behind the phrases 'sort of', 'I'm not sure' and 'so confused' — and the grip she had put on his fingers just then. Could those things suggest that maybe he wasn't completely out of the running — yet? No, knowing his luck with girls, that would be too much to hope for. He was devastated.

Even in the darkness, Sam could sense that Robbie was hurting. Feeling awful about what she was doing to him, she pulled their still intertwined fingers to her face and lightly kissed them. He could feel the tears on her cheeks and that tore at him even more. His musical ear-worm from just a few minutes earlier had already vanished from his mind. And when he tried to replace it with Mary MacGregor singing "Torn Between Two Lovers" the effort fell flat. That song just hurt — way too much.

—

And then their watches started their seven o'clock alarm rituals, one within seconds of the other. Rob got up and immediately began to dress. The doubled up sleeping bag was no longer the cosy, enchanted nest he'd awakened to.

"Do you want to gas up the generator or cook the oatmeal?" he asked, trying hard to get past, or at least get a handle on what had just happened.

"I bet you cook a mean bowl of instant oatmeal," Sam

replied as she hopped up and down, pulling on her flight suit. "I'll feed the generator." Hurriedly lifting her felt boot liners from the rack over top of the gas heater, she pulled them on.

"Oh, that's so nice to be able to pretend to have a warm floor underfoot, at least for the first thirty seconds.

"And Rob? Thanks. Friends for sure — good friends would be even better."

"I'm okay with that for now," he conceded, thinking at the same time, 'As long as I don't end up just being a big brother figure.' Then he added, "Sam? Don't quit ribbing me either, okay? I think you'd get awfully constipated trying to change how you communicate with me. I think it's just part of who you are." She smiled back, her eyes still wet and red, and she gave him a quick one-armed hug around his middle as she passed, heading for the door. A sisterly hug maybe, but it was better than having her avoid him completely.

CHAPTER 28

Fifteen minutes later they were sitting at the table over a breakfast of hot instant oatmeal, toast, orange juice and fresh perked coffee. And as they discussed their plans for the morning, McNabb was amazed at how Sam could slip into her professional pilot mode so seamlessly after the emotional episode she'd experienced just a little while earlier.

She had to top up the oil in the Otter's engine reservoir tank, she was saying, and even though she'd left the twenty-litre oil jug in the camp overnight, the heavy motor oil would pour as slow as liquid honey.

McNabb said he needed to refuel the two Ski-Doos and store them back in the shed, and Sam reminded him that after they were both done, she wanted to be introduced to the .30-06 rifle.

"Well, it's just like any other semi-auto Sam," he ribbed her lightheartedly. "You slap in the mag, cycle a round into the chamber, flick off the safety and start shooting." His attempt at humour fell flat and she threw him an exasperated stare before replying.

"Look, my dad let me shoot his bolt action .308 once and that's my entire experience with high-powered rifles. Other than getting a bruised shoulder, I don't have much to show for it. I wanted to take the firearms and hunter safety courses this winter, but none have been offered in Timmins when I've been available. Please, I need to know what to do with that thing."

He felt sick about pushing the wrong buttons so soon after this morning's bedroom confession. Repeatedly putting his foot in his mouth like that sure wasn't going to help win her heart.

"I'm sorry Sam. I was just pulling your leg but my timing's crappy … again. I'll...."

"Oh, don't sweat it, Robbie. Quid pro quo — I got you enough times yesterday," she interrupted, realizing that she'd overreacted to his dig.

"Well, I never took Latin, but I gather we're square now?" Receiving a smile for an answer, he continued, "Anyhow, I'll set up a range along the shoreline, with the point to the south of us acting as our backstop."

By the time they'd cleaned up the camp and finished their predetermined chores, the sun was finally up over the southeastern shore of the lake and the temperature had clawed its way up to -33°C. Carrying the rifle and the box of shells, McNabb walked down to join Sam where she was just finishing up tending to the Otter. He had already paced off a one-hundred-metre distance and placed a couple of cardboard boxes on the ice, each with a simple twenty centimetre black circle drawn with a marker on one side.

He started by showing Sam how to load, cock and unload the rifle.

"Always keep your finger outside the trigger guard until you are ready to take your shot. You never know when something, or someone you weren't expecting might show up either in front of or behind your intended target.

"Next, it's a big rifle for skinny people like you and

me. The recoil can really hurt your shoulder unless you keep the butt pulled snugly against it when you fire."

Sam hadn't thought of herself as skinny, and she wasn't really, but she took his comment as an awkward version of a compliment.

"And finally, telescopic sights are great for magnifying distant targets. And from here to these targets, whatever the crosshairs line up on at the instant you squeeze the trigger, that's where the bullet is going to hit. However, if you use the scope zoomed in to its maximum magnification, you are going to find that the image can be very unsteady. And if you haven't already got your target in sight, it is going to tricky to locate. My own preference is to stay zoomed out to the maximum wide angle until I need to bring the image closer.

"Now, I want you to aim for the centre of the dot on the left hand box, and first we'll have you dry fire, without a round in the chamber. That will give you a feel for the trigger pull and reduce the natural tendency to flinch."

Sam raised the rifle and after a moment's hesitation, there was the appropriate click. After three more cycles of dry firing, Rob handed her the loaded magazine. They put on their radio headsets from the plane to provide some hearing protection.

Sam fired her first round. Rob checked the distant target through his binoculars.

"Holy crap. I couldn't have done that on my first shot. That looks pretty well dead centre Sam. Let's see you do that again. Prove to me it wasn't a fluke." She did, and apparently it wasn't a fluke, because of the five rounds in the magazine, only one came within two centimetres of leaving the black circle. Ten minutes of instruction certainly wasn't enough to qualify her for her firearms licence, but McNabb was confident that her quick grasp of all things mechanical stood her in good stead for when she did take the course.

"Beautiful shooting Sam! And that's while wearing gloves. You ever plan on joining the competition circuit?"

"Yeah, and it starts right now. You shoot the other target. Loser buys dinner when we get back to Moosonee."

"Oh shit. I thought this would be embarrassingly easy," he lamented, but he was warmed by the thought that even in the midst of her torment over which guy to choose, she still wanted to go out with him when they got back to town.

His first four shots made a very close pattern near the centre of the target, but his fifth hole was punched a centimetre outside the target circle.

"Sure Robbie. Damned chauvinist. You just don't want to be seen having a woman take you out to dinner."

"Okay, here … beat this," he challenged as he reached inside his parka and drew the H&K pistol. Without pausing, he went into a shooting stance and put five rounds inside the black mark on his target.

"Wow! That's amazing," said Sam, watching his target through the binoculars. And after she'd had a thorough briefing on the semi-automatic handgun, Rob let her give it a try.

"Well, two in the target, and the other three all within ten centimetres of it, that's really good shooting too Sam. I think you've got 'the gift.' I qualified with guys who had to use two thirteen-round mags to make that many 'kill shots' at a hundred metres." Sam handed back the pistol and he switched magazines for a full one before slipping it back into the holster.

"It's a really long shot with a handgun. But they trained us for it because the hunters we deal with are carrying long-guns. And, while gun fights aren't exactly common in our business, the instructors want us to be confident that we can reach out and touch someone if we need to. Anyhow, I'm still buying dinner."

It would be another hour before the sun got high enough to minimize the shoreline shadows for proper aerial observation. Since they were both feeling the cold, Sam and Rob retreated indoors to sit by the gas heater, finishing the pot of coffee in the process. Nothing more was said about Sam's morning confession. All talk was of things professional, and she was the same high-spirited perky woman she had been the day before.

CHAPTER 29

At nine o'clock, Sam declared that they should get airborne. The available time when the lighting is most suitable for aerial searching is limited during the winter, so they would have to make the best of the time they had.

After loading their sleeping bags and personal gear back into the plane for the day's flight — standard safety procedure — Sam began the pre-flight checks on the Otter. At the same time, McNabb used his satellite phone to get a weather report.

Only when Sam was close to being ready to start up did they shut down the generator and remove the heaters and the engine tent. While those radial engines were amazingly robust when they were actually running in bitterly cold temperatures, getting them started in the minus thirties could be a real challenge. The Pratt and Whitney was on their side that morning and after some preliminary bucking and farting, it settled into a steady rumble.

McNabb heaved the ninety-pound generator up through the back door and climbed aboard. Sam beckoned him to the cockpit to make sure the plane didn't begin to roll while she went back to secure the Honda unit to her satisfaction. Rob made a mental note to check her tie-down arrangement so he could do it himself the next time.

By nine-thirty, they were in the air and headed across country on their predetermined search route. Since lakes are not placed on the landscape in a grid pattern, the route made for an unorthodox series of zigzags across the terrain.

Many of the lakes shown on the maps were little more than shallow ponds surrounded by subarctic muskeg, with no shoreline visible in their snow-covered winter condition. There would be no place to create a fuel cache, nor any identifiable landmarks to guide one back to it afterwards. So those lakes were quickly ruled out and required no attention save for the checkmarks made on the map to show that they had flown over them. Nonetheless, the whole route had to be flown and the Otter droned on hour after hour from one checkmark to the next.

"Rob, can you take it for a while?" Sam's voice came over the intercom at one point as she unbuckled her harness and prepared to leave her seat. "And you can do it from this seat. It's got the foot pedals."

While Otters could be equipped with a whole range of controls including dual yokes and pedals, theirs was equipped with a single yoke that could be flipped from side to side, but rudder pedals only on the pilot's side.

"Sure. I thought you'd never trust me with the old bird. Going for a walk?"

"No. If you really must know, that last coffee has gone right through me. I've got to go pee!" she replied, picking up a motion sickness bag from a seatback pocket on her way past him.

"Oh, you can do that? I mean into an airsick bag?"

"You don't know much about us women, do you?" She immediately felt a twinge of regret for belittling his lack of experience with girls. Still, she didn't want to keep leading him on — she was having a tough time as it was steering her own romantic thoughts without activating his.

"Hey, if lady truckers can do it into an empty windshield washer fluid jug *while they drive*, I think this little fly-girl can manage a wide open airsick bag in the back of a bush plane … a bush plane that is held *very* steady in the air by a student pilot who pays *very* careful attention to the view *out front* as he flies … *very* steadily."

"Yes, captain. Steady as she goes," replied McNabb, grinning as he slipped into the left-hand seat. He buckled himself in and took over the controls. This was his big chance either to impress her with his steady hand, or piss her off by hitting an invisible pothole in the sky somewhere ahead. He desperately hoped for the former, and when she returned to the cockpit, she took the co-pilot's seat, plugging her headphone into the intercom jack on that side.

"Very smooth, Flyboy, very smooth. Thank you. And because of the monotony of this kind of flying, I'm willing to split the flying time with you more or less half and half. *But,* I do all the takeoffs and landings and it all has to be logged in my name. You already caused enough bureaucrats to crap themselves when you flew this bird solo the other day."

"Thanks Sam. I'll be perfectly happy just getting whatever time you let me have, even though it won't count toward my hours. At least *I* will know I've done it."

—

One thousand feet above the James Bay Lowlands

McNabb had just switched the fuel flow from the nearly depleted aft tank to the unused centre one. Sam was looking down through the passenger side window when she spoke.

"Throttle back and trim it to start descending, Rob. Then when you've gone a couple more minutes in this direction, come around on the reverse course and I'll take over for the landing. I think you are going to want to take a closer look at those tracks down there." The tracks she saw were on a small lake just north of the Attawapiskat River.

"You've got it captain," he replied. It was almost one o'clock and his last coffee was working hard on his bladder now too. So it was either a trip to the back of the bus, or even more welcome, a stroll behind a tree by an unnamed lake.

The little round lake, less than a kilometre across, had a hundred-metre-wide ring of stunted spruce all the way around the shoreline. Beyond that, the trees tapered down into a fringe of tamarack and then the terrain returned to open, snow-covered muskeg.

After he'd made his turn and given the controls back to Sam, Rob could see the triple-ski tracks left by several recent ski plane arrivals and departures on the south side of the lake. This was the first encouraging sign they'd seen all day.

Normally, a pilot would perform a 'touch-and-go' landing and circle once to see if the tracks left by the aircraft turned grey, a sure indication of a sticky, slush-filled runway. But because there was no evidence of slush in the tracks left so recently by the other plane, Sam made her landing without the precautionary slush test.

Taxiing up to where the ski plane had parked, Sam shut down the Otter and they both climbed out. The silence was both welcome and deafening. There were snowshoe tracks leading into the trees, but since the snow on the lake was not deep, McNabb immediately headed for shore without his own snowshoes. In the bush, the snow was much deeper, but in the sub-zero temperatures the trail made by the previous visitors had set and frozen solid. He could walk on the tracks in his winter boots and not sink at all.

About thirty metres from the lake, he found what he was looking for. Returning to the Otter carrying the empty gas jugs, he unscrewed the lid on one and took a sniff.

"So, you won't accept a glass of wine from Gabby at dinnertime, but you don't mind sniffing gas. Robbie, what kind of guy did I take out on this first date anyhow?"

"It's the dry but fruity bouquet of 100-130 avgas, the stuff that Cessnas and Otters really like. Not the sweet, road grade fuel they allow small private planes to burn. But that's just the aircraft lover in me, Sam."

"You *are* a hopeless romantic, Robbie McNabb. Let's get going before our poor Otter loses all its heat and our daylight expires."

By 2:15 they were closing in on Attawapiskat, having flown from west of the Victor Diamond Mine all the way down the river toward the community. "We'll refuel here and then head back to Hawley for the night, checking the last string of lakes as we go," Sam declared as she began making preparations to land on the community runway.

"First thing tomorrow we'll peel a final strip off the west side of the map up here, and then concentrate on the territory between the Attawapiskat and Albany Rivers. After that, if we're still in business, it will be closer to fly out of Moose."

By the time they were closing in on Hawley Lake again, the shadows had grown long, and the last couple of lakes they checked showed no sign of activity.

Their second night in the Hawley Lake camp was far less eventful than their first. After several failed attempts to get the barbeque lit, Rob pan-fried a couple of juicy T-bone steaks on the kitchen range. To make it a proper meal, he also made up a pilaf of wild rice, mushrooms, onions, and red and green peppers that he'd brought from his own kitchen. After the main course, he broke out a small rum cake for dessert.

"You made the cake too, Robbie?" Sam asked.

"A recipe my teetotalling grandmother always made. 'There's more than one way to skin a cat,' she'd say in her later years. I think the dear old lady was a closet alcoholic — or would that make her a cake tin alcoholic?"

"I might not be allowed to fly in the morning if I have any of this you know. Mmm...." she managed, after he tucked a small forkful of the moist creation into her mouth. "Well, just a small slice then, please."

When they turned in, McNabb's nightmare did not return and they each slept on their own cots, the 5-Star bags remaining separate. It was a bit of a letdown for Rob, a reminder of Sam's unhappy revelations at the start of the day. But they'd made it through day two of their acquaintance in amicable fashion.

Sam had resumed ribbing him with her usual gusto, and he'd done his best firing back at her when he could come up with a quick reply. But at night, lying there on the cot next to Sam's, he still felt hollow inside. His thoughts alternated between his feelings of loss and those threads of hope that he'd salvaged from the morning's letdown — those phrases she'd used: 'sort of', 'I'm not sure' and 'so confused' plus the grip of her fingers, interlaced with his.

Something came back to him as he lay on the cot, waiting for sleep to come. As a teen when he was discouraged by his lack of success at attracting girls his mother had often told him, 'To the patient hunter goes the deer.' Mind you, the advice hadn't paid off on any of those occasions, but he still had faith in his mom's track record for handing out sage advice. Patience it would have to be.

Sam too, had a difficult time sleeping that night. She lay on her cot, tossing and turning as she tried to think back to those dates with Jack Colbrook last summer, but visions of Robbie McNabb kept interrupting. Robbie the likeable, gullible guy; Robbie the tall self-assured firearms instructor; Robbie, tormented by the nightmare; Robbie the tender T-bone steak chef — and rum cake baker.

Well, reviewing the past wasn't working, so how about thinking ahead to the May concert at the McIntyre. She imagined Jack enthusiastically applauding Shania Twain as she finished her rendition of "Blue Eyes Crying in the Rain." And in response, an image flashed into her mind. Robbie, was sitting alone in the rain, with tears flowing from his deep blue eyes.

With tears in her own eyes, she got up, dragged on her jumpsuit and boots and headed up the path to the outhouse. The Styrofoam seat allowed her to sit there for a few minutes, privately wrestling with her internal conflict.

"I really, really like you Jack. I want to be near you … to be *with* you. So why does my mind keep cheating on you?" she sobbed quietly in the frigid little building.

"I want to get to know you more. Please don't let him keep pushing you out of my thoughts."

CHAPTER 30

Friday, February 3 — Hawley Lake

Rob McNabb woke to find the camp already warm and his pilot sitting at the table, staring vacantly at a half-finished mug of coffee. He knew Sam had had a bad night because the camp door squawked each time it opened. And he'd heard it open quite a few times as the night progressed.

After making his own morning trip out back, he washed up and quickly threw together a bowl of Swedish pancake batter. Sam hadn't said a word up to that point, and wanting to respect her personal space, neither had Rob. She was obviously still struggling with her choices.

"Tough night, Sam?" he asked ten minutes later, as he set a stack of the thin, golden brown breakfast treats in front of her. "Did I poison you with something I cooked?" Gently resting a hand on her shoulder, he topped up her coffee then returned to the table a moment later with his own plate and mug. He sat down across from her. She finally moved her gaze up to McNabb's face. Her eyes were red from crying. But the tears were gone.

"Yeah, it was a bit of a bitch Rob. And no, it was nothing I ate … dinner was great. But thanks for asking …

and for giving me space too."

"There's no maple syrup, but we've got strawberry and raspberry jams and there's some hardened honey I'm softening up in hot water," he said. Sam opted for the strawberry jam. After several tentative bites of her breakfast, Rob thought she was about to push her plate away. But instead, she finally smiled and said, "These are great! Borrowed this recipe from your granny, too?"

"No, my cousin Neil makes these wicked things at camp when we go deer hunting. Only problem is, no one wants to leave camp until almost noon after we've had them for breakfast." And once the conversation got started, Sam managed to stow her mental baggage again and cheerfully meet the challenges of the new day. McNabb, still amazed she could do that, was immensely relieved. Watching her suffer kept his heart aching for her.

At -23°C the weather was mild by the standards of the two previous weeks. The problem with the milder temperature though, was that it meant there was likely some bad weather moving in. Their tracking campaign could soon come to an abrupt halt. After the relatively long stretch of calm air they had been enjoying, any tracks generated by the fleeing Cessna could soon be obliterated either by drifting snow or fresh snowfall, or both. As a result, they decided to get going even before the shadows shortened on the lakes.

As with the last run yesterday, the first leg of this day's search pattern would just be a cursory look on the unlikely chance that the Cessna had landed at Pine Lake or on the upper reaches of the Ekwan River, both lying substantially west of its most likely flight path.

—

One thousand feet above the James Bay Lowlands

Sam and Rob began the third hour of their flight checking out a string of small lakes between Mississa Lake and Ogoki Post, when McNabb's sat-phone began to deedle in his pocket.

"Hey James, what's up?"

"Morning, Robbie. We just got a call from one of the pilots at Air Creebec. He says that on Monday he saw what looked like a blue and white Cessna taking off from the first lake north of Pledger Lake, the larger of the two up there. There's a camp or trapper's cabin at the east end of the lake. You might want to take a look."

"Okay, we'll work our way over there. ETA in about another fifty minutes," he said checking the aeronautical chart on his lap.

"We'll let you know what we find. We may be euchred for any searches after today though. Cloud cover is beginning to move in up here, and the smoke from a couple of drill camps we've flown over is beginning to look pretty ragged and windblown. May not be any tracks left by tomorrow morning."

"All roger Robbie. Just remember, you be really careful if you see anyone who might have anything to do with this Eagle Feather character."

"We'll get back to you soon boss," he said, then pocketed the phone again.

"Let's work our way across the grid toward Pledger Lake Sam. Just north of it. Largest of several small adjacent lakes."

Forty-five minutes later they could make out the outline of the lake in question. While Sam flew the plane closer, McNabb left his seat. When he returned, he laid the

.30-06 between the pilot's seat and his own. The magazine was reloaded and he dropped it into Sam's parka pocket.

"Probably no one there," he said over the intercom. "But just in case. If the hair stands up on the back of my neck the way it did when I saw that poacher's open cabin door, I'd sure feel a lot more confident knowing that you were behind me ready to make a lot of noise with that thing."

"Oh, I've seen you at work too, McNabb. You'll probably drop any bad guys before I even get it up to my shoulder."

Before Rob was able to come up with a reply, Sam pointed down toward the lake on her side of the plane. "Someone's down there. Smoke's coming from that camp Rob. See it?"

"Yup, I do now," he said, straining to look past Sam out the pilot's side window. "And isn't that a three-skied track down on the other side of the peninsula there? Boy, the snow's already half blown over it. This will probably be our last chance to see tracks anywhere."

"Okay Rob, because the track's blown in and doesn't go right to that camp, I don't know what the slush is going to be like in the bay, so I'll have to make a preliminary touch-and-go. Unfortunately, between that and our thundering radial, this isn't going to be anyone's version of a surprise visit."

"Alright, you check for slush and I'll watch around the camp. If I see anything that looks even remotely hostile, we'll bug out fast and leave it for the police to investigate. But since the Cessna's not there and the tracks don't come from the camp itself, I'd guess it's probably just the trapper who belongs there. We'll be careful just the same."

Sam's touch-and-go on the lake felt good. There was

no telltale evidence of fishtailing to indicate deep slush while taxiing at speed, and after lifting off to make the return pass, only a couple of minor wet spots showed up in the Otter's fresh tracks. She went around again. Her final approach followed her original path, and she put the plane down exactly where she had the first time, this time cutting the power and idling up to within a hundred metres of the trapper's cabin.

CHAPTER 31

Small Lake north of Pledger Lake

Before the Otter's engine had clattered to a stop, a lone individual emerged from the trapper's cabin and started walking in their direction. The cabin door was shut and there were no windows on the front side, so McNabb felt that there was not much chance of someone lying in ambush for them. Not from inside the cabin, anyhow.

Exiting the plane, he walked cautiously toward the approaching man. At the same time, Sam descended from her door, rifle in hand. She squatted beside the wheel strut to watch from underneath the plane. Behind him, Rob could hear the magazine snap into the rifle's receiver.

As the two men neared each other, the stranger raised his hands and placed them on his head. That action raised an alarm in the officer's mind. Perhaps meant to allay his concerns, the move actually elevated them. Who, but a wanted man would put his hands up in surrender without knowing he was under suspicion?

Sam was also alarmed by the surrendering motion. She quickly chambered the first round. But she wasn't interested in the approaching man anymore; she was scanning the treeline along the lakeshore, looking for a third party.

She had watched enough westerns growing up, to know that the ambush doesn't happen from straight on — it's the bad guy you can't see hiding on the roof of the saloon who starts the shooting.

"Hey there, officer," the man spoke out when he was within twenty metres of McNabb. "I think you are looking for me. I'm Cyril Smith, and I was flying polar bear hides for Billy Joe Boyd and when that lunatic Eagle Feather shot him and hijacked the plane I flew him here four days ago and escaped. Only there were just three shotgun shells left in the camp and I used them up on a couple of grouse but I missed one, so I haven't eaten since Wednesday and...."

The man was in a hurry to get a big load of trouble off his chest and was probably suffering from a touch of cabin fever too. So it took McNabb a moment to halt the flood of information. With one hand held up in a police 'stop' signal and his other deliberately gripping the butt of his undrawn pistol, Smith finally fell silent.

But McNabb was still uncomfortable, not knowing if the man was alone, or maybe setting up an ambush. The hair *was* standing up on the back of his neck.

"Alright, Mr. Smith, just stand there for a moment please. Are you armed?"

"Just my pocket knife sir. Front left jeans pocket. Sorry, I should've left it in the camp. I wasn't thinking. I was just so glad to hear you guys coming in." The man was almost in tears, obviously glad someone had found him — either that or he was a really good actor.

"Who else is here with you?"

"No one sir. Eagle Feather took off with the 185 after

I hid in the bush, and I've been alone out here ever since."

Rob still wasn't convinced that all was secure, but he was beginning to feel that the man was not going to be a problem. Forty metres behind him, back at the plane, Sam was on edge. She could barely hear the conversation between Rob and the strange man, so she remained wary of the potential for an ambush.

"Okay, I want you to take your knife out and put it in the snow in front of you. You can drop it in a boot print so it doesn't get lost. Do it now," he ordered.

Smith complied.

"Okay. I need you to take off your coat and set it out in front of you, then step back five paces. Do it now."

McNabb advanced on the coat as soon as Smith backed away, and a check of the inner and outer coat pockets revealed nothing other than the man's gloves. Picking up the knife and pocketing it in his own parka, he moved forward and frisked the compliant Mr. Smith. No other weapons were found, and the photo ID in his wallet matched the man standing in front of him.

"Here, put this on again. I don't need my prisoner getting hypothermia out here. And yes, that does mean that you are under arrest for unlawfully transporting illegally harvested furs and also for your role, whatever it was, in the death of Mr. Boyd. Do you wish to say anything in answer to the charges? You are not required to say...." McNabb went on with the official police caution.

"Okay, we are going to walk to the cabin now. And since this snow makes for heavy going I won't cuff you until we get you inside, but I warn you, any unexpected moves will cost you dearly, do you understand?" McNabb asked as he looked toward the trapper's cabin.

"Yes sir."

"Trail up behind us Sam, eyes peeled," he called back toward the Otter. McNabb felt uncomfortable involving his pilot in an enforcement role. Despite her obvious skill with firearms, she totally lacked any enforcement training. But the young officer was increasingly confident that Smith was no direct threat.

When they got to the camp he instructed his prisoner to enter and walk to the middle of the room. McNabb stayed well back from the door until the man had complied and when there was no indication of Smith's signalling to anyone in the camp, he entered quickly, pistol drawn, and thoroughly scanned the darkness of the one-room building. The dirt floor obviously had no trap door to hide someone under and having seen no fresh tracks other than Smith's leading from the cabin, he was now confident that the man was alone. Sam arrived just as he was snapping the cuffs on Smith.

McNabb noticed a shotgun hanging on the back wall of the cabin. He took it down and inspected it. It was a single shot, twelve gauge Cooey. It was very old, but apparently still serviceable. It wasn't loaded, and there were no shells in view around the room, but McNabb broke the gun down into its three components and set them up on a shelf as a precaution.

"We're clear in here Sam. You can secure the rifle now. This is Cyril Smith. Pilot of the missing Cessna," he said.

"Mr. Smith, what is the U.S. registration number of the 185?" He wanted the American pilot to know right off the top that a Canadian game warden couldn't be hoodwinked by a simple identity switch.

"It's N74933."

"We checked and the Canadian registration you picked doesn't exist," McNabb replied, smiling. He queried

Smith on a number of other matters important to the investigation. The man willingly provided what answers he could but claimed to be in the dark as to Eagle Feather's whereabouts.

Then, pulling his sat-phone from his inner pocket, McNabb punched in the number for the police. "Sam, can you call James while I talk to Ballard? They'll both be pacing their office floors worried sick by now. Have a seat Cyril. We may be here for a while."

—

In his office at the police detachment in Moosonee, Staff Sergeant Ballard was relieved to learn that they had apprehended the pilot of the Cessna without incident. He had worried that if the poaching gang was actually there, things could get really ugly for the young game warden.

"Look Rob, if you can find out from the guy where the Cessna might have gone after it left … anything this Eagle Feather might have said or hinted at, it could make our lives a lot easier."

"I already asked him Staff and all he can tell me is that the guy headed east after he took off, and he should have run out of gas within a hundred miles of here. Possibly sooner. And for your info, the plane was registered in the U.S. The number is November 74933. Just as we had discussed, Boyd was using white shipping film to display the false registration.

"Anyhow, it looks like the weather's going to crap out soon, Staff, so we're leaving here with our prisoner in a few minutes."

"Okay Rob. We'll transport him to the detachment when you get back to Moose. In the meantime, don't let your guard down. Sometimes they play meek and mild just to lull their escort into a false sense of security."

"Yes sir. I don't think that's the case with this one though. You'll see what I mean when you meet him."

While McNabb had been on the phone with Ballard, Sam touched base with James Bird and also called for the latest weather. It was time to boogie if they wanted to get back to Moose before the coming snow blotted out the airport, and the Otter was strictly a Visual Flight Rules aircraft. VFR planes were not equipped for instrument landings in blinding snowstorms.

With Sam alone in the cockpit, Rob belted the handcuffed Cyril Smith into the first seat behind the cockpit bulkhead. He sat across the aisle, one row back where he could easily watch his prisoner and still see the pilot. The Otter was back in the air in minutes, plodding slowly eastward toward Moosonee.

—

Sitting alone in the cockpit, Sam thought back to the takedown of Smith. She was really impressed with how McNabb handled the situation. He had controlled events like a pro, and he wasn't mean or overly officious toward his prisoner. As a result Smith remained calm and compliant. 'Yup, I like the way he operates,' she thought as she tweaked the elevator trim. And then, 'Oh why do I keep thinking about the guy?'

She tried to push him from her mind once more with an image of Jack. Except when he reluctantly showed up, Colbrook's face wasn't completely filled in. Try as she might, she couldn't fully visualize him. 'Shit!' she thought. Two days earlier, she'd been able to picture every detail of the man — at least, every detail of him down to his bathing suit.

Swimming together in the hotel pool, when they attended the seminar, was as intimate as they had gotten.

'Oh Jack, what am I going to do?'

CHAPTER 32

Moosonee

The police were waiting to take charge of the prisoner when Sam taxied the Otter up to the fuel pumps in Moosonee. McNabb helped his pilot with refuelling and bedding the plane down in an empty parking spot on the apron. Then he called James to send a ride for them. Stopping off at the pilots' staff house to carry Sam's sleeping bag to the door, he suddenly felt awkward; he didn't know what to say. Despite developing a good working relationship with her, the last three days had been an emotional roller coaster.

"Hey Robbie," Sam saved the moment. "The Ecolodge in Moose Factory has great eats. Sunday night work for you?"

"Sounds good. I'll call and reserve for seven o'clock. And thanks for everything. I've really enjoyed working with you Sam."

"You sure know how to show a girl a good time Rob. That was some first date," she said as she swung her bags in through the front door. "See you."

Rob turned back to the waiting Suburban, throwing a

wave over his shoulder as he went. He was a little disappointed that nothing even slightly romantic happened at the door — not even one of her sisterly half hugs. But then Sam still needed time to sort things out in her mind.

He still hung on to the hope generated by those key phrases she'd used: 'sort of', 'I'm not sure' and 'so confused' — along with the grip she had put on his fingers. Surely those meant more than she realized. After all, they *were* going to be dining together in two days. And they were keeping that date at her suggestion.

McNabb went first to the office. After checking in with James, he took the Suburban and drove to the police detachment, dropping his baggage at home on the way over. The police had finished processing Cyril Smith for incarceration. Like Rob, the constables who met the man generally agreed that this was not so much a bad man as a man who'd gotten himself into a bad situation. When Rob arrived, Smith was eating a takeout dinner under supervision in the squad lunchroom — not in a cell.

A detective constable, due in for the evening shift, was lined up to interview him and take any statements he provided relating to the criminal aspects of his career with B.J. Boyd. McNabb had been invited to carry the interview into the area of polar bear running and other wildlife offences once the police had exhausted their inquiries.

During the interview, which lasted almost two hours, they got the complete unabridged version of B.J. Boyd's black marketing activities but didn't learn anything that would help them track down Eagle Feather.

Like the law-men, Smith didn't even know the poacher's real name but suggested that the man might not have any aboriginal blood in him. That fit with the information that Gabby Whitegoose and others from the

Hawley Lake settlement had suggested all along. It was obvious that Eagle Feather played his cards close to his chest in any exchanges he had with anyone.

During the interview, they learned several things about Boyd's techniques for working the black market that could be employed by Eagle Feather. Smith's boss had certainly opened up to the poacher as the liquid in the Canadian Club bottle had emptied that night. For one thing, Boyd claimed that exporting even lawfully harvested wildlife products to Russia and Asia was easier to accomplish through various means outside the law than it was through official channels — there was just so much less red tape.

The most common technique was to send the goods by container shipment directly to an agent in the destination country. The wildlife items were buried amidst clean plastic waste products supposedly headed to Asia for recycling. McNabb was quickly beginning to realize that it could be almost impossible to stop the movement of Eagle Feather's bear hides once they left the region. He left the police detachment that evening with the nagging feeling that if they didn't find Eagle Feather really soon, they might miss their chance entirely.

CHAPTER 33

Saturday, February 4

It was the first morning after McNabb's return to town. It was Saturday and supposed to be a day off. But new developments had come to light overnight in the search for Eagle Feather. So Bird called him to meet at the office at ten o'clock for a conference call arranged by Inspector Jones.

"Okay folks listen up," she began. "Item one: With the district inspector's approval, we've set up the joint task force that James suggested the other day. I'm farthest from the action, so using typical perverse government logic I've been put in charge. As far as I'm concerned, we'll all work more effectively together if we disregard rank and pay grade.

"Item two: My people here have managed to lift prints off the laptop and various household items from the camp. They belong to a man named Gerald Morgan, age forty-five. From accumulated records, and one old military ID picture, along with Cyril Smith's personal description of him, we have determined that this is our man. This morning, George put together a photo lineup including a copy of this one and Mr. Smith made a positive ID.

"Morgan has a long history of difficulty dealing with

authority figures," Jones went on. "Trained as a sniper with an elite Special Forces unit in the Canadian Army, he was dishonourably discharged after being court-martialed on a series of breach of discipline charges. After that, he disappeared for a while then resurfaced in connection with a string of luxury car and SUV thefts in Vancouver, LA, Dallas, Toronto, Boston … the list goes on … extensively. Each time the police in these cities were about to close in on him, he would vanish, only to surface weeks or months later in another part of the continent.

"Needless to say, for him to have avoided being caught as many times as he has, this man is much smarter than your average crook, and considering his Special Forces background, he represents a real danger to anyone he feels threatened by.

"I've got an old friend who is with the military police in Petawawa. I called him to ask if we could get any further background on the guy. As it turns out, he went through basic training with our Mr. Morgan before transferring to the MPs. He didn't much like the guy back then, and his opinion of him now is even lower … way lower.

"He has a collection of evidence, most of which dates back to the time of Morgan's discharge. But there's one item of particular interest that showed up more recently, years after he had disappeared off the radar. The whole collection contains some pretty graphic stuff that he can't let out of his office, but he says we really need to see it. And after he sent me a couple of screenshots, I have to agree.

"I've 'volunteered' Lloyd Macdonald to fly down there with our Turbo Beaver on Tuesday and I think Rob McNabb should go too. That is, if you are willing to give him up for two days, James.

"But I'll warn you both, the stuff he listed for me and

the pictures I saw could be really tough to look at … one item in particular, Rob."

"Can you give me a moment April?" Bird asked, and aside to McNabb inquired, "Are you okay with that Robbie?"

McNabb felt the hair standing up on the back of his neck again and his guts beginning to twist. But knowing that he'd hired on for the whole package and not just the easy stuff, he breathed in slowly and then spoke into the phone.

"Yes Inspector, I do need to learn everything I can about him, and if this will help, then let's do it. Where and what time do you want me to meet DC Macdonald?"

"He's got court in Fort Albany the day before and will overnight in the pilots' staff house in Moose. So you can pick him up there around 7:30 and drive him to the airport.

"George, is someone from your shop going too?" Inspector Jones continued.

"Yes Inspector, I've volunteered myself," Staff Sergeant Ballard replied. "Everyone else here either has court, or is on days off, and I can't afford to take anyone else out of the roster or the town will be lawless for those two days. I'll pick everyone up and get us to the airport."

"Thanks Staff."

The next item of business was a quick update from Ballard's new computer whiz constable. The report was not encouraging.

"All of Morgan's files are password protected and he doesn't use the common passwords that so many people think they can get away with. And he's backed up everything to the cloud," the constable explained. "So, even though we've got his laptop, he can still access his files from anywhere. We haven't put him out of business — yet. I'll keep working on it though.

"A friend of mine from Waterloo is a programmer,

and he sent me a password-breaking algorithm to try. That's where I'm at right now. I'll let you know as soon as I can get in Sirs, Ma'am."

After the call ended, McNabb sat there, deep in thought. Bird watched him from across their conjoined desks. After everything his young CO had been through in the past week he was concerned about putting him under more pressure.

"Robbie, if this evidence in Petawawa is going to be a problem for you, I'm not going to make you go."

"I'll manage, James. Inspector Jones says that she, and Macdonald and Singh have developed a perverse sense of humour to deal with stuff like that. It's not the kind of humour they share outside their immediate circle, but she said it helps. I'll get through it." He paused a moment, looking as if he wanted to say something else, but wasn't sure if he should. Bird waited patiently.

"James, you never did explain why the Sam Williams was in such a bad mood the day I flew Clark down in the Otter. It slipped your mind? Or was there a deeper reason?"

"It's a fair question. At first, I was planning to brief you on her situation, but then I realized that if you two were going to be working together, you should hash things out between yourselves, face to face. Was I right? You got it sorted out?"

"Yeah boss, we did, and I think that was the right thing to do. Only . . . are there any government rules against staff, uh . . . relationships?"

After Bird stopped laughing, he reassured him. "Not unless one of them is in a supervisory position over the other. So you're okay there Robbie, and I hope it works out."

"Yeah, me too. Mind you, there's another guy she

started seeing, but the way things sound, I think my arrival on the scene has put an awful knot in that relationship. I guess I'm on hold until she gets it all sorted out in her mind."

"I might end up owing Archie a bottle of Scotch," Bird mused.

Puzzled for a moment, McNabb soon caught the meaning of the comment. "Well there should be a rule against placing bets on employees' personal relationships," he said, grinning. The grin quickly became a wistful smile. Then he turned serious again.

"So, back to Eagle Feather … or Morgan, I guess. I've got some ideas on how we should work our side of this case, but I don't want to take a wrong turn. It's tough being the rookie on the team, and I don't want to come off looking like a wet-behind-the-ears city kid the first time I get assigned to a joint task force.

"From what I could learn of the black market fur business from Cyril Smith last night, we really have to find those bear skins before they leave our area, or they could easily be lost to us forever. But right now, I'm at a loss as to where he could be hiding … if he even survived his trip at all."

"Seeing as how he flew east from Pledger Lake on less than a hundred miles of fuel Robbie, how far would that take him? What is his logical next step from there, wherever 'there' is?"

"Well, he didn't land here … not at the airport, anyhow. And due east from Pledger Lake would have taken him to the winter road or the railway line somewhere southwest of town, with maybe a few miles to spare. If he flew any farther though, he'd have flown into the hinterland toward Quebec … and there's really nothing for him there.

"So I was thinking I should ask the train crew if they have any records, or remember anyone matching his description flagging them down or boarding somewhere down the line. And if he did, just how much stuff did he have with him. I can't see him getting on the train with a whole bunch of polar bear hides though.

"Do you know if the railroad guys would tell us if someone was obviously doing something wrong like that?"

"Well sure, most of them would, Robbie. I know a few of the guys, and they'd really hate having us seize their train for transporting illegal fur. That's been done in the past on other railroads, so most of them would be on the horn right away. I think that's as good a place to start as any. Go talk to them when the train gets in on Monday. It'll be the same crew."

"Okay, I'll start there."

"In the meantime, this was supposed to be your day off. So scoot."

Rob went for a long walk that afternoon. He found he could concentrate best during a vigorous walk. By the time he returned to his empty house just after dark, he had hiked out to the quarry and back. The fifteen-kilometre round trip had given him a brisk workout, but his mind was still in turmoil.

As anxious as he was to hear from Sam, he resisted the idea of phoning her. Even though he'd been tempted a number of times to give her a call, he knew she needed time and space. If she ended up not wanting to have anything to do with him, he didn't want it to be because of his impatience. If she wanted to talk to him, she had his number.

CHAPTER 34

Sunday, February 5

McNabb answered his phone. His heart warmed the instant he saw the red-headed pilot's name on his call display.

"Hi Sam, so are we still on for dinner tonight?"

"Hi Rob, I've got some bad news, and some other news. Which do you want first?"

"Should I hang up now and avoid a broken heart?" His sense of elation fell faster than it had risen. He quickly guessed what was coming next.

"Well, it isn't all *that* bad, but we'll have to do dinner at the lodge some other time. I've been told to take our Otter back to Timmins today. It's going into mothballs again. They're worried the engine might time out on us while we are airborne. It was already maxed out when they sent it north, so it's running on borrowed time. But later in the week I get to deliver the Moosonee Turbo Beaver back here. It's right out of the shop from its major overhaul … paint's not even dry yet."

"I'm really going to miss the Otter." And he'd miss Sam too, but he was glad that she was returning to town and still wanted to see him. "Is it safe to fly then? Should you even be flying it at all? They can always remove its wings up here and ship it down on the train."

"Don't worry. It'll be fine. I'll baby it all the way to Timmins, okay?"

"Okay, so what was the 'other' news then?"

"Well …" she paused. "I've been asked to take a transfer. They don't need me any more in Timmins, but I have my choice of two locations. First is in Dryden, training on the CL-415 water bombers. It would be a great opportunity for me."

"Sam, that's great … I guess. But that's almost out on the prairies!" His heart was sinking fast. This was his 'Dear Rob' letter, just done over the phone. "It's three quarters of the way to Winnipeg from here! Nice place, but gee, Sam...." McNabb was flabbergasted. He would never have a chance to build a relationship with her way out there.

"The other choice is a remote posting up north that they said nobody else wants. I kind of thought I'd take that one." His spirit slumped lower still. This was a disappointing turn of events.

"Can't they send someone else? Surely one of the more senior pilots would love to fly water bombers and you could stay in Timmins."

"No, I'm the most junior pilot in the air service right now. I'm the first person they get to kick around. They said it's either Dryden or the other one, so I agreed to take the other one. I'm moving to Moosonee!"

"Aw Sam, why do you torture me like that? I bet you pulled the wings off of flies when you were growing up."

"Oh, Robbie, you're just too gullible. I can't resist. Anyway, I'll see you late this week. And Sunday dinner at the lodge is mandatory."

"Well, thanks for the great news, even if you did leave me twisting in the wind. Need a ride to the airport?"

He was answered by the familiar whine of the inertial starter motor and the snarling roar of the Otter's engine before Sam disconnected the call. Ten minutes later their beautiful old ODL waggled its wings at him as it thundered past his house for the last time.

It being Sunday, he got busy with a binge of house cleaning.

CHAPTER 35

In the air bound for Timmins

Sam climbed the Otter to a thousand feet and trimmed it for level flight. Once she was satisfied that everything was running as it should, her mind wandered back to the decision she'd made on short notice this morning.

She'd just gotten out of the shower when her supervisor phoned and broke the news to her. It wasn't a pink slip by any means, he assured her. She was still very much part of the air service but the organizational chart had been reorganized again and she was now considered surplus to the needs of Timmins — not that anyone in Timmins had any say in the matter.

Having to make a major career decision while standing naked on the bath mat wasn't something she'd recommend to anyone. But, while the boss did say she could have the rest of the day to think about it, she had rashly chosen, on the spot, to move to Moosonee. Now, sitting at the big bird's controls, she still didn't know why she hadn't given more thought to the water bomber option. The pilots of those monsters made over a hundred thousand a year. As a co-pilot, she would have made close to that.

But either Moosonee or McNabb, or a combination of the two, had applied some kind of magnetic attraction to influence her spontaneously uttered decision. And that was it. Moosonee and McNabb.

Part of her glowed when she thought of him. All night Friday and most of Saturday, she had fought a battle of wills with herself, finally declaring in favour of Robbie over Jack.

All the way south to Timmins she kept running hot and cold over her decision. Half the time she was convinced that she should tell the boss that she had changed her mind. He might be disappointed to lose her from the region; but he *had* said she could think about it until the end of the day. And it was Sunday. Governments didn't make administrative changes on weekends. The other half of the time, Robbie kept leaping onto centre stage, making her feel all warm and fuzzy inside again.

As she taxied the Otter up to the hangar doors in Timmins, she was hit by the same nostalgia that had claimed McNabb. That lovely plane was finally ending its service life, but now it was part of her history — hers and Robbie's combined.

"Thanks for the memories old girl. I'll try to come and see you in the museum, or wherever you end up." She cut the fuel flow, shutting down the big engine. 'Oh why do I have tears in my eyes over a dumb old machine?' she asked herself as she made her final entries in the aircraft log.

Confused about how to proceed, Sam resolved to call Mother Jones when she got back to her apartment. But the inspector was coming out of the hangar just as Sam locked up the Otter's door.

"Hey Sam, I hear you are going to stay with us here in the northeast."

"Oh April, I think I've made a terrible mistake," Sam

sobbed.

"Come on inside and tell Mother all about it," April Jones said, wrapping a comforting arm around Sam's shoulder.

"I think there's still some dreadful coffee left, and we've got the whole place to ourselves." They sat at the big table in the hangar lunchroom and nursed their coffee while Sam poured out her concerns to her mentor. And the coffee was terrible.

"So I've not even known Robbie for a week … worked with him for just three days. Why would I let a fleeting attraction to him make me decide to transfer close to him, rather than going to fly with the big boys in Dryden?" The inspector let Sam vent and after five or six minutes, she finally ran out of steam.

Mother paused for a moment, and then began, "Sam, those were three days that were full of the work you love to do. You got to fly your beloved Otter and you lived and worked in close quarters for three days and two nights with Rob. I think you may have gotten to know him better than you realize. In fact, the way you describe him as constantly pushing the other fellow out of your mind, I'd say he'd won a place in your heart before you knew it."

"That's what really worries me, April. The last guy I thought was Mr. Right turned out to be a real jerk, a possessive, demeaning jerk. And the guy before him still makes me gag whenever I think about him. So how can I trust my own judgment with Robbie McNabb? I want it to be him, but I'm terrified I'll be wrong again."

"Sam, the way you've described the previous men in your life, I just don't see that in Rob. I see a resourceful, hard working young man who's fallen head over heels for you. He's just too open … too transparent to hide the wicked traits those others exhibited. Don't be afraid to test the waters. You can always back away if he doesn't work out.

"And unless I miss my guess, choosing to transfer to Moose was probably influenced at least as much by your love of the lowlands and the Natural Resources family that calls Moosonee home. Remember, that's where you cut your teeth in the air service. McNabb is probably only a portion of what led to your decision. And if it was a decision of the heart, so be it."

"Thanks April. I think you're right. I do feel a magnetic attraction to Moose … and to Robbie," she smiled. Moosonee and McNabb it would be.

The two women hugged before dumping their cold coffees into the sink and locking up the hangar doors.

CHAPTER 36

Monday, February 6 — Moosonee

The Monday train from Cochrane arrived in Moosonee at 1:55 on a bitterly cold afternoon. It was only five minutes late, an uncommon and amazing feat during the harsh conditions of a northern winter. While the conductor was busy detraining the passengers, McNabb climbed up to the locomotive cab to speak with the engineer. He asked him if he had seen anything of a large man with long black hair — but not a regular on the line — waiting, or boarding between Moosonee and somewhere south of Onakawana any time the previous week.

"He'd probably be taking the southbound, and he may or may not have had some white commercial fur bags with him," he explained.

"Hmm, that rings a bell … the man, but without the baggage. Just let me think back," he paused, staring momentarily at the cab ceiling. "We don't get many pickups there this time of year and my logbook for last week is down in Cochrane now, so I'm guessing here. But yeah, on Tuesday, I think, a guy sounding like that flagged us at Onakawana … tough looking customer … or was it

Wednesday … just a minute. Ray will know," the man paused to pick up a radio mic. "Ray, it's KC, do you copy?"

Less than fifteen minutes later, after a free coffee in the dining car, McNabb had the information he was looking for. After thanking the train crew, he drove back to the office, made a phone call. When James got off the phone from a call of his own, Rob gave him the latest news.

"He boarded at Onakawana with no baggage on Tuesday night, leaving his snowshoes on a peg on the outside of the old section house. Stayed to himself the whole way south and Ray, the conductor, says he saw him head into the Station Inn as soon as he got off. And the snowshoes are still hanging there. Oh yeah, he also said he'd give us a heads up if the guy shows up again.

"So I'm thinking he has stashed his furs somewhere up here near the rail line and must have some way planned to come back and get them out. I'll tell the police what I've learned. I'm sure they'll be willing to watch that stretch of the winter road even closer for signs of odd comings and goings."

"I agree Robbie. And I'd also have the Cochrane COs check the hotel. Maybe he's set up housekeeping there for the time being."

"Already done that and they promised to get back to me before coffee time. They said they'd also let the local police know he might be in town."

—

Timmins

Gerald Morgan was waiting for a delivery at the Timmins rental storage yard. The transport truck was due to arrive early that afternoon; the poacher was in a hurry to move his project to the next stage.

It was 2:15 when his shipment arrived and he watched as the transport driver rolled the two, twenty-foot shipping containers off his flatbed and placed them side by side in the storage yard. Two containers might be considered a bit of overkill, but he was not going to trust his entire inventory to just one. Those things had a nasty habit of falling overboard on transoceanic crossings and he didn't want to risk losing everything to one fluke accident. It wasn't exactly the sort of cargo you would buy insurance on. He would hold one container back for several weeks to ensure they sail on different ships.

Another thing that might appear to be overkill was buying twenty-foot units. After all, the whole lot of his furs had just been flown down from Sutton Lake in a six-seat bush plane. A gut feeling told him that a small eight- or ten-foot container was more likely to raise the curiosity of customs or port inspectors somewhere along the way. Since most major shipments were made in twenty, forty or fifty-three footers, his would more easily blend in with the crowd. At eighteen hundred dollars per unit, it was a small investment for the extra peace of mind. Besides, the nearly new containers had only one trip behind them and he knew that he would easily recoup the cost of them on resale in Asia. There was always a shortage of them on that side of the Pacific.

His next step involved a carpentry project. Using rental tools and lumber delivered by the nearby Home Hardware store, he built a wooden bin into the far end of each container. While he could have brought everything over from the store in his own truck, he had left the vehicle in a public parking lot several blocks away. There was no point being seen with all his acquisitions in one place. If the truck suddenly came to the attention of the authorities, he didn't want them putting two and two together and discovering his shipping plans.

Each of the wooden bins was capable of holding half of his furs. In case of bad weather along the way, the bottom of each bin was built two feet off the container floor — the built-in ventilation in the containers was supposed to exclude water, but again, Morgan was taking no chances. The hides could not be completely sealed for shipping or they might begin to develop mould or mildew. They'd be ruined. So they had to stay high and dry and be free to breath in the fur shipping bags.

Morgan did not like being idle, and the time he had spent waiting for his containers to arrive had not been wasted. In need of packing material to conceal his bins, he had visited several recycling facilities in the region and bought up enough bales of waste plastics to fill both containers to the doors.

The waste management companies were delighted to help him out, because despite government-mandated plastics recycling, the current market for their product was spotty at best. They weren't quite giving the material away, but it cost him only a few dollars per tonne. And they would deliver whenever he was ready.

Morgan knew that his packing system wouldn't stand up to the x-ray technology employed on containers arriving in North American ports but these were outbound, headed for an Asian port where he knew that little attention was paid to light loads or empty containers deadheading to that part of the world. The recyclable plastic filler was primarily to deter low-paid, light-fingered dock workers and corrupt officials in the port of arrival.

What better way to discourage pilfering, than for potential thieves to face a wall of discarded plastic after breaking into an incoming container. Whether or not there was any market for the plastic waste when he got it over there would remain to be seen, but he certainly wasn't losing any sleep over it.

CHAPTER 37

Tuesday, February 7 — Moosonee

It was 7:30 on another crisp winter morning in the lowlands, but the overnight low had only dropped to -30°C. It was a definite improvement over the deep freeze of the previous six weeks. Rob McNabb stood waiting at the end of his driveway as morning twilight worked to overtake the night.

Minutes later, he was sitting in a warm police cruiser with the staff sergeant and Lloyd Macdonald headed for the airport. It took the three of them no time at all to ready the police Turbo Beaver for its flight. Even with a pause for an airport coffee, they were airborne by 8:15.

Ballard deferred to McNabb, allowing the 'honorary' Otter pilot to sit beside Macdonald, who enthusiastically introduced the young CO to the world of the turbo-prop aircraft. The route to Petawawa took them southeast, over a substantial portion of western Quebec. And if McNabb had thought northern Ontario was a vast, lake-dotted stretch of Canadian shield, then that part of Quebec had to be every bit as beautiful.

About halfway there, Macdonald looked back at the

dozing staff sergeant and keyed the intercom. "If you don't tell Mother, I'll let you take it for a bit. The old fellow back there can't touch us … we're air service."

"I heard that," came from Ballard.

"Thanks Lloyd." They both grinned at the staff sergeant's retort and McNabb took the right-hand flight controls lightly in his hands. He made a couple of gentle sweeping turns and altitude adjustments to get a feel for the plane.

"Like the Otter, it handles really smoothly … at least that's the word I'd use. Yeah, this is really nice. I'm used to the Cessna trainers … if there's a puff of wind two miles ahead, the little beggars bounce all over the sky." He settled back on course at the altitude Macdonald had established.

"But I'd sure like to know what it is Sam likes so much about these planes. The smell in here is like sticking your head inside the exhaust pipe on a diesel bus. Do they all stink like this?"

"Not the newly rebuilt ones Rob. They've got longer exhaust stacks. But this one isn't due for its major overhaul yet, so the exhaust seeps through every gap in the fuselage. It gets even worse when we are banked in a tight turn."

"Just the thought of worse is beginning to make my skin crawl," McNabb looked a touch pale. "I could picture decorating the inside of an airsick bag really easily if this stink got much worse. Aside from that, it *is* a real beauty to fly." After a quick glance toward Macdonald, he added, "Don't tell Sam about the weak stomach thing. She'd do donuts in the sky the first time she got me into one, just to watch me suffer."

"Knowing Sam, she'll probably do that anyhow, Rob."

"You're probably right."

It was 11:30 when they landed at the Canadian Army base in Petawawa. They were met by Inspector Jones's contact, Major Wilson. He took them first to have lunch at the officers' mess and right after they finished eating, he drove them to his headquarters.

"What you gentlemen are about to see, is not for the faint of heart. I'm going to show you a couple of home videos that were collected as evidence against Gerald Morgan. Both were filmed by Morgan himself. A sick mind with a bit of an ego issue, I'd say.

The first one is part of what led to his court-martial, and has to do with animal torture and mutilation. Primarily, he used domestic rabbits, cats and dogs as targets, but it wasn't as simple as that. And as much wartime destruction as I have seen inflicted on humans and animals during my tours in Bosnia and Afghanistan, these still make me sick."

The major turned on the video. Displayed on a large flat screen mounted on the conference room wall, the images came with sound but no narration. The three visitors in the room were transfixed by the disgusting action taking place in the video. It showed Morgan releasing his various victims, usually one at a time, into a steep-sided sand pit located somewhere in a remote forested area.

His objective was to shoot them with small calibre rifles and handguns and see how many times he could injure them before they succumbed. The more injuries an animal sustained before death, the higher his 'score.' He kept the score tallied on a whiteboard placed within view of the camera. The images of the pitiful, terror-stricken animals were sickening, and the frightening efficiency of the atrocities was beyond description. Worst of all, he appeared to be having fun doing it.

The three visitors sat aghast as Major Wilson ejected

the tape from the video recorder. Even Constable Macdonald, who had investigated more murder scenes than he cared to keep track of, found that this animal cruelty ranked with the worst of them. McNabb just sat there shaking his head.

"You can understand why we didn't want that kind of sick mind mixed in with our troops. We train them to take lives alright, but not like that.

"This next video, we found only recently. It was stashed with some of Morgan's personal effects that turned up during a cleanup of unclaimed lockers. This is the one I warned Inspector Jones about. It solves a previous cold case — the rape, sexual torture and savage beating of a fifteen-year-old girl from just outside of Pembroke over twenty years ago. Morgan grabbed her while she was walking the quarter mile home from where the school bus dropped her off. After he'd finished what you'll see in the video, he left, taking the tape with him. We think he intended to come back for more, except the MPs were doing a sweep of the area that day to clear it of civilians. There was a live-fire training exercise due to start the next morning.

"The girl was found unconscious and chained to steel rings bolted into a wall. She never regained consciousness and died a couple of days later. He didn't leave any useable prints, and DNA testing wasn't then what it is now. No one had any idea he'd been the perpetrator until the tape showed up.

"So in addition to all the active, continent-wide arrest warrants issued for this guy, he is of particular interest to us. And while this is a joint murder investigation between us and the provincial police, we have retained jurisdiction over the security of the evidence. I just pray we get to use it on the sick bastard one day soon … if something deservedly horrible doesn't happen to him first.

"Now … Officer McNabb, the inspector says that this may hit you pretty hard … for reasons which will become almost immediately obvious. Please understand that we'll not think any less of you if you need to step out while this plays." And with that, he snapped the second VHS tape into the player.

Like Morgan's first tape, there was no introduction and no narration — just the sound recorded at the time. The opening image was of a naked and sexually aroused Gerald Morgan starting up the camera, then turning and moving across the room in what appeared to be a hunt camp. He approached a figure huddled in the corner and grabbed his victim, now obviously a girl. Holding her by the arms, he dragged her to a mattress on the floor close to the camera.

McNabb froze. The shock of what he saw left him horrified. If the video hadn't been taken twenty years earlier, the girl could have been Samantha Williams as a teen. The face, the curly red hair, the build — they could have been twins. The instant he saw the poor girl, he felt the blood draining from his cheeks and his guts tighten.

He didn't stay for the whole video. The initial horrors that he did see inflicted on the girl and her terrified screams were more than enough to convince him of the raw evil he would be facing if he ever did track down the man who called himself Eagle Feather. He had neither bargained, nor been trained for anything like this. All he wanted to do was catch a plain old garden variety polar bear poacher.

When Ballard and Macdonald emerged from the conference room, McNabb was walking unsteadily out of the major's washroom, where he'd left his lunch. They too, looked badly shaken.

CHAPTER 38

Petawawa

When they boarded the Turbo Beaver to head toward Timmins — they weren't going all the way back to Moosonee that day — McNabb chose a seat in the back of the plane. Still sickened by the small part of the video that he had seen, he wasn't feeling too chatty. The dark humour used by the CSI team couldn't even begin to be applied here. Lloyd Macdonald would attest to that later.

George Ballard, giving an unseen nod to the pilot, took the seat beside the CO rather than the vacant one up front beside Macdonald. Chatty or not, the rookie ought not to be left alone to brood. Mother Jones had warned the staff sergeant of what they would see in the video, and passed along the essence of a private talk she had had with Sam, after McNabb's nightmare at Hawley Lake.

"The inspector was concerned that you had to see that, Rob," Ballard's voice came over the intercom. "It made my skin crawl too, and in my years on the job, I've seen more rape and abuse victims than I'd care to remember. But we all agreed that since this guy moved into your patch and is the primary suspect in your bear case, you really do need to know what he's about.

"Just remember, you aren't alone in wanting him brought down. One mention of his name on the phone or radio and we'll move heaven and earth to get there. So if you catch so much as a whiff of the bastard, you back off and wait for the cavalry to arrive. Understand?"

McNabb nodded. He already knew that the members of the police force supported him, but after what he'd seen today, the reinforcement of that message was important.

"And if by some twist of fate you end up facing the man, use your training. From what I've seen of a CO's self defense training regime, most of you could outdo many of our members on the shooting range.

"I was entirely impressed with the level of skill and the standards expected of your people when I went through one of your ministry's qualification matches. I just barely scraped by, and in police circles I'm considered a pretty good shot. Anyhow, James tells me you were the top scorer at your most recent shoot. So, as I said, follow your training.

"As for Samantha Williams, as long as you don't introduce her to Morgan, I very much doubt their paths will ever cross. She's airborne and he's normally ground-bound. But we'll watch out for her too. She's flown most of my detachment members in one direction or another since her first contracts started with the air service and she's a favourite of ours. We won't knowingly let anything bad happen to her."

"Thanks Staff."

They landed in Timmins that night and stayed at the Comfort Inn. Ballard had reserved ahead and anticipating that the young game warden would have a rough day, he had booked him into the same room. Macdonald went home to his own family for the night, promising to pick them up first thing in the morning in order to get them back to Moose before noon.

Rob had hoped that Sam might be in town, but when he tried her cell phone, she answered from Hearst where she had just finished another day of moose surveying.

"We had great conditions, Robbie," she said, enthusiastic about the fact that she was now flying moose surveys as a full-time employee, no longer a contract pilot with no benefits. It was her dream career come true.

"The guys saw loads of moose in an area that's been almost barren of them for nearly twenty years."

McNabb tried to mimic her enthusiasm, but she easily detected his subdued spirit.

"What's wrong Rob? Are you okay?"

"Sorry Sam, it was my first time in a diesel Beaver … sweet thing to fly … Lloyd let me take it for a while. But God, do those turbines ever stink. And then we hit some bad turbulence on the way back. I'm still feeling a little green," he lied. He didn't want her to know what he'd seen in Petawawa — didn't want her to know anything about that evil son of a bitch.

"When are you coming back up to Moose? More importantly, when are you moving up?" he asked. On that topic at least, he could show genuine enthusiasm.

"They said any time I want to start moving my stuff up, I am okay to use the bird on deadhead flights. They know I live mostly out of boxes so moving furniture isn't going to be part of the package. If I take a couple of boxes each time I'm flying home from another district, then they won't have to pay for a commercial move. Perfectly symbiotic relationship, wouldn't you say? So I'm figuring I should be all done in Timmins by the end of the month. That's when I'm paid up to with the landlady anyhow."

"Sam?" He paused, then decided against his next question. It would be better if she lived in the staff house, at least for a while, he guessed. He'd ask her to move in with him later if things went well. "Sam, will I see you Friday?" he asked instead.

"Maybe Thursday even. There's supposed to be some weather moving in shortly. That'll put the kybosh on our survey for the rest of this week."

"I'm really looking forward to seeing you, whenever you get there."

"Me too, Robbie."

"Bye Sam." As much as he ached to end the conversation with 'I love you,' he didn't dare. Even though she had chosen to transfer near him, he still was wary of scaring her off. After the ups and downs of their few days working together, he was deathly afraid of rejection.

"Bye Flyboy," she finished, and he could almost 'hear' her heart-warming smile. At least for now, the Petawawa experience had been eclipsed by more pleasant thoughts.

CHAPTER 39

Wednesday, February 8 — In the air over Onakawana

Lloyd Macdonald had McNabb and Ballard airborne and bound for Moosonee before 8:30 that morning. The CO had reclaimed his seat beside the pilot, and Ballard sat in the back in relative comfort, relieved that the night in the hotel had gone without incident. McNabb had dropped off to sleep even before the eleven o'clock news was over and there had been no wild dreams to wake the senior officer as the night progressed. Rob's phone conversation with Sam Williams apparently had a settling effect on him. He no longer wore the tormented look he'd had when they left Petawawa.

As agreed before they left Timmins, Macdonald flew the Turbo Beaver along the railroad line when they got closer to where Morgan had boarded the train. They looked for snowshoe tracks in the bush on either side of the line.

They also did a couple of passes up and down the winter road in the immediate vicinity of Onakawana but saw nothing. In one place they thought they saw moose tracks along both sides the road, but there was just one set and they were partially snowed in, not fresh.

—

Timmins

Finally finished his preliminary arrangements in the city, Gerald Morgan headed north out of town in his Chevy truck. His new sheet-metal airtight stove and smoke pipes were stacked in the back seat and his used Polaris was tied in the cargo bed. It was 9:45 a.m. and he was getting anxious to start moving his bear hides out of the Cessna and into his containers. As much as he was in a hurry though, he knew that he had to stay with the pace of the traffic and not draw any attention to himself.

Near the top end of Highway 655, a police cruiser caught up and began following him. It was a long straight stretch with plenty of room to pass, so the longer the vehicle tailed him, the more he tensed. This could be a problem, he thought and he felt for the familiar .45 lying under his jacket on the seat beside him.

Soon however, the car pulled out and passed, the officer apparently not concerned by his presence. So the guy whose truck he'd bought hadn't yet raised the alarm about not getting his licence plates back. This was good news. If the guy hadn't thought of it by now, the plates were likely Morgan's for the duration.

—

Moosonee

The moment McNabb arrived back at the office, James Bird gave him some news they had been hoping for. Ballard's computer-whiz constable had called just minutes earlier. He finally cracked the passwords to Morgan's files. So Rob and James immediately drove over to the detachment where they joined Ballard and the police members of their task force. The group worked through the lunch hour and well into the afternoon, poring over the poacher's files.

The computer records included a bonanza of material for any police force investigating his auto-theft activities. But everything was filed alphabetically in one single massive folder, with randomly assigned file names that gave no clues as to their contents.

The group in the conference room had to open every file individually to determine if it contained material relating to the current case. A clerk catalogued each file as the person opening it determined its significance.

"Bingo!" At 3:35, James Bird finally opened the first file directly related to their investigation. From it, they learned that their wanted man had recently rented space at a storage facility in the west end of Timmins.

George Ballard got on the phone immediately and made arrangements to have a plainclothes member from the Timmins detachment interview the facility owner and discretely find out what Morgan was up to. Half an hour later they learned from that source about the two containers the poacher had obtained.

The storage facility owner, being a little nosier than some of his clients might like, told of the do-it-yourself building projects Morgan had engaged in. He didn't know exactly what was being built, but he did say that other than lumber, nothing had been loaded into the units yet. They were however, conveniently parked in front of one of his hidden security cameras. And yes, he'd let them have the password to monitor his cameras through the Internet. That job was turned over to the city police. They had more bodies available.

"Okay, we know that Morgan landed somewhere near Onakawana with a planeload of fur," McNabb sat, thinking aloud. "And we know he went down to Cochrane by train, empty-handed, and somehow got to Timmins, where he now has two containers, ready to receive something … obviously his furs. So if nothing's been delivered yet, why don't we just set up a round the clock welcoming committee and grab him when he arrives at the storage place?"

"I'm sorry to have to rain on your parade, Rob," the computer-savvy constable broke in, "But from what I've been reading of his auto-theft enterprises, police agencies that thought they had him boxed in like this before, regularly got fooled. He had a habit of setting up more than one shipping arrangement. A number of times he loaded his goods into a set of containers totally unknown to them while they waited at the original set. Transports moved in and picked up the load and left the police standing around slack-jawed, wondering why he hadn't shown up. He appears to have an uncanny knack for knowing if one of his options has been compromised."

Ballard and Bird sat silently letting the two youngest members work through their own ideas. The supervisors had both seen situations where the unfettered minds of rookies came up with truly inventive solutions that more experienced officers, already set in their ways, missed entirely. Unless the young lads wandered off topic, the old guys would hang back for now.

"Crap. Then we're back to having to get him here on our own turf," McNabb acknowledged. "So, this may sound a bit like wishful thinking George, but do you guys by any chance have a long range UAV somewhere in the province? A drone that could fly for hours would be the ideal thing to park in a circular orbit over the Onakawana area, watching for him to arrive."

"Rob, the units our traffic-crash investigators use are all we've got. They are battery operated, and only last about twenty minutes in the air. Resources like what you are talking about are still pretty much in the realm of military hardware," Ballard said.

"What about this Major Wilson you guys met yesterday?" James Bird joined in on the brainstorming. "I doubt Canada has any big drones yet, but if the army wants Morgan as badly as we do, maybe he could talk the Americans into joining the search with one. He's wanted in the States too, after all."

"I doubt the federal government would want to invite U.S. Homeland Security — they being the owners of the nearest drones — to fly over vast stretches of our country, even if they were willing to help," said the computer whiz. He was a recent transfer in from a federal government contract job.

For the next few minutes the conversation drifted back and forth from one idea to the next with no positive results. Partway through the brainstorming session, Rob McNabb found himself only half paying attention. There was something troubling him. Something he'd seen, or thought he'd seen but he just couldn't quite put his finger on it.

"Rob?" Ballard asked, trying for the CO's attention. "Rob, you've got that faraway look, like you had in the plane yesterday after we saw the videos. You okay?"

"Yeah … the plane … that's it … this morning Staff. Remember those moose tracks we saw beside the winter road?"

"Yes I remember. What of them?"

"There weren't any other tracks there, other than that

set, or at least we didn't see any, not for miles either way from there. And the pattern was *almost* random like moose, only more of a *regular* zigzag, not quite as random as a moose might really make. Like, maybe … they were man-made. If we could find that spot on the ground and verify that they are or aren't moose tracks, then the next step, if they are man-made, is to draw a line on the map from Onakawana, across the road at that spot and it would possibly extend to near where the plane is. What do you think?"

"It's a long shot Rob," James Bird said. It was the first time he'd ever called his rookie anything but Robbie. "But it will be dark before you could get down there today and I don't want you rambling around down there on your own. You know what Morgan is like. George told me what you saw yesterday." He was troubled about putting the brakes on his budding detective CO, but he didn't want to expose him to unnecessary danger, either.

"Can you lend me a constable tomorrow, George?" McNabb knew that James would be testifying in court in the case of a delinquent licence issuer and wouldn't be available to go.

"We could drive down, look along the roadside for those tracks and if they aren't moose or caribou, then we might have narrowed our search area by a wide margin." McNabb was warming more to his own idea the more he thought about it. "And if we find the Cessna, we should still be able to follow his tracks to wherever he stashed the furs. There hasn't been enough wind or snow in the bush since the day he landed to completely cover his tracks."

"Okay. I'll set it up with the shift sergeant. But plan on an early start, there's snow moving in tomorrow afternoon. Be here by seven. You'll never find the tracks, let alone figure out what made them once they get snowed over.

You okay with that James?"

"Yes that's good with me.

"I do have one last question George, though on another aspect of the case. About B.J. Boyd. There's been no media coverage at all about his unfortunate passing; how'd you manage that?"

"Well, I'm delighted with how airtight our two organizations are James. And the inspector spoke personally to Gabby and Edna, who spoke with their neighbours … obviously nothing's leaked from there yet either. Anyhow, we'll try to keep a lid on it for as long as it takes to get this guy. Again, after what we saw in Petawawa yesterday, I'd hate for Morgan to get nervous. With his skills, he could hurt a lot of good people before we get him corralled.

"Oh, and your friend, Agent Sturgis; he agreed to say nothing. He put it something like, 'until the eviscerated corpse of that hick poacher lands in my parish, the media here ain't got no questions to ask'."

CHAPTER 40

Airborne near Hearst

Sam Williams and the Hearst fish and wildlife technicians only got a couple of lines flown before the weather began to interfere with the moose survey. By 11:30 a.m. the sun was obscured by cloud cover, so the rest of the survey would have to wait for another day. The observers depended on bright sunlight to make contrasting shadows of the moose tracks in the snow, otherwise they were just about impossible to see from the air.

After dropping the technicians back at the Hearst airport, Sam headed for Timmins. Maybe if the timing worked out, she'd get to take the freshly overhauled Turbo Beaver back to Moosonee today — to her *new* home. She was looking forward to that.

However, when she landed, she was third in line at the fuel pumps, with some rich guy in a Challenger business jet just ahead of her. He must have come in on fumes, because it seemed to take forever before he finished refuelling and taxied away.

Sam finally took her turn at the pumps, and after

parking the Beaver she'd been using, she tied it down and pulled on its covers. By the time she was done, the late hour made a Moosonee flight imprudent. Besides, the chief pilot had some things he wanted to discuss with her before handing over the keys to the Moosonee Beaver. So the trip north was out for tonight, but with a major snowfall due to arrive tomorrow afternoon, she would be heading out in good time in the morning.

—

The Moosonee winter road

It was mid-afternoon as Morgan drove toward his destination on the winter road. At each place the seasonal road crossed a stream or river, the snow-packed road surface would slope down the riverbank, sometimes steeply, and the traffic had to drive across the frozen ice surface to the other side, then climb back up to level ground. There were no bridges. And some of the riverbank snow ramps had developed heavy moguls despite the road crews' best efforts to keep them graded. Negotiating the crossings at a dead-slow crawl was the best way to keep control and minimize the chance of bottoming out the suspension.

On the other hand, the road surface between the stream crossings was amazingly smooth and kept wide by constant grooming. He could easily roll along at eighty or ninety km/h.

As he drove farther north, Morgan began watching for a winter road maintenance yard he'd been told of. It was supposed to be near the Onakawana section house. He found it just a couple of kilometres from the railway stop and he pulled into the broad snow-packed parking area. In addition to the road maintenance equipment sitting in front of a portable office trailer, several trucks with American plates and enclosed snowmobile trailers were parked off to one side. This was perfect. Parked beside the visiting vehicles, his truck would look like that of any other snowmobile tourist sampling adventure on the 'James Bay Frontier'.

After backing his snowmobile off the truck onto a high snowbank, he headed out along the road toward the Onakawana section house where he retrieved his snowshoes. They were still hanging on the outside wall.

Back at the winter road works yard, he loaded up the rest of his gear and headed off to the bush. As he snowmobiled out of the yard for the second time, Morgan followed an old survey line cut through the bush as straight as a ruler. When he felt he was far enough from the winter road, he turned in the general direction of his tent camp and began weaving through the black spruce and tamarack forest, navigating now by GPS.

By 4:30 he was hooking up the smoke pipe to his new stove and getting ready to settle in for the night. The weather reports he'd listened to before his truck radio lost reception indicated some stormy conditions. A few centimetres of snow were expected overnight, but they were mainly calling for high winds. That wasn't so bad, but a major snowstorm was forecast to move in tomorrow afternoon. He wanted to be on his way back to Timmins before that one hit.

As the evening wore on, the weather changed as predicted. Not much snow fell, but the wind really got up. Even in the shelter of the spruce stand his tent would go into spasms of flapping canvas from time to time. But he stayed warm. His new stove was perfect for the job.

During the night however, a tall spruce tree standing

just upwind from the damaged Cessna snapped off several metres above the ground. It fell across the white plastic tarpaulin that covered the aircraft. The shelter was split wide open. As the night wore on, the wind shifted direction several times, ravaging the damaged cover from different angles.

By morning the tarp lay badly shredded, its remnants still tied to the spruce trees bordering the plane. Nothing was left of the camouflage. Other than the spruce top lying across its fuselage, the aircraft was fully exposed. And while a white airplane with blue markings, surrounded by a snow-covered forest doesn't beg to be spotted from the air, it was no longer invisible.

CHAPTER 41

Thursday, February 9 — Moosonee

Just before 7:00 a.m., Rob McNabb pulled into the Moosonee police detachment parking lot. Puzzled by the lack of police vehicles out front, he went in to see who was going to ride with him out the winter road. The receptionist was the only one there.

"Hi Barb, where is everyone?" he asked.

"Bad night, Rob. A big hockey fight with a visiting team led to a stabbing in Moose Factory. It has everyone tied up over there for the day. Even the boss is there trying to help sort out who did what to whom. And our one spare body took an appendicitis attack during the night, so he is also over on the island getting knifed, although in a far more productive way, I hope. I'm afraid we don't have a ride-along for you to borrow. The shift sergeant sends his apologies."

"Oh … well, thanks anyhow. I sure hope things improve as your day goes on. See you 'round."

"Bye, Robbie."

Back out in the Suburban he pulled out his cell phone and tried calling James at home. The boss could get one of the technicians to go with him. But Bird wasn't answering, so he decided to go to the office and wait for him to show up.

Then, two blocks later, he started hearing a whining sound from under the hood of the SUV. He knew that sound. The power steering fluid was running low, so he looped back around the block to hit the gas station and buy some. It was no big deal. Only, when he opened the hood to add the new fluid, he saw that the power steering pump had sprung a major leak.

"Aw, c'mon Murphy! How come you always show up at the worst time?" Frustrated, he parked the vehicle, handed the keys to the mechanic and hoofed it back to the office. Now he needed James to find him a ride-along technician *and* another vehicle.

There was no sign of Bird when McNabb entered the office. To fill time until his arrival, Rob decided it was about time he checked his voicemail — it had been a few days since he had responded to his messages. The sixth message he listened to, left at ten minutes to seven that morning, was from the boss.

'Hey Robbie, its James. I just spent an awful night with this bad tooth, so I can't do court today ... I'll leave a message for Marion, and she can call the Crown Attorney when he gets in. I called Doc. Martin at home and he's going to fit me in to do the root canal first thing this morning. If you hear this before you leave, you guys be careful out there, okay?'

McNabb had been bugging his boss for several weeks to get that tooth looked after. Intermittent as the pain had been, it was obviously bothering him. Rob's father, from personal experience, had always said that as gruesome as its name implied, a root canal was like a Caribbean cruise compared to enduring the misery that led up to needing it. Anyhow, between James and the police, there'd be a lot of pain on Moose Factory Island this morning. 'Good place to stay clear of,' he decided.

The sky had already clouded over. The temperature had quickly risen from an overnight low of -29°C to -15°C. It looked as if the snow expected for later in the afternoon could start just about any time, and Rob wanted to get down to Onakawana to check those tracks before they got buried. That is, if they were even there anymore; the wind during the night could have already obliterated them, but he felt it was still worth a try.

Making one last attempt to find a passenger, he stopped by the DM's office just as he arrived for work, but Archie Foulton had to let him down too. "Sorry, I haven't got anyone to go with you, laddie. All the field staff are finishing their first aid training today, but you can take the lot of them tomorrow if you want." If the normally hands-off administrator had known of Bird's orders not to travel down there alone, he would have forbidden Rob from leaving the office. But he didn't know.

'Fat lot of good tomorrow will do me,' McNabb thought, so he stopped at the front desk and let Marion know where he was headed and then walked back to his house.

Groaning at the job ahead of him, McNabb cleaned six week's worth of snow off his silver Dodge quad cab. He'd drive it down there on mileage. It wasn't a new truck by any stretch, and it sure wasn't fancy, but it started up immediately, and by 8:20 a.m. he was headed southwest, out of town and up the winter road.

—

Near Onakawana

Gerald Morgan emerged from his tent to find the snow drifted in entirely new patterns and the trail his snowmobile had made yesterday was completely buried. That was good. It eliminated the chance of anyone discovering his location. It was almost 8:30 a.m. and he had a lot to do today.

Taking his rifle from the tent, he strapped on his snowshoes and headed back toward the Cessna. He wondered how his temporary camouflage had weathered the overnight winds; he hadn't thought to buy a backup tarp in town. So he was disappointed, though not entirely surprised when he arrived at the plane to find the cover destroyed. If anyone was looking, the plane would be recognizable from the air.

There was nothing left of the tarp aside from strips of shredded plastic, so he knew that he could no longer store his hoarded furs there. But with a major snowstorm promised for later in the day, this was the perfect time to move his stash. By tomorrow there'd be no sign of the considerable tracks he would make while he relocated the goods.

Before getting started, he took the time to gather the remnants of the tarp and bury them in the deep snow. Even though it was white on white, he was concerned that a loose end flapping in the wind could be noticed from the air, drawing unwanted attention to the Cessna before he'd abandoned the site.

CHAPTER 42

Timmins

Sam Williams finally got through the administrative details involved in signing out the Moosonee Turbo Beaver. The plane had been test-flown by the chief pilot several days earlier and was fuelled and ready for her trip north. Sam and the chief air engineer went over the bird in a final 'pre-delivery' inspection.

Modified with a stretched body, the now eight-seat bush plane was a thing of beauty. Its bright yellow paint shone from just back of the propeller, all the way to the tip of its swept-back tail. The top of the engine cowling was flat black and made for a crisp contrast with the yellow fuselage. The hunter-orange marker strips on the leading edges of the wings were as yet untarnished by aerial contamination and bug splatter. New OPAS logos stood out proudly on the passenger doors. It was as good as a brand new aircraft.

She'd never had the pleasure of flying a new or newly refurbished airplane before and was bursting with pride as she went through the start-up procedures. Though it was the same as starting any other Turbo Beaver, for this first start-up she spoke out loud, as she went. She saw it as 'bonding with the bird.'

"Master switch on … fuel boost pump on … engage starter … eleven percent rpm … fuel on." The familiar dull roar of the burning fuel taking over from the starter motor was her signal that she had ignition. As the engine ran up to operational revolutions, she moved the propeller setting from fully feathered, to neutral pitch and the freewheeling prop became an invisible blur.

At 9:43 a.m. she called in her request for departure, and Timmins radio cleared her for takeoff. The Turbo Beaver with full fuel but no cargo, other than Sam's overnight bag and first two boxes of worldly possessions, left the runway no more than two hundred metres from its starting point. She was on her way to the next phase of her life. Even though she'd used Moosonee as a base many times before, now it would be her home.

She was pretty sure too, that she was on her way to a new relationship. The heart of that matter — McNabb himself — still had to be tested. If a relationship was to develop, she expected to be a partner, not a possession, as her previous short-lived affairs had ended. Would Rob, could Rob, provide that kind of relationship without screwing it up? She really hoped he would be the one. The emotional battles she'd waged with herself over the past eight days had left her drained. She didn't normally operate like that — not with one side of her brain in conflict with the other. The left side normally ruled, leaving no room for argument.

Well, for better or worse, she was going to follow Mother Jones's suggestion and go with her heart. 'I'll take it slow, and at the first sign of him turning to the dark side, that will be the end of it,' she concluded.

She quickly turned her mind back to the business at hand and climbed the plane up to two thousand feet. The wind was already blowing from the east and the sun shining weakly through a veil of increasing cloud cover. The snow was on its way. Rigged with wheelskis, the six-hundred-and-eighty horsepower bush plane could easily cruise at one hundred and forty knots. She would be at her destination in about an hour and a quarter.

—

Near Onakawana

At 10:40 a.m., Gerald Morgan was several hundred metres from the Cessna. He was snowshoeing back toward his tent camp with the first two bags of fur slung over his shoulders. He would bring the snowmobile back to move the rest of them, but in the deep powdered snow, he first needed to pack a firm base using the traditional native technology. On the snowshoe-packed trail, the Polaris, with its powerful engine, wouldn't be as likely to dig in and bury itself in the deep powder.

Just then he heard the familiar whine of an approaching single engine turboprop aircraft. It was coming from the southwest and sounded as if it would pass overhead.

'Shit. Government bird, most likely,' he told himself, knowing that the most common single engine turboprops in northern Ontario were the MNR Turbo Beavers. And at that moment he was in the centre of an area of sparse, stunted tamarack trees — the one species of conifer that sheds its needles in winter. It was not a clearing, but the denuded branches made for inadequate concealment. If he started toward the heavier spruce canopy, still over a hundred metres away, his motion over the ground could draw the attention of anyone watching from above and the approaching plane was already quite near.

He dropped his load and unslung the rifle from his shoulder. It was a Winchester .300 magnum — a weapon preferred by many police and military snipers, and one of the models that he had trained on in the army.

He stood perfectly still and waited. The plane was several thousand feet overhead, and it would pass a little bit to the east of his position. It was at an altitude that wouldn't normally be used for an aerial ground search, so Morgan relaxed and picked up his load again.

—

Two thousand feet above Onakawana

Between moments of checking the aircraft instrumentation and scanning the sky for other aircraft, Sam Williams casually looked down toward the winter road, two thousand feet below. Traffic was sparse as usual, and the only vehicles she could see were a couple of pickups. As she glanced down at a spot a little west of the winter road, she realized that passing under her portside wing, was the barely distinguishable shape of an aircraft, mostly white. It was sitting amongst the trees at the east end of a small lake. She'd flown this same route numerous times and she couldn't recall ever seeing a plane wreck down there. And that got her wondering: could this be the bird that had been the object of all their recent searches. She knew the guys hadn't found it yet.

Easing back on the power and increasing the propeller speed, she began a wide sweeping turn. Her power adjustments were equivalent to gearing down the transmission in a car or truck to descend a steep hill. With flaps slightly lowered, the plane gradually slowed and settled to slightly less than a thousand feet above the ground.

Sam dug her smartphone out of a breast pocket and powered it up, intending to get a picture of this new discovery. A little more power applied to the turbine halted the Beaver's descent.

The plane she had seen came into view more clearly now. It had to be the missing Cessna. The wing-top registration was partially snow-covered, but the last two letters matched those they'd been looking for. As she passed over top of her find, she hit the 'Mark' button on the Beaver's GPS to fix its position. She'd have to make another pass to get her picture.

—

The moment he heard the turboprop engine note change overhead, Morgan cursed his luck. The Cessna had been discovered. There was only one way to remedy that. He dropped his load again, braced his rifle against a nearby stunted tree and waited.

Everyone has seen the images on TV of thousands of rounds of anti-aircraft tracer raking the skies over Baghdad or some other conflict zone and none of it hitting a single airborne object. And it is true that hitting a moving target is not easily accomplished, but Gerald Morgan had trained with the best and had become the best of them. To take his skill to an even higher level, he had designed his own personal training program and learned to hit those terrified animals multiple times. The cats were the biggest challenge as they dashed, panic stricken, around the confines of the steep-sided sand pit.

He only had to lead the plane by the smallest amount,

because on its present heading it appeared almost stationary in the sky. And the slow-flying Turbo Beaver approaching him was no match for the .300 magnum round leaving the rifle's muzzle at over three thousand feet per second.

—

It was 10:47 a.m. and Sam was approaching the downed plane to get her picture — her finger was poised on the phone, ready to capture the image. Just then, a sudden but brief cacophony of tortured metal screamed from the other side of the engine firewall. The loss of power was instant. The plane began its inexorable descent toward the frozen landscape.

The small lake the Cessna had landed on was upwind and already a mile behind her. The rest of the terrain so near to the Moose River was almost completely covered in a spruce and tamarack forest. And the river itself at that point was a field of jagged ice ridges.

Having no idea what could have happened to cause such a catastrophic engine failure, Sam immediately put the plane into a gliding turn, hoping to make it back to the lake, but a sudden squall, blowing in with the advancing storm, was bleeding off too much of her forward ground speed. She knew right away that she was going to come down in the trees.

Her only consolation was that with the stiff headwind, and lowered flaps, her impact speed would most likely be survivable, but the plane would probably be a write-off, or at least be out of service until long after she was fired. That thought left her cold. To have worked so long and so hard to get here and then have it taken away in an instant — that went beyond being just a cruel twist of fate.

At six hundred feet she began emergency shutdown procedures. With the fuel turned off, she was about to kill the master power switch when she realized she hadn't even taken time yet to make a Mayday call on the VHF. And even as she keyed the mic with one hand, her other was flipping the EPIRB manual arming switch to the 'on' position.

While in flight, the device was always set to activate automatically in the event of an impact, but Sam worried that if the impact turned out to be no more than one experienced in a heavy landing, the device might not trigger at all. Should she end up injured or trapped and unable to reach the switch, rescuers might not be able to pinpoint her location for some time — possibly days — particularly in the coming snowstorm. But now it was transmitting full-time, even before her flight ended.

"Mayday, Mayday, Mayday, this is Oscar Echo Yankee, I have lost engine power just west of the Moose River approximately fifteen miles upstream of Moose River Crossing. I'm only a couple hundred feet above ground now. Ditching in the trees. Also, probable sighting of the wanted Cessna 185 close by, over." She didn't have time to repeat her message; the more the winds buffeted the plane the lower it sank — she needed all of her attention to control its descent.

"OEY, Moosonee," came back surprisingly fast. Marion, the receptionist in the district office, was on her toes as usual. "OEY, Moosonee we are receiving your message, and will get help to you as soon as possible."

Seconds later, a male voice said in a calm controlled tone, "Sit tight when you get down Sam, and don't forget to activate your EPIRB. Help may be closer than you think." James Bird's voice came through clearly. Just hearing it gave her a sense of calm. He always had that effect on folks. She clicked her mic twice in acknowledgement and then she ran out of sky.

The disabled Turbo Beaver met the treetops at less than forty knots, and the long slender spruce trees cushioned the initial impact as Sam Williams kept it level for as long as she could. The crash was happening to textbook standards, if such was even possible and it looked as if she'd be okay until the stub end of a dead broken spruce, resting horizontally in the forest canopy, came smashing end on, through the pilot's windshield.

Even if she'd had time to twist out of the way, the pilot's safety restraints wouldn't have allowed her that much movement. And even though the plane had slowed to fifteen knots, the tree stub slammed hard into her left shoulder, a severe blow so painful that she passed out.

—

Gerald Morgan smiled at the fact he'd brought the snooping government plane down with just one shot. He hadn't lost his touch. It came down in the trees with an audible smashing and drumming of wood on aluminum as it mowed down a section of forest just over a kilometre from where he stood.

Though tempted to snowshoe over and eliminate any survivors, he quickly decided against it. Now that the Cessna had been located, the government plane's EPIRB was probably sending out its distress message. He had to move his furs farther and faster than he'd originally planned. And anyone who lived through the crash would be fully occupied with the more urgent matter of survival. So for the time being at least, they'd pose no threat to him.

CHAPTER 43

Near Onakawana

When Sam regained consciousness, the wind was whistling through the broken windshield and her shoulder was pinned hard against the seatback. The plane was sitting almost level and appeared to be suspended in the broken trees, the skis just inches above the snow surface below. She managed to undo her seatbelt harness but she couldn't move and she was in agony from the pain in her injured shoulder.

She wasn't able to grasp the seat adjustment lever from her pinned position, so she strained to reach the kneeboard in her flight bag. It too was almost out of reach, but she eventually managed to pull the bag closer with her finger-tips and extract the metal clipboard. Using that, she was able to extend her reach and work the seat adjustment. By sliding the seat farther back, she was finally able to free her shoulder and get up.

Opening her flight suit to check her injury she felt nauseous and she knew that she needed to get out of the plane immediately in case it caught fire. She didn't remember turning off the master power switch, but it was already off. Both front doors were jammed. Without taking time to grab her parka or mittens, she headed back through the passenger area and tried to exit there.

The starboard door was lodged up against a broken spruce tree, but the portside door opened easily and she stumbled out, more or less falling to the ground, badly twisting an ankle between the ladder rungs in her hurry to escape. That brought on a new wave of nauseating pain, and after a fit of vomiting and retching she passed out, collapsing forward into the deep snow.

—

Moosonee

In the district office, James Bird was peeved. No, it went way beyond that — he was royally pissed off. And he was desperately worried at the same time. He'd just returned to the office following his root canal procedure — at least that had gone better than expected. But that's when he learned that contrary to orders, his young conservation officer had gone looking for Gerald Morgan without any backup. And now the new district pilot had just been in a plane wreck.

Picking up his phone he hit the speed-dial for McNabb's sat-phone. He was hearing ring tones only — the thing had rung seven times with no answer and he was just about to hang up when the CO came on the line. It was 10:55 in the morning.

"Hey James, what's up?"

"What's up with you, young fella? I gave you explicit instructions not to go tracking that man without backup, but here I get back to the office and Marion tells me that's exactly where you've gone. I thought you had more sense than that Robbie. When you get back here, we are going to have a long and serious talk. Look, I don't want my number one detective CO going down at the hands of this Morgan guy. Understood?"

"Uh … I'm sorry James, I just…." But there was no point bringing up a string of excuses, and he certainly didn't want to get any further into the bad books with his supervisor. He had never heard Bird raise his voice before and felt terrible about upsetting him.

"I'm sorry James. I'm on my way back to the office now. And I couldn't find those tracks. They must have gotten blown in during last night's high winds."

"Well you aren't the only one in trouble. Where are you now?"

"I'm just leaving Moose River Crossing."

"You got snowshoes with you? And survival gear?"

"Yes … Why?"

"Well …" and this was the part James Bird wasn't looking forward to telling him, "Robbie, Sam's plane lost power just a few minutes ago. We haven't heard from her since she made her Mayday call, but she said she's found the missing Cessna. It's somewhere near where she went down. The Search and Rescue Centre puts her EPIRB signal down around Onakawana."

"Oh, shit! I was just there a little while ago," McNabb was stunned by the news. It left him in a cold sweat.

"Fire up your GPS Robbie and I'll give you the coordinates. The SAR folks say that they are getting too much snow to send up any air assets. It's snowing here now too, and we don't want to leave her out there on her own overnight. Especially with … well, you know what I mean. What's the weather like there?"

"It started snowing here about fifteen minutes ago. It's getting heavier by the minute, and the wind's picking up too. James, your signal isn't very good. Give me the numbers quickly before we lose the connection."

Just as Bird was reading off the last decimal of the coordinates for Sam's location, the satellite phone's signal was lost. At least the last digit represented tens of metres, not hundreds. McNabb tossed a mental coin and entered a '5' for the missing value.

—

Moose River Crossing

With his heart in his throat, McNabb threw his Dodge into a bootleg turn in the middle of the winter road. Engaging four-wheel drive he headed back south as fast as he could, but was stopped by a road maintenance crew five kilometres along.

"I need to get through right away," he told the foreman. "We've got a Turbo Beaver down in the bush near Onakawana."

The maintenance crew had just arrived to begin repairing a soft section of the road. What had been open road fifteen minutes earlier was now piled with fresh snow they would pack down to build a firm base.

The foreman recognized McNabb as the officer who had given him a warning for littering. Without hesitation he had the bulldozer operator make a temporary path for the Dodge to pass over.

Back on the road again, Rob kept telling himself that Sam had to be okay. But why were there no further communications? Sure, the plane is damaged, the radios out, but surely her sat-phone would have still worked, at least until the weather had deteriorated. He dreaded the thought that something bad had happened to her.

As he drove by the entrance to the winter road maintenance yard his GPS showed he was just under three kilometres from Sam's position. This was as close as the road would get to her crash site. No, he refused to call it a crash site. He kept telling himself that she just had to make a forced landing out there somewhere.

Turning his truck around again, he wheeled into the maintenance yard and pulled up to the office trailer.

Pounding on the door brought no response. Everyone would be out plowing or packing or grooming or whatever they did to a winter road during a heavy snowfall. 'Everyone' would probably be the maintenance crew he'd just passed down the road.

He moved his truck over to where three vehicles were already parked — judging from the enclosed trailers behind two of them, he guessed that they were visiting snowmobile tourists. He parked beside a brown Chevy pickup that was even older than his 2003 Dodge.

Hauling his personal 3-Star sleeping bag from the back seat, he stuffed it inside his big backpack and added standard emergency items packed in waterproof bags. It was a tight fit, and it would be bulky, though not overly heavy to carry through the bush.

After strapping on his snowshoes, he dug out his compass. If sat-phone signals were failing in the heavy snow, then his GPS would probably soon follow. For now at least, the satellite-based device was still pointing the way.

As he crossed the clearing toward the edge of the forest, he was walking over crusted, windblown knee-deep snow. The snowshoes kept him nearly on top, so the walking was easy. That was for the first hundred metres.

As soon as he entered the black spruce forest the

snow became deep and powdery. Without snowshoes it would have been at least thigh deep, and even on his winter walking wear he was sinking to his knees nearly every step of the way.

Worse still, a thin crust near the middle of the snowpack would almost hold his weight but then give out just as he was in mid-stride. The sudden letdown he endured on every single step was aggravating and it slowed his pace to a crawl. It felt to him the way one feels when being chased in a dream — his legs just wouldn't move freely or fast enough, no matter how hard he tried to run or walk. Only this was no dream.

As time dragged on, the snowfall became more intense and when the forest canopy over his head thickened and became covered with new snow, he lost his GPS signal. The final bit of information he received from the unit showed that he was moving at just over one kilometre per hour. It was discouragingly slow progress.

Now without the GPS, he had to follow a compass course and pace off the distance as he went, but he had to recalculate the number of steps he took for each hundred metres he covered. His usual stride in easy walking over bare ground came out to about a hundred and ten paces, but looking back at his slow progress through the deep snow, he estimated that he would have to double the count — at least.

As McNabb struggled on it began snowing so hard that he was walking blind, his compass giving him the only hint as to his direction. And even then he had to keep wiping the snow from the instrument. Keeping the wind on his left cheek was the best way he had for staying on course.

When he eventually came to a bit of a clearing and the snowfall eased momentarily, the GPS gave him several minutes of readings, though with only a sixty-metre range of accuracy. It showed him to be a hundred and ninety metres from the plane, except now it was lying off to his far left.

He rested a moment to catch his breath, and standing there, he thought he caught the faint sound of a snowmobile engine. Between the wind and the heavy veil of blowing snow, the sound gave no clue as to its direction, but it left McNabb with the unsettling feeling that it could be Morgan. The snowmobile tourists would have headed out toward the Moose River — not inland toward the endless muskeg. He immediately tried to dismiss the thought, knowing that a trained but wanted commando wasn't going to be riding noisily through the forest on a whining snowmobile. Was he?

Having regained his breath, McNabb urgently struck off in the new direction indicated by the GPS, hoping against hope that it wasn't sending him on a wild snow-goose chase. Now struggling in the new direction, his face was being stung by sharp wind-driven snow pellets. At the same time, inside his parka he was overheating and perspiring freely. The heavy going through the deep snow was getting harder with every laboured step, but he refused to give up. He was desperate to find Sam.

He paced off two-hundred metres with no sign of the Beaver. He began to fear he might have missed the plane completely. But just when his spirit was on the verge of breaking, he saw some freshly broken branches and pieces of treetops sticking out of the snow and hanging from the trees around him. He knew then that he must be getting close.

From the time of James's phone call, it had taken him two and a half hours to get this far — way too much time if Sam was badly injured and in need of medical assistance. The very thought drove him forward despite his burning muscles.

CHAPTER 44

Near Onakawana

The instant McNabb saw the downed aircraft through the heavy blowing snow he noticed the tree stub jammed through the pilot's side of the windshield. His heart sank. He doubted she could have survived an impact like that. And as he made his way to the starboard side of the Beaver's nose, a cold hand closed firmly around his heart. Raw hatred flared inside him as he stared at what was an obvious bullet hole in the bottom of the newly painted engine cowling.

With tears in his eyes, Rob McNabb struggled through the tangle of broken treetops and deep snow, to get around the plane's nose to the other side. From there, he saw the open passenger door.

"Oh, thank God. *Sam*!" he called out. But just as his hopes began to rise, he looked down and saw the very image that had haunted his nightmare in Hawley Lake just a week earlier. There, with the snow blowing through it, and over it, was a tangle of curly red hair. Just her hair. She was gone. How could a cruel dream ever foretell such a tragic event?

Grief-stricken, he dropped his backpack where he stood and plunged exhausted, staggering the final yards through the snow and broken branches. He dropped to his knees beside the cluster of orangey red locks. When he reached out to touch them, his vision blurred by tears, he felt Sam's head immediately beneath. Further probing down into the deep snow revealed her entire body. But it was small consolation to learn that the nightmare had simply gotten the details wrong. The plain horrible fact remained that he had lost her. Heartsick, he leaned forward and began to dig out the body of the woman he'd fallen in love with, now lying face down and motionless in the snow. He rolled her over and brushed the snow from her sweet face. Then he pulled her to his chest in one final tearful hug.

He might have missed it, his body wracked as it was by his own heart-rending sobs. Not once, but twice he thought he felt the smallest flex of movement in Sam's otherwise lifeless form.

Desperately clutching at any chance that she might still be alive, he began mentally kicking himself for handling her so roughly. Not knowing what injuries he might have aggravated, her body should have been immobilized, not rolled over and hugged. It was entirely possible she could have spinal cord damage. Switching his mind back into rescue mode he searched his memory for the appropriate first aid response.

Between his own anxious heart pounding and the fact that Sam was in an advanced state of hypothermia, McNabb couldn't feel any pulse. But she *was* occasionally stirring, ever so slightly. Doing a preliminary examination in thigh-deep snow in the middle of a raging snowstorm was almost an exercise in futility. With his mittens removed, his hands were getting cold and numb, and Sam was dressed in her bulky winter flight suit. Even worse, the suit was unzipped from neck to waist and partly filled with snow.

However, because of the soft snow he was able to feel around underneath her enough to satisfy himself that he couldn't detect any apparent external bleeding. And he was encouraged that he couldn't feel any unusual deviations in her long bones or spinal column. It made for a pretty sketchy triage, but he felt that hypothermia was now the greatest threat to her survival.

Desperately hoping that he wasn't making a mistake, he carefully lifted her up and laid her up on the floor of the broken Beaver. Sam couldn't have weighed any more than a hundred and twenty pounds fully dressed in her snow-filled winter gear.

Fortunately, the plane's back seats were stowed and the passenger area was clear of clutter aside from an inch or two of blown-in snow. Climbing in after her, McNabb quickly swept out the accumulated snow with his mittens. Then closing the door, he urgently looked around to see what he could do to warm the place up a bit.

He knew that the little emergency camp stove outside in his backpack had only enough fuel to cook a couple of quick meals, not heat the cabin of a bush plane for an extended period. And there was no portable generator on board the plane, so the electric heaters lying in the baggage compartment were of no use. He grabbed the engine tent from behind the folded rear seats and went forward to the pilot's seat. Unable to push the spruce tree back out through the shattered windshield, he did his best to wrap the canvas cover around the intrusion and close off most of the incoming wind and snow.

Next he knew he had to start getting some warmth back into Sam's cold body. Her sleeping bag and the emergency kit were stowed in the back compartment behind the seats, so the bag was the next thing he deployed.

Just putting her into the sleeping bag without adding extra heat wasn't going to help other than stopping any further heat loss. But until he'd taken care of a few other things, that would have to do.

Being as gentle as he could, he worked her free of the flight suit, releasing more snow to be brushed out the door shortly. She stirred restlessly as he worked the garment off her left shoulder and he figured that must have been where the tree stub impacted her. But through her long underwear, the arm appeared to have a normal range of motion and there was no sign of even minor external bleeding. And when he got down to working the suit past her right ankle, a similar restless response was triggered. Again, the offending joint appeared unbroken and her flinching gave him reason to hope that she hadn't suffered any major spinal injuries. He finished by laying her inside the sleeping bag and bundling the wide edges around her.

In reality, the floor of the plane was as cold as everything else, but it sure felt a lot colder, and McNabb knew that it would be a continuous source of heat loss unless he got another insulating layer under the sleeping bag. He quickly exited the plane and went forward to pick up his backpack while watching the surrounding forest for any sign of Gerald Morgan.

Before re-entering the plane he dug the satellite phone from his coat pocket and turned it on, but the dense cloud cover and the heavy falling snow still blocked the signal. Since there appeared to be no fuel leaking from the Beaver, he would have to risk trying the aircraft radios.

Meanwhile, in case that didn't work, he needed to send a signal of some sort to let the outside world know that he needed help. From inside his pack, he pulled the portable EPIRB unit that the ministry had issued to him with the warning, 'You'd better be on death's door before activating this thing.' Apparently a whole lot of government paperwork and interagency cooperation was required before anyone would respond to the distress call from this particular device.

'Well, Sam *is* on death's door,' he reasoned, 'and her aircraft EPIRB is already activated, so if by any chance the signal from this unit can get to a satellite, then they will know that I have arrived at the same location, and that this really *is* an emergency.'

Placing the EPIRB on the roof of the plane, McNabb climbed back into the Beaver. Once closed inside, he locked the door behind him. The thin aluminum skin and lightweight door latch wouldn't begin to keep out either an intruder or his bullets, but McNabb hoped that any attempt by Morgan to open the door would at least give him a chance to start pumping .40 calibre rounds out through the fuselage.

Next, he leaned forward into the cockpit and flipped on the main power and radio master switches. The radios both came on and he immediately started transmitting on one after the other. After waiting for several minutes, he received no response to his calls on either set. Little did he know that the antenna for the ministry VHF had been ripped from the roof by broken tree parts as the plane mowed down a swath of forest. And with the storm raging outside, there would be no aircraft flying overhead for some hours to come and no aircraft close enough to pick up his calls on the general aviation set, so he shut off the radios and set about arranging for his patient's care.

He had to start getting some warmth into Sam if he was to have any chance of reviving her. He began by sliding her, in her sleeping bag, to one side of the cabin and unrolled his 3-Star flat on the floor. Gently again, he lifted her back toward him and set her sleeping bag over top of his own.

That was the only mattress they would get, but it would help. Then, quickly shedding his parka, boots, snow pants and uniform, he climbed into the sleeping bag with her, closing the snaps behind him with some difficulty. The 5-Star was big, but with two occupants it was crowded.

'So far, so good,' he thought. As slow as her respirations were, he could hear that she was still breathing. But when he began feeling about on the outside of her long underwear, the only place he could detect anything at all resembling warmth, was between her thighs.

'Aw shit. This won't work. I'll never be able to transfer enough heat to her through two layers of longjohns.'

There was only one way to solve this problem. He'd already gone outside the box when he flew Gord Clark to medical help in a plane he was neither licensed nor trained to fly, so it was time to go out on a limb once more — and according to the first aid training he'd taken, this *was* a legitimate treatment.

"Sam, I just hope you understand, and don't hate me for this," he apologized, as he began to strip off his own underwear. That manoeuvre was tough enough to execute in the crowded sleeping bag, but getting the injured, unresponsive pilot free of her remaining clothes without letting any cold air into the bag involved major feats of dexterity.

Fortunately, she wore an old-fashioned style of men's one-piece long underwear, buttoned down the front with an 'escape hatch' at the backside. The buttoned front made it much easier to remove from her injured shoulder than a pullover style would have. Even so, each time he moved either her left shoulder or her right ankle she would flinch. Finally kicking her discarded underwear to join his own at the bottom end of the sleeping bag, he lay on his right side and pulled her back up against his chest and her bare buttocks into his lap.

He gasped when her cold skin met his. Lying together, nested like spoons in a drawer, he held her close to him.

"Sam, we're going to get you warmed up.," he began quietly. "Think warm thoughts. You're safe now, sweetie. We're going to pull you through this, you and me. I've just barely gotten to know you, but we get along so well I just can't lose you now," he said, close to tears. "You *have* to warm up. You've still got so much to do with the rest of your life. I'm *not* going to lose you now."

In total contrast with the gentle sensitivity he showed the woman, his .40 calibre pistol lay between the layers of bedding. Held loosely in his right hand, it was aimed at their one opening door, just in case Morgan should drop by.

CHAPTER 45

In the wrecked Turbo Beaver

There was nothing erotic about the naked man clasping the naked woman lovingly to his chest. The bare body in front of him was cold and McNabb was getting colder by the minute. His own body heat was being bled off to replenish Sam's. After the first half hour, he figured that she wasn't likely getting much benefit from his front side anymore, so he slipped over top of her, and while lying on his same side again, he backed his butt into her lap this time. It was a position no more erotic than the first. Although he could feel her small firm breasts pressed against his back, they were ice cold. He lacked any sensation of lust; but rather, felt a burning love, and he desperately hoped this beautiful, feisty woman would survive and help him build on that love.

After another interminably long half hour Sam began to shiver. From what Rob could remember of his first aid training, the human body going into hypothermia stops shivering below a certain temperature. So it stood to reason that she was finally warming up to that temperature in order for the shivering to start again. By now his back was chilled but his front had warmed considerably, so it was time to reposition again.

This time, with his right shoulder getting sore from lying on the hard floor of the plane, he changed the arrangement. Lying on his back, he pulled Sam onto his chest and they lay front to front, with her head lying on his chest just below his chin. She was noticeably warmer now — not hot — but no longer like a slab of meat, fresh from the cooler. And her shivering was more intense. He hoped that was happening because she had regained more of her energy. He remembered reading that shivering was supposed to generate as much as a couple of degrees of body heat each hour, so he lay there with his left arm around her and his right hand still pointing the pistol through the sleeping bag at the door. He continued talking, in what he hoped was a reassuring voice. He at least, was beginning to feel reassured.

Sometime during the next hour Sam's shivering stopped and she lay comforted by the relative warmth of her rescuer lying beneath her. At the same time, he had drifted off to sleep, exhausted by the afternoon's exertions. Sam couldn't see him because it was dark, cocooned inside the sleeping bag — just as dark as it was outside now in the storm. But she knew it was him. She'd had a dream that he'd saved her life, stripped her naked and climbed into bed with her. She lay there enjoying that thought until she suddenly realized her situation.

"Oh my God! You really did," she exclaimed, waking McNabb with a start. "Robbie McNabb, you sneaky devil, you're in bed naked with me and it's only our second date."

"Sam, I'm really sorry, but I wasn't going to be able to warm you enough through our longjohns and...."

"Robbie, you saved my life," she cut him off, hugging him with a one armed embrace. "Don't you dare apologize for doing *that.* I was just surprised that you'd actually done it. I mean, I thought I'd dreamt it. I was in a dark tunnel, then you were there, crying! Then in the dream you took me to bed and when I woke up, it was real … you were real."

"Oh Sam, am I ever glad you're okay." He was ecstatic that she had pulled through. And he let go of the pistol, long enough to return her hug. He told her about experiencing the rerun of his Hawley Lake nightmare when he first saw just her hair in the snow by the wrecked plane and she tightened her hug.

"How are you feeling?"

"I still feel cold, especially my feet, but I'm a lot better than when you found me. I hardly remember any of that. My shoulder really hurts. But I don't think anything's broken. I think it's just badly bruised. My ankle doesn't hurt until I flex it hard one way or the other. We'll have to see how it is when I try to stand on it."

"Well we should probably break open the survival kit and make some supper. I'll get into my longjohns and my chef's outfit and whip up a feast of roast beast or Kraft Dinner or whatever they've packed in there for us. But first I need to take a bladder break," he said, exiting from the top of the sleeping bag — still naked.

"Me too Rob. Can you please hand me a … thanks," she said, appreciating his quick grasp of her needs — and his quick grab for a nearby airsick bag. "You're learning fast, Flyboy."

"Hey, it is much milder out now Sam," he said as he opened the door to relieve himself. "It's still snowing hard, but the wind has died down a lot."

"Here Rob," she said a moment later, an arm reaching out of the sleeping bag. "Water the lawn for me too please. I'm still feeling a little shaky and I'd like to warm up in here a while more … with your help. Supper can wait."

"Actually, no it can't. I've lost a lot of body heat too, just warming you up. So a hot meal and a cup of tea will help both of us. Just let me back in there for a few minutes," he said, shivering. She shrieked as she pulled their naked bodies together again. His skin had chilled quickly during the brief intermission.

"Now you have just the tiniest idea how it felt for me the last few hours," he said as the two of them began to struggle back into their long underwear. "Anyhow, carrying forward what someone told me recently, 'It isn't the bridal suite at the Chelsea Hotel, but then this is only our second date'."

He gradually warmed again, and with Sam snuggled next to him, he dozed off briefly once more, only to wake moments later when he heard her quietly weeping beside him in the sleeping bag.

"Hey Sam, what's wrong? You're safe now and I'm here with you," he tried to reassure her. "And if one of us is always going to be crying, we're going to need to get rubber sheets for these sleeping bags."

"Oh Rob, I worked so long and so hard to get this job," she sobbed. "I haven't even passed my probationary employment period, and now I've wrecked the plane. It hasn't even got three hours on it since its major overhaul and I've *destroyed* it. They're going to fire me for sure and I'll *never* get another flying job again, not after being fired from the air service." The weeping climaxed into a full blown outburst of sorrowful crying.

"Oh Sam, Sam, Sam. It wasn't your fault honey." He had a difficult time breaking through her grief.

"It wasn't your fault, Sam. Sweetie, you were shot down. It had to be Morgan. Your last message said you saw his plane near here. Somehow he managed to put a round right into your turbine! I saw the bullet hole myself, honest."

'Honey' and 'sweetie' might not have been words that a modern, independent career woman wanted to hear, but she quieted shortly and held him tight for awhile. He figured that if she hadn't liked his selection of endearments, he'd have heard about it pretty quickly. Again, they drifted in and out of sleep.

—

Waking with a start, McNabb checked his watch. It was almost 7:00 p.m. He knew that they'd have to get some warm food and drink into themselves really soon. His feet still felt cold, and he knew that Sam would be worse off than he was. Leaving the relative warmth of the bag, he quickly climbed into his insulated snow pants, parka and felt boot liners, skipping the thinner uniform layer for now. Their immediate need was for hot food.

He hurried to set up his Sterno stove, a small portable camp stove that burned a gel type of fuel. From the storage area behind the plane's passenger compartment he retrieved the emergency survival kit and pulled out several bags of dehydrated meals. Reading the labels he asked Sam, who was still inside the sleeping bag, "What's your pleasure Captain Williams, beef bourguignon or chicken cordon bleu?" Waiting on her answer, he poured bottled water from her portable cooler into a cooking pot from the kit.

"Dead cow please," came back. Her witty spirit was beginning to re-emerge.

They ate hungrily in darkness and silence. McNabb was still worried about a potential visit from Morgan. Several times during the evening after the wind had subsided further, they definitely heard the distant sounds of a snowmobile engine. All the CO could think about was what he'd seen on that second video in Petawawa. And now that vicious son of a bitch was so close they could hear him.

They tried their satellite phones again after they ate, but it was still snowing too much to connect to the system. And after a futile attempt to use the aircraft radios once more, McNabb thought to ask Sam if she knew where the Cessna was in relation to their plane.

"I couldn't say for sure, but I marked it with the GPS as I flew over it. Do you think the unit will give us a reading?"

"Well, even after my sat-phone quit this afternoon I was still getting some readings on my handheld GPS. It can't hurt to try, although I'm not quite sure I'm ready to discover that we're parked just one campsite away from the guy."

When the Beaver's GPS indicated 'No Signal,' he asked Sam where her broom was. Just like cars and trucks in the north, every bush plane carried a broom or a snow brush in the winter. Still dressed in his outerwear, Rob stood in the open door and swept the broom in wide arcs across the plane's roof to expose the built-in GPS antenna. Before he was back inside, Sam got a signal and plugged in a 'Go To' command for the waypoint she had marked.

"Fifteen hundred metres isn't quite next door," McNabb said, only somewhat relieved. "But he's not over on the other side of the river either." As far as he was concerned, they were still uncomfortably close to Morgan's activities, but he didn't want to stress Sam out, any more than she already was. He kept his concerns to himself. If the murdering poacher hadn't come looking for them yet, maybe finding them just wasn't in his plans.

Warmed by their meal, they returned to the sleeping

bag in their longjohns and cuddled together for mutual warmth and security.

—

Near Onakawana

It had taken Gerald Morgan until long after dark to get all his furs removed from the disabled Cessna and set up a new campsite three kilometres south of his first location. The first half of his load he had taken by snowmobile directly out to his pickup and locked them in the cab before returning to the plane for more. It had taken three trips just to accomplish that much.

He was curious about snowshoe tracks that he had crossed on his way out to the truck, but they were largely snowed over and he was too pressed for time to check them out. At that point, he still had to relocate his tent to a new campsite, and because of the heavy snowfall, each trip almost required the Polaris to break trail all over again. It all took time, and he wasn't finally ready to head for Timmins until after 9:00 p.m.

Driving down the snow-covered winter road was a real challenge too. He didn't dare drive any faster than 40 km/h for much of the trip. Even then he almost ended up in the bush twice and briefly got stuck climbing one of the steeper riverbanks. As a result he didn't get into the city until early the next morning.

—

Friday, February 10 — Timmins

It was 4:20 a.m. when Gerald Morgan kicked the snow aside and opened the doors to one of his two shipping containers. Little did he know that security cameras were capturing his every move. The owner of the place had gone to great lengths to conceal his seven cameras from prying eyes.

—

The sergeant in charge of the night shift at the Timmins city police department had been given the task of watching for any action at the storage yard. The owner had given them the password for his camera system so they could watch it online from their office rather than having to put bodies on a round-the-clock, live stakeout. And the arrangement would have worked out too, except for the arrival of a pair of rowdy drunks brought in by two constables.

One of the miscreants insisted on puking all over the floor at the cell entrance. His buddy slipped in the mess and went down hard. When the drunken idiots began yelling a stream of obscenities at the attending constables, the sergeant had to leave his desk for twelve minutes to help settle the commotion. As a result, by the time he was sitting by the monitor again, Morgan had already driven up, opened the container, stacked eight polar bear hides in the bin, locked the container and driven away. The motion detector security lights at the facility had gone out the instant before the sergeant came around the corner to return to his desk. The fresh tire tracks in the snow were invisible in the darkened image on his screen.

CHAPTER 46

In the wrecked Turbo Beaver

Rob McNabb awoke just before 5:00 a.m. All he could hear was silence. There wasn't even the subdued hiss that falling snow makes on a still winter night. It had stopped snowing at last. In fact, he could see stars poking through the broken forest canopy outside the Turbo Beaver's windows.

Activating his sat-phone finally brought results and lying there in the dark he hit the speed dial for James Bird's desk phone. He suspected his boss would still be at the office.

In fact James had been too worried to go home for supper and Margaret, his wife, had brought him a plate of hot food during the evening, staying to make sure that he ate.

Between repeated phone calls to the rescue coordination centre passing along weather conditions each time, the worried man sat staring at the silent phone and the VHF radio, desperate for news.

Marion and Archie were each feeling guilty about letting Rob leave the office that morning even though they'd never been told about Bird's admonition to the young officer. They had spelled each other off, keeping James company throughout the night. At the moment, both of them were there — both subdued, both mentally exhausted. All three jumped, startled, the instant the desk phone warbled. Bird picked up and seeing the call display he immediately put it on speaker for the benefit of the others.

"Hi James, she's okay … we're okay. But it was close, we almost lost her … That bastard shot her down … Yeah, he put a round right through the turbine. Sam's really upset about the plane. It's a mess, but I keep telling her it wasn't her fault … No, nothing's broken but she's got a badly bruised shoulder and a twisted ankle … The sky's clear here now and I'm sorry we didn't call sooner but we fell asleep after we tried the phones the last time around midnight … We don't know if the guy's still around or not. According to the Beaver's GPS, the Cessna is only fifteen hundred metres southeast of us. It might be unsafe for any rescue flights."

"It's okay Robbie, George Ballard is on it, so rescue choppers *will* be arriving at some point in the morning along with the transportation safety board accident investigators.

"Oh, and thanks for activating your personal EPIRB. It put us somewhat at ease knowing you'd made it to the site, but of course, without voice communications we were all still at our wits' end worrying about you two."

After exchanging the important details, James instructed McNabb to stay on his toes until Morgan was ruled out as an immediate threat, and he told them both to call their parents.

"The lid was blown off the story just in time for the six o'clock news last night. So your folks are worried sick and have been on the phone with me several times during the night."

"Okay James. Thanks. We'll call them right now."

—

Moosonee

At 6:40 a.m. the Canadian Rescue Centre's big Bell 212 search and rescue helicopter arrived in Moosonee. The pilots had skirted wide around the site of the downed Beaver. They had no desire to fall victim to Morgan's sharpshooting even though they were passing in the dark of night. Landing at the airport, the rescue chopper immediately began to refuel. They would wait for the police to secure the crash site before risking an approach.

A large contingent of reporters was booked to head north on the morning commercial flight from Timmins to cover the rescue of McNabb and Williams. Archie Foulton was given permission to ride the chopper out to the crash site. He wanted to brief the two of them on how to handle questions when the cameras and microphones converged on them.

—

Timmins

At 7:50 a.m. pandemonium broke out in the Timmins police station after receiving a phone inquiry from the owner of the storage facility. He wanted to know what they did with the guy after he showed up at his shipping containers during the night.

Furious that they'd missed him, the chief chewed on the staff sergeant's ear, and the staff sergeant chewed on the shift sergeant's ear, and the shift sergeant had to explain why he wasn't glued to the monitor all night long.

Word was sent to Moosonee that Morgan had left the bush and come to the city, so the emergency response team bound for Onakawana stood down. It would be safe to send in the SAR and crash investigators' choppers. A police chopper would be sent up from the south to work on the criminal investigation once the others were clear of the site.

The Timmins storage facility owner came to the police station and showed them how to review the images recorded any time the motion sensors picked up activity in the yard and turned on the lights. As a result, they got a good screen shot of a late '90s Chevy pickup, including a licence plate number. But the camera was aimed just inches too low to capture Morgan's face.

When they contacted the registered owner of the pickup, he explained that he'd sold the truck but forgotten to remove the plates.

—

Morgan's motel room in South Porcupine

After watching his careful planning unravel on national TV news, Gerald Morgan suddenly had to go to ground. He also had to eat the loss of the eight bear skins in the first shipping container, and both of the containers as well.

The one container had been opened in front of media cameras, and the furs were seized by the local conservation officers on nationwide breakfast TV. It was real a piss-off, losing over a third of his inventory.

But he'd gotten himself out of tight squeezes before and he'd do it again. Only, he'd have to do it with a badly shrunken bottom line.

He made some immediate changes to his living and parking arrangements. In keeping with his policy of always staying one step ahead of the law, he had previously scouted out a single-car garage for rent on a side street off Mountjoy South.

It took no time at all to come to an agreement with the owner and Morgan had the Chevy truck out of sight before anyone clued in to its being a vehicle of interest.

An hour later, he moved into a downtown rooming house where his fellow residents preferred anonymity over celebrity. He'd be safe there for the time being.

CHAPTER 47

Near the wrecked Turbo Beaver

By the time the heavy thumping of the Bell 212 rescue helicopter reached his ears, Rob McNabb had packed a crude landing pad in a clearing he found a couple hundred metres from the Beaver. Without snowshoes, he would have been up to his waist in snow. Even with them on he had been at it for almost forty minutes and he was exhausted. After setting off a smoke flare just downwind of the landing zone, he stepped back into the trees to avoid the blizzard that the chopper created with the downwash from its heavy rotor. It was just after 9:00 a.m.

Three search and rescue technicians, Staff Sergeant Ballard and District Manager Foulton emerged from the big red machine even before the rotor came to a stop. While they were still strapping on their snowshoes, McNabb came out of the trees to greet them.

"Hey Archie, George, am I ever glad to see you guys. What a night!" Both Foulton and Ballard were quick to return the greeting, and they immediately introduced the SAR Techs.

"Sam tried on her snowshoes but her ankle is too

tender this morning to bear much weight and she was afraid she'd lose her balance. So she's waiting back at the Beaver. We might never find her if she tipped off the trail in this snow. It's the deepest snow I've ever seen in my life. So anyhow, I need a hand getting her to the chopper."

"We've got that covered, Officer McNabb," replied the woman SAR Tech in charge. One of the others pulled a stretcher from the cabin of the rescue bird and they all followed McNabb through the shattered trees to the downed aircraft.

Sam, sitting in the open doorway of the Beaver, was grateful for the arrival of her rescuers, but felt a little humiliated at having to be carried out on a stretcher.

"You can bring your personal gear and such with you, but the accident investigators will want any cargo, the emergency kit and everything else that belongs with the plane left onboard," the SAR leader instructed. "Part of their job is to determine emergency preparedness of any aircraft that goes down. They'll be here within the hour, but we won't wait for them. Our job is to get you back to town. They can conduct any interviews they want with you, there."

Everyone wanted to take a look at the damaged Beaver before they left and they were all amazed by the single bullet hole in the engine cowling. The staff sergeant didn't voice his thoughts that if the plane had been hit several feet farther back, the pilot herself would probably have taken a direct hit. Unlike military aircraft, there is no armour plating to protect the pilot of a bush plane.

Sam was given a quick check-over in the heated cabin of the 212 before they took off, and once airborne they made a low, slow pass by the damaged Cessna. During the brief flight to Moosonee, Archie Foulton explained how they would deal with the waiting army of media.

—

Moosonee

When Rob helped Sam step down from the rescue chopper at 10:15, they were greeted by a mob of hungry reporters wielding every imaginable type of audio and video recording device. The media people had been given a prepared press release prior to the arrival of the new celebrities, and their initial questions were spawned from that document. Of course it wasn't long before they began probing for the sensational juicy stuff — the headline-grabbing meat of the twenty-four-hour news cycle.

"Officer McNabb, how does it feel to become a national hero overnight?"

"Well, I'm hardly the hero here. All I did was hike in to where our plane went down and help out with a little first aid at the scene. It was Pilot Williams whose sharp eyes found the poacher's plane. Now, with her sighting, we'll be able to pick up the trail and have a much better chance of finding whoever is responsible for killing all of those polar bears." Rob stuck to releasing only the information that Bird and Foulton had written up earlier in the morning.

"Ms. Williams, did the poachers really shoot down your government plane? Or was it a mechanical failure or maybe pilot error?"

"All I can tell you is that I was just about to take a picture of the missing Cessna when the turbine powering my aircraft quit … suddenly and violently. Officer McNabb showed me what certainly appears to be a bullet hole in the nose section, but it will be up to the accident safety investigators to determine the actual cause of engine failure." She felt hurt by the suggestion that she might have been at fault, but said nothing in rebuttal.

The quality of queries soon got worse. "Ms. Williams what was it like to get shot down by a wanted criminal?"

"You mean, as opposed to friendly fire?" Sam parried back. She just couldn't resist.

"Officer McNabb, how did you treat Ms. Williams for her hypothermia?"

"I made us a dinner of beef bourguignon on my little camp stove and we washed it down with a cup of hot, sweet tea," he replied without missing a beat. He got an appreciative sideways glance from Sam.

"Is it true you two are going together?"

Seeing that the press conference was rapidly degenerating into a media feeding frenzy, Archie Foulton broke in. He ended the questions with the parting comment, "I'd like to thank you all for your interest today, but Officer McNabb here has an important investigation to wrap up and we have to get Pilot Williams fitted for a new aircraft."

Shepherding the two beleaguered survivors toward the airport terminal building, he couldn't help chuckling. He was still chuckling when he got them loaded into the crew cab and started driving back into town.

"Friendly fire, lass?" he finally asked.

"Fitted for a new airplane?" Sam queried back, hoping that what she'd heard was for real.

"Well Samantha dear, assuming you pass whatever you have to pass to be declared still fit for flying, there's a district here that still needs its new pilot. And we just got word that the transportation safety inspectors have already agreed with McNabb's conclusion. You didn't wreck the aircraft. The 'wanted criminal' did. Yes we still need your services, lass." He reached across the seat and gave her a gentle fatherly pat on the knee.

Back at the office ten minutes later, the rest of the staff, who'd willingly remained 'locked up' during the press conference, broke out in congratulatory cheers. But as raucous as their fanfare was they made a far easier audience than the media scrum had been out at the airport.

Sam refused to go for medical attention immediately. "Look everyone, stop bugging me. I'm not mortally wounded. I've just got a bruised shoulder and a twisted ankle. I need to get things squared away with the accident investigators before I worry about minor stuff like that."

She spent the rest of the morning answering the transportation safety inspectors' questions. Rob was allowed to sit in and lend moral support, but aside from describing the accessibility and condition of the Beaver's onboard emergency gear, they needed little from him.

James Bird brought in a takeout lunch for everyone so they could wrap up their initial investigation quickly.

It was not until after lunch that Marion finally got to drive Sam to the Emergency Room in Moose Factory to have her injuries looked at and some X-rays taken. She was still grumbling about all the attention she didn't need.

At the same time, McNabb caught a ride with one of the police constables down to Onakawana to retrieve his truck. He had just finished clearing off the night's accumulation of snow when a chartered Hughes 500-D helicopter landed beside him. It was the chopper that the police had sent to handle their part of the investigation. Lloyd Macdonald got out of the passenger side and waved Rob over.

"Hey Rob, glad to hear you two are safe. Are you both okay?"

"Yeah. Nothing broken. Sam's got a couple of nasty bruises she won't let anyone look at, but one of the Moose

Factory doctors is checking her over right now.

"It was a long tense night though, Lloyd. I just kept thinking about what we saw in Petawawa the other day. I think the knurled pattern from my pistol grip is going to be permanently moulded into my palm." He looked down, flexing the fingers of his right hand.

"I'm glad you didn't stay through the whole show that day, Rob. It was … uh … no, I'm just glad you didn't see it all. I've never seen worse. It made the most graphic horror movies I've ever seen look like bedtime stories for small children.

"Anyhow, I've got two boxes here from the Beaver. They've got Sam's name on them and we don't need them for the investigation. Also her overnight bag and her flight case too. Can you get them to her for me?"

"Sure can. Thanks Lloyd." Five minutes later he was on the road. Heading back to town he had the sound system cranked, playing some of his favourite hits from the 1960s. John, Paul, George and Ringo were singing "Love Me Do" as he left Moose River Crossing. It wasn't his favourite Beatles tune, but he smiled. It felt right for the occasion.

CHAPTER 48

Moosonee

After stopping for a quick shower at home, McNabb got back to the office around 3:00 p.m. and he found James busy at his desk. Sitting down across from him, he wondered how he could smooth things over after yesterday's indiscretion.

"James, I'm sorry about going off on my own like that yesterday. I...."

His boss raised his hand to stop him. "Robbie, yes I was really ticked off, and I had a whole bunch of things I was ready to say to you about it, but in light of what happened out there, I just can't do that.

"You saved a life last night. It was a very brave act. You are fast developing a reputation around here for your quick and resourceful thinking and I'm betting that there are things you learned out there that can't be taught by any means other than first-hand experience. I think there are times when things work out for the best without any supervisory intervention."

"I just got lucky this time, James."

"Whether it was good luck or good management, we'll close that chapter here and now." James smiled and sat back, his body relaxed. "We've each learned something about the other's abilities and expectations Robbie, and that's most important of all. And I'm glad you came to me without waiting for a summons." He paused a moment before continuing.

"Next item. The critical incident counsellor isn't available to see you two until Monday in Timmins."

"Aw c'mon James. I already talked to them less than two weeks ago. I know this was a separate event, but it's all to do with the same guy and they'll just go over the same things I heard before. I already know what kind of after-effects to expect. I'd get more benefit out of finishing this case off than I would wasting two days in town, hearing some psychologist telling me all over again what I'll feel like after a traumatic experience. Yeah, Sam's got to go, but please leave me out of it this time, okay?"

"Are you sure you are going to be alright … especially after what you've just been through?" Bird asked, waiting to measure McNabb's reply.

"Yeah, I'll be fine. If I had to go, it would really worry me, having to talk in front of Sam about what I saw Morgan doing in that video. I just couldn't bear to put her through that. She doesn't need to know. George and Lloyd have both talked to me about what we saw, and as hideous as it was, I can move on.

"Besides, the situation last night finished with a happy ending. Sam and I are really beginning to get close and it's not just a 'hero' worship thing on her part either. I mean, even before what happened yesterday, she had already chosen to transfer here, rather than to Dryden where she could have been driving 415 water bombers. It's just a feeling I have, but it's a good feeling James."

"Okay then, I'll talk to the higher-ups and see if they'll

let you by with a pass this time. But if you have any second thoughts, *or* if I see you beginning to unravel, all deals are off. Okay?"

McNabb agreed.

"Now," James began his final topic, "I understand Sam is planning to stay in Moose this weekend. When she got back from her checkup this afternoon, she told Archie that since she still has her job — and there was never any doubt about that except in her mind — she wants to get settled in here as soon as possible. But we're concerned that after a traumatic experience like that, she shouldn't be left rattling around alone in the pilots' staff house all weekend.

"If you don't feel it's the right time yet to ask her to stay with you, then you tell her that Maggie and I would like to have her spend the weekend with us."

"Thanks James. You can't believe how much I want her to move in with me. But even though things seem to be going really well between us, I'm scared to move too fast. I mean, after last night, she might want some time without me … just to be sure. So I'll see if she'll stay with you."

"I think she's upstairs in the pilot's office. Archie told her to make it hers."

—

McNabb found Sam hooking up a computer on a big oak desk in a small upstairs room with a view of the river. Despite her shoulder and ankle injuries, she had just finished dragging the desk around and shoving it against the window to face the river. Rob scanned the room as he placed her pilot's flight bag on the desk.

"How do you like my new office Robbie?" Sam asked, pausing before she went on. "And the answer is yes."

"Yes? You mean, 'yes I like your new office?' I don't know, Sam. It seems to me it lacks the personal touch I thought someone like you would give it. Where are the flowering rhododendrons and the portraits of your championship horses?"

"No, I mean 'yes' to the question you *didn't* ask me the other day when you flew back from Petawawa. The day you sounded so shaken. To that unasked question the answer is yes."

"You mean...." As tired as he was, McNabb needed no time at all to recall what he had wanted to ask but hadn't dared.

"Yes, Rob. It was obvious what you wanted to ask, and yes, I want to move in with you. I'm tired and I've had a crappy week and I need a hot bath; this way we can see if we can get along under strained circumstances."

"You mean last night wasn't a good enough test?" Despite being dead tired, she broke out laughing and wrapped her arms around the man she finally acknowledged she was in love with.

But McNabb wasn't finished. He needed to know for sure.

"So … we're okay then … you and me?" he asked. He cupped his hands on either side of her head, tilting it up so they were face to face. "I mean … you're no longer torn between two lovers?"

"Yes Robbie. You won, and I'm so sorry I put you through all of that." Her eyes watered up and he could see that in addition to being tired, the past week had left her emotionally fragile, quite in contrast to her normal feisty self.

"Sam, no. You got the worst of it," he said, tenderly kissing the tears from her cheeks.

"As agonizing as the past week has been for me, all I

had to do was wait for your decision … and you even left me with a couple of encouraging hints. But I can't even begin to imagine the torment you went through, having to choose one guy over another. You are a woman who thinks with her head, but for this decision you had to trust your heart."

"What … hints?" she asked cautiously as she searched her memory for any unintended comments she might have made. She didn't realize she'd been so transparent until he told her about the phrases 'sort of', 'I'm not sure' and 'so confused' that she'd used that first morning in Hawley Lake.

"And the way you gripped my fingers, Sam, I just had to believe that I still had a chance to win your heart. Those were the things that kept me going through the week and again yesterday after I found you by the plane. That is, after I realized that you were still alive," he went on, a lump forming in his throat at the memory of Sam's red hair in the snow. "But now you're mine."

"As partners, Robbie," she emphasised. "I will not be a possession of anyone's. And you *will* face a probationary period, you know," she said with an impish grin breaking through — her tears quickly drying.

But she was dead serious when she told him of her previous screwed-up relationships.

"Robbie, I don't want you to ever change — to turn cruel and possessive like those guys did."

"Sam, I could never do that to you, and if there's ever anything that bothers you … anytime … please tell me right away. The last thing I'd ever want to do is spoil things between us."

"Well, young Robert McNabb, I *think* you should be able to pass your probation without any problems if last night was any indication," she said as she placed one thigh between his and raised it provocatively.

"I originally thought yesterday afternoon was a long dream that paralleled reality; I realize today, it was a series of slightly more lucid moments I had, running from the time you found me in the snow until I woke up with you at the end. And what I do know is, that although you had plenty of opportunity to do inappropriate things to my naked me with your naked you, you didn't. To be able to resist that kind of temptation takes a lot of respect — and I really love you for that. Or … am I maybe … not tempting enough for you?" she asked. Smiling, she continued to press her thigh tighter and higher.

"Oh, you are more and more tempting every second Sam," he said, pulling her closer in response. "Luckily, if we factor in all the overtime I put in yesterday, it's quitting time and TGIF; let's go home and you can tempt me there — all weekend long." They reluctantly broke their embrace and he helped her down the stairs to the main floor of the building.

"We're going home James," he said as they looked in on him before heading out the door. "Thanks for the offer, but I didn't even get a chance to ask her." The two of them, tired but happy, left the building arm in arm. Sam was still limping badly but Rob had parked his truck close to the main entrance and they were at the house in less than a minute.

To his boss, McNabb looked a little flushed and a lot pleased with himself. James smiled, satisfied. Reaching into the bottom drawer of his desk, he pulled out a liquor store bag and headed down the hall toward Archie Foulton's office. This was one bet he was more than pleased to have lost.

—

Timmins

Gerald Morgan felt like a caged lion. Pacing the floor in his rented room, he didn't dare go out until the public furor over his seized polar bear skins and his narrow escape from the law died down.

The cops and the game wardens were buzzing around like hornets whose nest had just been kicked in. His only consolation was that the rest of his inventory remained undiscovered. Given a few days, he'd be replaced on the news by some other headline story. But he'd have to lay low until the excitement was over.

CHAPTER 49

Moosonee

As soon as they arrived at McNabb's house — now their house — Rob carried Sam's two boxes of possessions inside and she limped in with her overnight bag. She declined the offer to be carried over the threshold.

"That's a little old-fashioned Robbie, and I think even then, it just applied to newlyweds, not probies."

She was immediately impressed by the relative tidiness of his place, 'man-cave' though it was. Setting her bag down in the front hallway, she asked, "Could you please show me the way to the bathtub? I ache all over and I want to soak for an hour."

"Sure Sam. Would you like a Tylenol to help with the pain?"

"Oh, you're way ahead of the curve, Flyboy. That sounds like a great idea. Just don't let me fall asleep in the tub though, or I'll drown and you'll have to rescue me all over again."

"Not a chance, Sam. All I seem to be doing these days is medevac and rescue work. I'll find you a rubber duck to hang onto instead." She stuck her tongue out at him and turned on the hot water.

Half an hour later, just as McNabb was starting to thaw a container of 'Warden Stew' in the microwave, Sam called out from the bathroom.

"*McNaaabb* ... where are the bath towels?"

"Oh shit," he said to himself heading double time down the hall toward the linen closet. "Sorry Sam, I threw them in the laundry the other morning just before work. Here's a clean one." He held a big, fluffy towel through the door without looking in.

"It's okay shy boy. You *can* come in you know. I mean we spent half of yesterday naked together in the plane."

"Yeah, but I never actually *saw* you Sam. I kept you wrapped in your sleeping bag cocoon the whole time," he said as he tentatively began to open the door. "It wouldn't have felt right ... I mean, in first aid training we're taught ... Oh, Sam! You're so beautiful now that you've emerged from your cocoon, my pretty butterfly."

"I'm not your pretty *anything* right now. Look at me!" she exclaimed, standing naked in the tub. Pointing at her shoulder she said, "Look! Big ugly purple and yellow shoulder and a yucky black swollen ankle."

"Yes, but butterflies are *supposed* to be colourful," he replied smiling.

"Oh Robbie, you're a hopeless romantic." Ignoring the proffered towel, she wrapped her wet arms around him instead. Human nature took over immediately. Any serious pretense at modesty had been dissolved the day before and Sam was every bit as curious about discovering him as he was about her. They made their way to the master bedroom, both working to get Rob free of his clothes. Then they settled onto the queen-sized bed together, Sam lying on her back in the middle of it, her legs spread slightly apart. Her red hair, still wet from the tub, lay in floppy curls on the dark blue duvet. Rob knelt beside her, his knees by her hips.

For a moment he did nothing — just looked — taking in the beauty of the woman lying there. No, she was not skinny. He'd been wrong to call her that. She was absolutely beautiful. Small round breasts, a gentle womanly flare to her hips, the most perfect thighs and her bright orange pubic hair which she'd trimmed to a small chevron, an alluring modification to an already erotic image.

Sam lay there looking up at her guy. Robbie's lean muscular body was poised for action, his erection a straight arrow eager to get started. His wide-eyed innocent gaze was turning her on more and more as the seconds ticked by. The anticipation was driving her insane. She was a woman of action, and action was what she wanted — right now.

"It's okay, Robbie," she prompted. "Go ahead. You can touch me … anywhere … everywhere. I'm not fragile, honest."

Eagerly encouraged by Samantha, his first sexual experience was even more exciting than he could ever have imagined. He began to tenderly explore all of her womanly places — those places he'd had access to the previous afternoon but did not, because such touching would have been a violation of a first aider's trust.

Now he thrilled as he leaned over her and eagerly began to kiss her, his lips, his tongue and his fingers moving down to begin a tentative exploration of her breasts and erect nipples.

"Not much there, I'm afraid," Sam confessed, a little shyly.

"They are just perfect Sam. Small breasts mean I can get even closer the lovely woman behind them."

His hands continued downward, gliding across her flat belly, and on down, caressing the smooth milky skin of her inner thighs. Finally, sitting back up to watch, he cautiously slid a couple of fingers inside her — into the place in a woman where no man can begin to imagine the feel of it until he has actually been there himself.

Sam shivered with the pleasure of his gentle touch — gentle, but almost electric. In return, she played with his rock hard erection while he explored and manipulated her. Tentative though he was, this man was bringing her closer to ecstasy than her previous boorish partners had ever done — and he hadn't even entered her yet. In her own excitement, she continued eagerly working his penis with her fingers.

"Sam, if you keep doing that, it's going to happen before it is supposed to!" he pleaded, not sure whether to let it happen anyhow, or try to hold back.

"Oh, Robbie, just let it flow," she said as she pushed him over on his back and rolled up on top of him. Straddling him and gliding her vulva along the length of his erection, she urged him on. "Then you'll last longer when you are inside me, and maybe we'll get to come together." And after the space between their abdomens became suddenly wet and slippery they both relaxed, savouring the moment. Any thoughts of embarrassment on Rob's part dissolved under an onslaught of passionate kisses from Sam and he quickly became hard again.

On top this time, he slowly entered her, pausing briefly to take in that exquisite velvety sensation for his very first time. It wasn't wild passionate sex they had — he being concerned about aggravating her injuries, and she, putting up with the discomfort of them. But for Rob's first time, wild passionate sex would have been overkill. It was still the greatest pleasure his mind and his body had ever experienced.

And Sam's fantasy of simultaneous orgasms came true. She and Rob arrived there at almost exactly the same instant. It was the most beautiful experience she had ever had too. She knew then that with her previous so-called lovers she'd just been 'laid' but with Rob, she had truly made love. Now she knew for sure that he was the man for her. She knew she had made the right choice.

"Sam sweetie, that was wonderful. No … that doesn't even begin to catch it … words just can't describe it," he said as they lay there in sweet exhaustion, their naked bodies still intertwined.

"Robbie, you've made me happier than I ever thought a guy could. I love you, Flyboy. And the terms, 'honey' and 'sweetie'," she held up a hand to cut off the hurried apology she could see coming.

"They *used* to kind of grate on me. But I seem to remember hearing them in the foggy hours of yesterday's hypothermic recovery. And because you used them in such a touching way, they have a special meaning for me now."

His reply was a happy smile and a prolonged kiss. They lay in each others' arms, Rob watching her as she dropped off to sleep.

As he lay there, the pleasures of his new experience were unwillingly interrupted by darker thoughts. Before he could sleep, he had to push the images of Morgan ravaging Sam's young look-alike from his mind. That horrible re-run was becoming a nightly occurrence for him. But exhaustion eventually overtook him and cuddled close to his sweetie, he too finally slept.

CHAPTER 50

Saturday, February 11 — Timmins

Gerald Morgan was only slightly disappointed to learn from the TV news that the pilot of the plane had survived. But what really shook him when he first saw it on TV was the woman's face. For an instant he could have sworn it was the girl he'd taken to the abandoned hunt camp years earlier in Petawawa, but of course he knew it wasn't. Just the same he was haunted by the fact that it had happened so long ago. He'd really enjoyed himself that day.

What he *couldn't* stand each time he watched the same news clip repeated, was the smug look on the hero game warden's face as the reporters hurled their stupid questions at the two of them. The guy was probably getting it off with the pilot chick.

But his eyes kept returning to the redhead. 'I'd love to meet you face to face, baby. What I'd do with you....' And that fresh fantasy aroused him once again. 'Yeah, someday we'll make that happen little girl.'

However, not allowing his erotic thoughts to completely distract him from his situation, he was fully aware that Eagle Feather had to disappear completely. Although the police hadn't mentioned the rescue and subsequent arrest of Cyril Smith, they had used the pilot's description of Morgan to doctor his twenty year old military photo to show the long black hair.

He'd already prepared for just such a contingency, so when he emerged from his Timmins rooming house that morning, Gerald Morgan looked like a different man. It was the only way he was going to be able to move freely about the city without attracting unwanted attention.

He'd shorn his hair down to a conservative businessman's cut and given it a dark-brown dye job with grey highlights at the temples. It was a more appropriate look for a man of his age than the long black style he'd used to establish his Eagle Feather persona.

He had done a good job of his makeover too. Not many folks can, while looking into a mirror, coordinate either scissors or electric shears well enough to create a hairstyle looking like anything other than a chop job. But a man of Morgan's talents, with so many followers — albeit of the law enforcement variety — needed to be able to slip past his fans unnoticed if he planned to stay in the profession for long.

He headed out the door, starting across town on a mission. He just needed that one last set of items to keep the law at bay for his final foray up the winter road. He needed to find the right set of licence plates for his truck.

The knee-jerk reaction of most criminals would be to ditch the truck and find another. But he knew that's just what the police would expect him to do. No, the same truck with a fresh identity was what he needed.

Only when everything was arranged to his full satisfaction would he make that one last trip to Onakawana. Then he would pick up his stash of furs there and head out to the west coast.

He could export the goods from British Columbia just as easily as from northern Ontario — in fact, probably with even greater ease. The remaining furs in his Sutton Lake drying shed would have to stay in hiding until he could fly back for them in the open water season.

In the meantime, he had a lot of ground to cover before he would find what he was looking for.

—

Monday, February 13 — Moosonee

Rob and Samantha had thoroughly enjoyed their first couple of days of cohabitation just relaxing.

She was walking without a noticeable limp when he drove her to the airport to catch the Monday morning commercial flight to Timmins. Her shoulder was pretty stiff yet and the ugly bruise suggested even worse but she knew it wouldn't be long before she would be back to normal.

Following her appointment with the critical incident counsellor and passing a brief flight medical, she was booked to finish up the moose survey flights out of Hearst District. Already looking forward to the next weekend, she was due to fly back home to Moosonee with a replacement Beaver on Friday.

Her Timmins flight was called and their parting embrace was one made by two people totally in love. Sam was about to head to the departure gate when Rob handed her a thin paperback book.

"Not a very romantic gift after our first weekend together, and it isn't even gift-wrapped. But if you have time to study it in the evenings this week, Bert de Groot said he'd let you challenge the test with the rest of his students next Saturday afternoon."

Sam looked at the book. It was the study manual for the Canadian Firearms Licence examination. It wouldn't qualify her for a hunting licence, but with the permit, she could legally carry a rifle with her in the aircraft. She could take the hunter safety course independently as the winter progressed.

"It's the perfect gift for the girl who has everything," she said, giving him a quick one-armed hug. "Only, I don't have anything to give you," she ribbed him.

"This weekend was everything I could ever have hoped for Sam. You don't need to give me anything. Just make sure you get back safely on Friday."

CHAPTER 51

Thursday, February 16 — Timmins

Gerald Morgan was pleased with himself. It had taken five days of systematic walking back and forth and up and down the length of every street in almost every Timmins neighbourhood before he found what he was looking for. Finally, there it was. Sitting buried under a winter's worth of snow was a light brown Chevy truck the same age as his and it still had licence plates. The fact that there were no motion detector yard lights on the houses on either side of the driveway would pay off too, when he made his move.

Two doors up the street, an elderly woman was sweeping a dusting of snow off her sidewalk. Morgan, now presenting a very respectable image, approached the woman and asked, "Excuse me, but does Harold Johnston still live in the blue house over here?"

"Oh, no, you must be mistaken, there's never been anyone by that name living there; not in the fifty years I've been here anyhow. No, Pierre and Yvette Boudreau live there. Just moved in but five years ago, or maybe it was six years. The time goes by so quickly now don't you find?

Pierre's the manager at the Royal Bank. Are you sure you have the right address?"

"Yes, it's 1812 Cedar Street, isn't it?"

"Cedar North?"

"North? Oh, I forgot about that. No, he's on Cedar South. Thank you very much. I'm so sorry to have bothered you dear." What a delightful lady. Now he had a name he could use along with the plates after he borrowed them from good old Pierre. But he'd only do that when the time was right

For the next few days, Morgan laid low in his boarding house room. He followed the news carefully in order to get a feel for his present state of 'wantedness.' And the very lack of news, indicated that he had pretty much faded from the public's immediate memory. Neither the local paper nor the northern Ontario CTV network had mentioned him for three days and he'd been replaced on the national news four days earlier by suggestions of administrative chaos in the American government leadership — something to do with fire and fury. He would soon be good to go.

—

Friday, February 17 — near Onakawana

Rob McNabb and James Bird had spent most of the week near Onakawana, both on and off the winter road. Like the police, the CO and his boss were hoping for a return of Morgan's Chevy pickup or a likely replacement. They worked three overtime night shifts watching the road, spelling off the police whose numbers were already stretched thin because of a search for a missing snowmobiler north of Moosonee.

When they weren't watching the road they were snowshoeing through the deep powder snow in the vicinity of the abandoned Cessna, trying to pick up Morgan's trail. But following the heavily snowed-in tracks left by the poacher was close to being an exercise in futility. As good as modern snowmobiles had become, their machines just couldn't cut it for trail breaking in the waist-deep snow, so they never left the garage. Instead, every metre of the way had to be gained by human leg power.

They had been able to pick up the poacher's trail in the bush just metres from the abandoned Cessna. But even where it was visible Morgan's path showed up only as a very slight trough in the otherwise uniform white surface. And every time they hit a clearing or a slight thinning of the forest cover, the trail was completely blown in. At that point they would have to split up. Each man would traverse a wide sweep on the opposite side of the assumed route in the hope that one of them would pick up the slightly indented trail in the next spruce stand. Then they could follow it once again. Sometimes that worked, but all too often it didn't.

"Oh Robbie, I've been spending way too much time pushing a desk. I'm just about licked," Bird complained on one of their numerous rest stops.

"You and me both, James," McNabb panted as he came up to meet him, "I'm using muscles I didn't know I had." He paused, leaning against a spruce tree while catching his breath and surveying the area around them. "I sure hope we find something in here soon."

It was 2:15 that afternoon when they finally came across a promising location. They'd actually been within a hundred metres of the spot on two separate passes earlier in the week.

In the midst of a particularly thick spruce stand they

found definite signs of recent human activity. Snowed in though it was, a small rectangle of trees was missing from the natural random pattern of the forest. James noticed it the instant he saw it.

As tired as he was, Rob stepped down off his snowshoes into the waist deep powder and started kicking around trying to find something under the snow.

"We've got recently cut stumps," he said, as he cleared the snow from the first couple he found. "What's this? Hmm, a stove and smoke pipes. They're almost new by the look of them." He stopped to rest and looked around the area as he did.

"Okay, so he camped here, and kept his furs either here or in the plane. Then Sam came along and after he...." The memory of what had happened that day sent shivers up McNabb's back. "Yeah … anyhow … so he knows the forest will be flooded with rescuers and he moves his treasure … half of it to Timmins, but where's the rest?"

".300 Winchester magnum," James interrupted, as he carefully pulled a spent shell casing from a tree branch it had been slipped over. "Why would he hang his empty brass here, not just leave it in the snow?"

"Don't snipers like to clean up after themselves, so they don't give away their hiding spots to the enemy? Maybe carrying it back here, from where he took the shot was just a reflex response to his military training. But then, why leave it stuck on a branch stub for an eagle-eyed Indian to find? That's just plain careless," McNabb speculated.

Bird smiled benevolently in response. Despite all the politically correct terms in use for indigenous people, many of the Cree still referred to themselves as Indians, at least some of the time. After all, they were still governed by the archaic Indian Act of Canada. And James wasn't above occasionally ribbing McNabb about his 'paleface' origins, so a bit of good natured payback from the young fellow was okay.

In fact, Bird saw it as further evidence that his southern Ontario rookie was beginning to feel at home in the north. The change in him had become obvious starting the day the bear runners' case had landed in his lap. The 'kid' had found his stride, and his boss was pleased.

After they bagged the spent cartridge for evidence, the search for the 'buried treasure' resumed and they didn't stop until they'd kicked through, and used their snowshoes to shovel aside every cubic metre of snow in that clearing. The poacher's remaining furs were not buried there. Nor were there any other evidentiary hints left on the forest floor.

A possible trail, leading to the south, showed promise — more so than any other portion of the faint trail they'd tracked to the abandoned campsite. This time it was very obvious as it wound through the thick spruce stand. But just as it had before, the poacher's route quickly disappeared as soon as the forest canopy thinned enough for the wind to pass through the trees.

The afternoon was getting on and both men were sweat-soaked from their exertions, so after saving the campsite location as a GPS waypoint, they headed back out to the Suburban, ready to call it a day. Following the stale trail would have to wait for a fresh start on another day.

CHAPTER 52

Moosonee

Sam arrived back in Moosonee after the office had closed, so she called Rob at home. He drove his own truck out to the airport to pick her up. During her first weekend with him, she had expressed a desire to apply a woman's touch to the main living areas of their house. McNabb assured her that he would make the place ready for her magic by Friday.

Her call for a ride came as he was organizing the closet in the back bedroom in preparation for setting up a computer room. Rob was one of a dwindling number of his generation who preferred a desktop PC over a laptop or tablet. With an interest in landscape photography and the acquisition of a large format colour printer, it made sense for him to keep his new hobby confined to one part of the house — one room where he could leave things in moderate disarray without upsetting Sam. They still had the third bedroom at the front of the house to use as a guest room.

"Come and see my new bird," she urged after they unlocked from a firm hug. Arm in arm, she led him around to the front of the airport terminal building.

The Turbo Beaver, parked across the apron from

where they stood was the most tired, beat-up looking aircraft that McNabb had ever seen in the government fleet. The dirty faded yellow paint was contrasted by two fuselage panels displaying lime green metal primer — temporary patches repairing of some recent body damage. Parts of the last registration letter on the underside of the wing had peeled, so that the M in C-FOEM could have been misread as a V.

"Did they pick that up for you at a thrift store?"

After Sam stopped laughing, she swatted him hard. "They said that's all they'll trust me with now." She went on to explain that it was a short-timer, due for a major overhaul very soon. "But hey, in the meantime, if I get a few scratches on it or make an occasional crash landing, no one will be any the wiser."

Her next plane would be ready for the float season — it wasn't getting a full refit, but it would look much smarter than this one.

"As for poor old OEY, after they fetch her out of the bush, the guys say she will live to fly again. But it will be one of those projects that only gets attention when they have some time to fill, so they said I might get to fly her again just before my retirement party. I'm thinking in thirty-five years, she'll probably be solar-powered for her first flight."

—

That night Rob made his deluxe lasagna — a recipe borrowed from his mom. The only thing Sam didn't like about it was the cleanup afterwards. It seemed to her that he'd used every pot, bowl and cooking utensil in the kitchen to prepare the heavenly creation. So she resolved to tackle that job later, after they sat together on the sofa to watch the evening news over an Irish coffee.

"Sam, I've signed out the 30-06 for you," Rob told her during a commercial break in the newscast.

"And I got instructions from the air service guys on how to mount a rifle case for an all-terrain vehicle in the back compartment of the Beaver. The ATV case saves them having to engineer some kind of permanent storage container. They weren't resistant to the idea seeing as how you are flying alone up here at times, and I think partly because of what happened last week too."

"Thanks Robbie. I just hope I pass the test tomorrow."

"You'll do just fine Sam." He planned to get out his own long-gun collection the next morning, to show her the various types of firearms she would be expected to know for exam purposes.

"I also found this in the spare bedroom when I was cleaning it out after work today," he said. He was holding up a 'like new', Kevlar body armour vest. It had been left by the previous officer when he'd retired and moved away. The man was one of the old guard who figured he'd only put on the vest if he got into a tense situation. Of course, that was about as practical as trying to fasten your seat belt just before you are in a car crash. Rob was from the new generation of officers; he wore his vest daily as a normal part of his uniform.

"Until Morgan is caught, I want you to keep this with you in the plane. And if there's anything going on that involves him and if it's happening *anywhere* near you, I want you to wear it. It won't stop rounds from his 300 magnum, but remember what Cyril Smith said about him having a .45 calibre pistol too."

"Robbie, don't be silly. I'm not going to wear that

thing. It was just a freak coincidence that our paths crossed last week. I'm never going to see him again."

"Sam, I keep telling myself that too, and I'm sure you're right. But we're convinced that he still has furs hidden up here somewhere. And unless he's caught first, he'll be back for them. Honest, sweetie, I wouldn't ask you to do this if I hadn't seen what they showed us in Petawawa that day.

"Evil doesn't have enough synonyms to describe what he...." Rob stopped short. He'd already said too much. The memory of what he'd seen that day was sickening. The things he saw Morgan do to that poor girl still made his blood boil. To think that a man could do those horrible things to any person let alone an innocent young girl was beyond comprehension. And now that vicious animal was lurking in his territory.

"What did you see down there Rob?" Sam muted the TV volume before turning to face him. "I know it's been haunting you, whatever it was." She could easily read his distress. She had sensed that something had been bothering him off and on, ever since the day he'd talked to her on the phone after returning from Petawawa. She was concerned about the effect it was having on him.

"You need to tell me, *please*. Whatever it is, it won't let you go until you do."

"I don't want to scare you any more than I already have Sam. I shouldn't have said anything." Now he felt really uncomfortable.

"If I know about it too, then we can face it together. You said you felt better when I was with you after your nightmare at Hawley Lake. You'll feel better if you share whatever it is that worries you now."

"That was different, Sam. That was just a bad dream, but this guy...." His mind was spinning, half-paralyzed by the thought of her hearing the story. At the same time, he knew deep inside that if he didn't tell her now, he would be putting up a barrier between them, and he simply refused to do that.

So reluctantly, the story came out — at least enough of it for her to understand his torment. First he told her of the video of Morgan shooting the poor animals in the sand pit, and she thought that was terrible.

"That was nothing Sam, compared to the short bit I saw of the second tape. I left before it finished. What I did see was the start of a video he'd recorded of his gruesome sexual torture of a teenage girl he'd kidnapped. And the major said that a couple of days later, the girl died.

"Sam, the worst part for me was that...." at this point, he really didn't want to finish. He was afraid that the rage he felt toward the murderer would show her a side of himself that she wouldn't like — a rage he could barely contain.

"Sam, the girl looked just like you. She could have been your twin." His hatred toward Morgan flared inside him as he kept transposing the girl's image onto Sam and Sam's image onto the poor tortured girl; and the memory of Sam being shot down by the man just fueled the fire more.

Sam wrapped her arms around him, crying for the torment he'd endured while trying to hide his knowledge from her. He returned the embrace, holding onto Sam while he tried to make the horrible images fade. And she was right. Once he'd told her the horror of the videos, he had nothing to hide from her any more. But it really bothered him that she had to hear about it at all. They cuddled on the couch awhile, and then went to bed early. Sam left the dishes until the morning.

And those images of what he had seen Morgan doing to that poor girl — they were burned in his memory forever and had a habit of flaring up at the least opportune times.

CHAPTER 53

Saturday, February 18

Four days earlier, Sam and Rob had each received a personal email from Archie Foulton and his wife Jeanie. It was an invitation to their annual 'Mid-winter Blues Cheer-up Night' on Saturday — today. All fourteen ministry staff and their spouses or partners were invited, and as usual, it was a potluck supper.

It was always well attended — the only excuse for absenteeism that Jeanie would tolerate was contagious illness or a death certificate. Even advanced pregnancies were not excused. The retired midwife always said that if anyone went into labour during the meal, she'd turn the banquet table into a delivery table and they'd party on.

For Rob and Sam it meant for a busy day. Right after breakfast, and before reviewing for her firearms licence test, Sam launched into washing up the pots and pans from last night's lasagna. She became alarmed when she saw Rob starting the spare ribs he was doing for the potluck. He was getting more pots out from under the oven.

"Aw jeez McNabb, I'm going to be doing dishes until I'm ninety if you keep this up. How many pots do you need for this creation?"

"I can do ribs in just two, sweetie. This pot now and the big lasagna pan later on." He carried on talking, oblivious to the look Sam was giving him. "As soon as I've got them simmering, I'll go and lay out my rifles and shotguns so I can give you a crash course on firearms handling."

"Why did I ever give you permission to call me sweetie?" she interrupted. "I thought it was to be used for intimate moments — not as a lash for the galley slave."

Rob looked up just as the wet dishcloth smacked him in the face. That set a playful tone for the rest of the day.

The one exception to that was during his firearms training session. Gun safety was a serious affair and Sam paid close attention all the way through. The guns were all unloaded of course but she still handled them with respect.

She really enjoyed learning from him and with her strong mechanical aptitude she had no difficulty mastering the technical details.

—

When they walked to the Foultons' place at 5:40 that afternoon, the redheaded pilot was still bubbling over her firearms test results. She'd aced the multiple choice written exam and surprised even de Groot by passing the practical gun handling portion without even a minor error.

Rob was carrying the rib pan, wrapped in a blanket to keep it warm, and Sam carried their bottle of rum and the Coke. The district manager's rules were simple. 'If you're drinking then you're walking.' Oh, and shop talk was not permitted at the party.

"I'm so proud of myself," she told McNabb as they walked. "Tonight I'm really going to party."

Not sure yet of the social protocol — it was his first

ministry party in Moosonee — he asked Sam if it was wise to party it up in the boss's own home.

"Aw c'mon Robbie, he's Scottish, and these little shindigs of theirs are the one time we are allowed to cut loose as a family." Sam had attended one of the Foulton events the first year she was on contract with the air service.

They were welcomed at the door by Jeanie Foulton. "Aye, it's the young laddie and his sweetheart," she called out as she led the couple down the basement stairs to where the other guests had gathered. Born in Montreal, she was no more Scottish than Williams or McNabb, but living with Archie for over forty years, she had adopted a significant accent of her own.

The dinner offerings were laid out on a trestle table on one side of the basement. Another longer table, spanning more than half the length of the big room, was laid with enough place settings for everyone. A beat-up wet bar under the stairwell appeared to be sagging from the load of BYOB liquor bottles on it. Dancing flames from a cheerful fire glowed through the glass front of the wood stove in the far corner.

Rob and Sam were a little embarrassed by all the attention lavished on them — McNabb's two successful rescue missions and Sam's survival after being shot down had destined them to be the celebrities of the night. Sam quickly mingled with the group and within minutes was already halfway through a beer someone had offered her.

Archie came over to Rob and offered him a Scotch. He was about to decline, the rum he'd brought with him being his drink of choice. But the DM insisted.

"Ach, laddie, it's you I have to thank for this nectar. I won it fair and square from your naive supervisor." He grinned, winking at James Bird who was sampling the appetisers just a few feet away.

Realizing that he might end up having to carry Sam home — now she was drinking something pink from a tall glass — McNabb decided to accept the scotch. Having never acquired a taste for highland whiskey, he knew that he'd be able to make one or two shots of the stuff last all evening. He didn't feel like drinking much tonight, anyhow.

He was just pleased to be among friends, and meeting some of their spouses for the first time. Marion gave him a hug as she introduced him to her husband, the loans officer at the bank. Others were introduced to him in turn, and then it was time to eat.

The dinner was great. All the contributing cooks were congratulated on their various specialties and the big centre table was being dismantled to make room on the 'dance floor' when the phone began to ring.

"Aye, just let it take a message love," Archie called to Jeanie as she was about to pick up the basement extension.

From where McNabb was standing, talking to James and Maggie, he could hear only snatches of the Foultons' cheery greeting. But the incoming response was spoken with the obvious intent of catching someone's attention.

"It's Sergeant Black calling. Sorry to interrupt the party, but I need to get in touch with CO McNabb, immediately. It's urgent!"

"Aye, we can't hide you from the law here laddie. Not when he's our next door neighbour. You'd best pick it up."

McNabb's first thought was that there was a family emergency back in Brampton, so it was with an ominous feeling of dread that he took the phone from Jeanie's hand.

"McNabb," he answered cautiously. Sam suddenly stopped in the midst of a conversation with Bert and his wife, and the room soon fell silent. All they heard, of course, was Rob's end of the conversation.

"Where did they see him? … Just the truck but not his face? … Where are they now? … Uh, yeah … I guess I can. Can you pick me up here? We'll still have to stop at my place for my vest and hardware … Okay, I'll see you out front in a couple. Bye."

"Sorry everybody. Duty calls."

James and Archie converged on him immediately and Rob could see an uncertain look come across Sam's face as she crossed the room to join them.

"The Smooth Rock Falls ghost car is tailing a light brown Chevy pickup headed north toward Otter Rapids. Until Moose detachment can get all hands on deck, Blackie wants me to start out with him to help set up his 'welcome wagon' as he called it, near Onakawana."

Sam knew that the brown Chevy meant Morgan. "I'll get my coat and catch a ride back to the house with you," she said.

"No Sam sweetie, why don't you stay here and party on?" he urged, giving her a reassuring hug. "You'd go nuts waiting for me alone at home while everyone else is here partying. They're the closest we've got to family up here." She stood there a moment, looking almost lost.

"Are you sure? I mean, you don't mind?" she asked. He nodded his confirmation, and then, just as quickly, the fun-loving party girl of minutes earlier, reappeared.

"Okay everybody. Let's party on," she said to the rest of the room. McNabb gave her another quick tight hug. "Love you," he whispered to her as he disengaged.

To James, who accompanied him upstairs, he quickly explained, "Last night I told her about the videos I saw in Petawawa. Last night it was the right thing to do. But right now, I really wish I hadn't. It's going to be too fresh in her mind."

"Don't worry Robbie. We'll watch her, and we'll see she gets home safely when things wind down here. Now, you stop worrying about her and remember your training. Talk with Blackie on the way there. Get to know him and I think you'll get a pretty quick grasp of what he expects of you.

"I worked with him down in Toronto once when the police helped us on a wildlife commercialization raid. I assure you, you can count on him having your back. But you need to have his too, okay? Now go; your ride's here."

McNabb stepped out the door into the bitter cold, still pulling on his parka. He could hear Trooper's 1970s hit, "We're Here for a Good Time, Not a Long Time" blaring in the basement. At first he smiled, and then on reflection, he hoped Sam wouldn't pick up on the significance of the second phrase in the title. He hoped too, that it wasn't a harbinger of what was to come.

CHAPTER 54

Moosonee to Onakawana

Climbing into the big Ford police truck, Rob shook hands with Sergeant Simon Black. Like the staff sergeant, Black was a tall man but he had more of McNabb's slender build. They'd met several times in the detachment but not yet had the opportunity of working together.

Blackie, as everyone called him, had been a Special Forces soldier before he switched to policing and then a SWAT team member in Toronto before he moved north in search of a slightly quieter lifestyle. He had a reputation for his cool-headed approach to high-risk enforcement encounters and had dealt successfully with many bad-assed criminals during his career. On the short ride to McNabb's house he told him he had some new high-tech gear he wanted to put into service that night.

"One question: have you been drinking?"

"Oh yeah, about a third of a sip of Archie's scotch." That drew a quick laugh from the sergeant.

"Oh. Is that the bottle you won him?"

"Sergeant, are there no secrets around here?"

"Good thing you left him some. He treasures that

stuff. And I need you dead sober tonight. We'll get your gear at your place and then we'll talk about this poacher of yours on the way out there."

McNabb was in and out of the house in less than two minutes. He hopped back into the police truck carrying both his service pistol in its shoulder holster and the .30-06 he'd signed out for Sam's plane. Racing through the house, he'd thrown his vest on over his head without bothering to do up the Velcro straps, and he was starting to make those adjustments as Blackie backed out of the driveway.

"Nice rifle," the sergeant commented. "What is it?" After McNabb told him, he continued, "Okay, behind you in the back seat is a laser sight that will snap on to the top of the scope. It's quick and easy to adjust, especially at night so we'll do that as soon as we choose a spot to set up.

"There's also an ultra-light headset and boom mike on the same frequency as this one," he said, tapping the unit already fitted to his head. "Get that on and adjusted for comfort as we go so it won't be a new distraction for you when things start happening out there.

"Now, fill me in on everything you know about our Mr. Morgan. I've already been briefed, but I like to hear everyone's impressions. You never know when someone hears or reads a different meaning into a perpetrator's background or his M.O."

McNabb was impressed by the man's efficiency. He had the hallmarks of a true leader and he knew that the sergeant was highly respected by all the constables he worked with. He gave Black a summary of everything he'd learned about Morgan so far. And after relating what he'd seen on the Petawawa videos, he went on to tell Black his concerns about having told Sam about the man just last night.

"Well, you were pretty much between a rock and a

hard place there, Rob. Police spouses can be tormented just as easily by being kept in the dark as they can if they have the whole story. And from what I know of Sam, she wouldn't put up with being kept in the dark. But it's a fine line you have to tread. And since she is, I gather, your first life-partner, there's going to be a steep learning curve ahead for both of you. If you want the relationship to last, just remember you have to keep the lines of communication open. Work on any perceived problems when they first develop. That's true in all relationships of course, but in couples where one is in law enforcement, the tipping point can be a lot more hair-triggered."

Blackie seemed to be an encyclopedia of information on law enforcement tactics, human psychology and just about any topic he touched on. But he was a good listener and didn't present as a know-it-all. He'd obviously gone through his career with his eyes wide open. This was the kind of guy McNabb could really enjoy working with — and the action hadn't even started yet.

It was almost 8:15 p.m. when they stopped to reconnoitre a suitable intercept location south of Onakawana.

It took only minutes for Rob to snap the laser site on his rifle and adjust it so the red dot it projected showed dead centre through his scope.

—

Moosonee

As the party at the Foultons' place ramped up, almost everyone was dancing. Sam knew just about everyone there from her days as a contract pilot and she circulated freely, dancing with most of the men.

She had stopped drinking after supper, her party mood somewhat dampened by Rob's sudden departure. She knew that his work could interfere with his leisure time. That was part of the life of a CO, but she just hadn't expected it to happen tonight — not so soon after they'd formed their new partnership. It left her with a strange feeling that she'd been through this before but she couldn't recall anything like it happening in her past.

Then she began thinking about the horrible man that McNabb was out to apprehend. And only then did it begin to dawn on her that this must have been what her mom had felt each time her dad stepped out the door to go on a night shift when Sam and her sister were small. Although it wasn't expressed openly to them, their mom's fear was easily picked up by two perceptive little girls. For Sam, now it was a frightening feeling.

The basement, with almost thirty active people circulating, was getting noticeably warmer. In an overpowering sensation, the hot, crowded room and the four stiff drinks she'd had earlier magnified her sudden concern for the safety of her man. She began to feel light-headed, but not wanting to make a scene she tried bravely to carry on as if nothing was wrong. She tried at least, until the room began to spin. She was dancing with Abe Koostachin, the wildlife biologist, when she began swaying unsteadily, the colour rapidly draining from her face.

"Robbie," she gasped as she lost all sense of balance and her knees began to buckle.

"Sam, what's wrong?" Abe asked. He caught her just as she sagged toward the floor. "*Need help here*!" Koostachin was quick to raise the alarm as he gently eased her down.

"Poor wee lass." Jeanie Foulton's midwifery kicked in

as if she'd been expecting a patient to walk through the door at that very instant. "Blanket here Archie! Let's lay her over there on the pullout, then. Everyone give her some breathing space. Poor thing's just fainted, that's all.

"Someone get me a cold wet cloth please. There are clean ones over by the laundry. I wonder what's brought this on?" she puzzled as she fussed about, tending to her patient.

"She's been through a couple of rough weeks, Jeanie." It was James Bird who spoke as he came over to offer help.

"Having her plane shot down was bad enough, but there was some personal turmoil she went through before that. And the poacher her man has gone after tonight, well he's a real piece of work."

"I'm guessing she's worried sick about Robbie right now," Maggie Bird contributed. "I went through that more times than enough when James was working in the field."

"Can one of you strong men please carry her up to the spare room?" Jeanie requested.

James had the limp pilot in his arms before anyone else could act. Moments later, Mrs. Foulton was sitting beside Sam in the cool quiet of their guest room, prepared to nurse 'the poor wee thing' back to health.

CHAPTER 55

Near Onakawana

It was 8:20 when Sergeant Black and Rob McNabb prepared to take down Morgan on his approach to Onakawana. They chose a spot where the winter road made a steep stream crossing. It was far enough south of the original site of the poacher's activities that they were confident the man would be driving right into their hands.

The massive F350 police truck was a crew cab; it could easily accommodate five fully uniformed officers. A custom built, low-contour camper unit was installed over the truck bed, its roof just inches higher than the truck cab.

Inside the camper was the core of the high-tech stuff. An ultra-quiet gasoline generator powered a bank of sixteen high-intensity floodlights that could rise from inside the unit to project a blinding field of light in any direction the operator chose. That was all operated by a wireless remote control.

That same control unit could also manoeuvre the truck while the operator took cover in the nearby terrain. Before giving McNabb a demonstration, the sergeant called the ghost car to determine its present location. The word was that the subject had just descended into another creek crossing ten kilometres south of their location.

"So, this is how it goes, Rob. You and I will stand at the edge of the treeline on opposite sides of the road. I'll take the side of the oncoming driver and you will provide backup and cover the passenger side. The guys didn't see any indication of passengers but you can never be too sure.

"Now here's where the quarter-million-dollar toy comes in." Blackie took control of the truck while standing there on the roadside, remotely driving the Ford down the road and over the lip of the stream bank. When it was about halfway down the sloping ramp, it stopped. Before the next step was initiated, they each donned a pair of sunshades, more like fashionable welding visors than standard sunglasses. McNabb could hear electric motors whirring, and seconds later, in addition to the truck's regular headlights, the sixteen floodlights rose up and turned the small valley into daytime. With the lights all slightly fanned outward from each other the whole place became a dazzling winter wonderland — even with the shades on. Blackie turned the floods off again almost immediately.

"I aimed it down the hill so Morgan won't think the sun is coming up as he works his way out of that valley south of us. And I only gave us a few seconds so our night vision will recover quickly. Leave the shades down for a couple of minutes and you'll re-adjust faster." The big pickup backed sedately to the top of the riverbank, and continued backing up the road for another fifty metres.

"What we will set up here, Rob, is a progressive barrier. Our truck will be completely in darkness until he first comes over the lip of the creek bed. It will be back there where I've stopped it, and we'll be hugging the treeline on either side." They strolled back up the road toward the pickup as the sergeant continued his briefing.

"When the subject vehicle crests the lip, I'll activate the headlights and the regular light bar. Over the loudhailer, I'll give him the order to stop. If he does, then the next step is a normal high-risk takedown. In that event, I'll order him to shut off the engine and put his hands on the wheel and then I'll approach. You hang back and cover me.

"Once I've established control in close, you move in, clearing the passenger side of his truck on your way. Your side arm will be best once you get near. I understand you were top qualifier, both day and night shoot on your last time through the mill."

"I wish people would stop bragging that around for me. Now I've got to hit whatever I draw on." McNabb's reply was made in all seriousness.

"Don't worry Rob. I've seen your training record ... can't keep any secrets around here. You'll do fine. Just follow my lead.

"Now, back to the takedown sequence. If he doesn't stop on command, I'll call 'blinder' and you'd better lower those shades fast, because right after that, I'll light up his life. If he still doesn't stop… and he'd be driving totally blind by then … I'll move the truck in on him. And with those steel bull-bars on the front of our beast, a normal pickup doesn't stand a chance. We'll jam him into a snowbank and take him down by whatever means necessary.

"And finally, just remember: while we know him to be a real badass son-of-a-bitch, he doesn't know squat about us. That gives us an edge over him."

—

Moosonee

McNabb arrived back at Foulton's place around 10:50. He'd called from the takedown scene to let everyone know that it was a false alarm. The truck had been a GMC pickup with a Chevy tailgate. It was an understandable mistake, because the tailing vehicle never got to see the GMC logo on the front of the truck. The First Nations elder they'd pulled over was a little shaken, but he'd stopped on the first command so he didn't get the blinding light treatment. When he was told who the police had been expecting, he said no apology was needed and he wished them good hunting.

Archie had told Rob on the phone what happened to Sam. That had shaken him pretty badly. He'd not been comfortable leaving her when he had. Now he was really kicking himself for telling her about Morgan's videos.

"Don't beat yourself up about it, Rob," Black told him. "What's done is done. We'll help you move forward from here." Just hearing that reassurance gave him the encouragement he needed.

Among his many other duties, Sgt. Black was the local detachment's critical incident team leader, and consistent with his other qualities, he had a reputation for successfully helping police members and their families through rough spots. He would take Williams and McNabb under his wing for the time being if he was needed.

When Rob arrived at their door, Jeanie Foulton assured him that Sam was okay and that she had given her a Gravol so she'd get some sleep. "Do you want to stay with her here for the night, perhaps?"

"Thanks Jeanie, but I'd really rather get her home tonight. Blackie suggested we get some undisturbed quiet time together."

Rob and the Foultons got Sam up and bundled into her parka. He thanked them again for taking care of her, and apologized for messing up the party by leaving when he did. Then he directed her, wobbling groggily, out to the police truck. She promptly fell asleep during the two-minute drive back to the house.

She remained asleep as he carried her inside and straight to the bedroom. They'd both slept naked together since she had moved in — all four nights. But the house was cool, down to its nighttime temperature and he wanted her to get a good sleep so he looked through her dresser drawers and found a nightshirt to put her in. After putting on his own pyjamas and turning out the lights, he climbed into bed and snuggled her close. But he couldn't sleep.

He lay there worried, hoping desperately she'd be okay in the morning — hoping she hadn't slipped over some irredeemable emotional edge. The Foultons had said she kept repeating 'Robbie' from time to time after she'd fainted. This wasn't the feisty Sam he knew. He was in uncharted territory now.

CHAPTER 56

Sunday, February 19

When Sam awoke it was still dark, but morning twilight was just beginning to chip away at the blackness. Robbie was snuggled close with an arm around her waist and she was surprised to find herself wearing a nightshirt. She had the unsettling feeling that he had had a bad night, but it took her a moment to remember why.

'Oh, shit. The party. Morgan. Robbie left and survived and I stayed and flamed out. As if he didn't have enough to worry about already.' As daylight slowly crept into the room, she lay there trying to make some sense of what had happened.

'So why, when Robbie makes me feel more secure than I've felt in years … maybe more than I've ever felt … why would I suddenly feel insecure last night?'

Gradually it came back to her. She realized that it was her mother's problem, not her own that had flared up. With relief beginning to settle over her mind, she realized that her bladder needed some relief now too.

Lowering the toilet seat, she smiled. 'That's my guy.' Sitting there, she began to realize that the house felt cold. It was just past eight o'clock and she hadn't heard the furnace running since waking almost an hour earlier. The thermostat in the hallway was programmed for 21°C, but the thermometer read only 11°.

She hurried down to the basement. After a quick discussion with the 'smart' oil furnace, Sam did a quick tour of the rest of the basement. There was a sturdy workbench, but no tools. "Shit!" She flew back up the basement stairs.

—

"McNabb! Don't you have any tools in this place?"

It was ten after eight. Rob woke with a start to find Sam standing by the bed. She was wearing his housecoat and a toque and mittens. And the house felt awfully cold.

"Sam, are you okay?" His first thoughts were not for the condition of the house — not after having lain awake most of the night, worrying about his loved one's mental state. And dressed as she was, he could be forgiven his initial impression that she was still off-balance.

"I'm just fine Flyboy, and I'd love to hop in there right now and shag you raw for getting me through the night, but I think my womanly parts have frozen shut! The furnace quit. Now, back to my original question: Do you have any tools?"

"Out in the truck," he said as he quickly rolled upright and struggled to pull his jeans on over his pyjama bottoms.

"Hurry, I'm *cold*!"

"Here, lie down on the warm spot I left." He swept her off her feet and dropped her on the bed. Following a kiss and a big hug to show he was glad she was back, he threw the covers over top of her and asked, "Who do I call to get a serviceman to come and fix this thing on a wintry Sunday morning?"

"We don't need a service*man* Robbie. What have you got for tools? Mine are still in my car in Timmins."

"Sorry sweetie … dumb male chauvinist question; and I grew up with natural gas heating so an oil furnace is a mystery to me. You can fix it? 'Nother dumb question I suppose," he said, checking his pockets for his truck keys.

"It's a really simple machine Robbie," she continued from under the duvet. "Just think of it as a gas turbine engine without the turbine. We've got spark and combustion air … there's just no oil getting through. It says so on the digital readout."

When he returned to the house, lugging his bitterly cold seventy-five-pound tool chest down the basement stairs, Sam was already there examining a high-pressure burner nozzle. It had been left sitting on top of the furnace by the last person to service it.

"Boy, that's really helpful Robbie. I'm going to get frostbite working with these tools. Maybe from now on you could leave them in the house, except when we're travelling. Even then, if we had a breakdown, a CAA membership would be more useful. You know there are almost zero parts you can 'fix' on your own at the side of the road on a modern pickup. Even one as old as yours!"

"Which side of the bed did you get out on this morning Sam?" he asked. In reply, she stuck out her tongue. He knew she was back in full stride.

"When they service these things they always leave the old nozzle on site as a backup," she said, turning her attention back to the sick furnace. "We just have to switch out the plugged one for this old one, and then call them on Monday morning. This happened a couple of times when I was staying in the staff house," she explained as she quickly disconnected the oil supply line and dismantled the furnace burner unit.

"If you watch carefully, I think even a city slicker game warden could learn to do this in a pinch," she grinned at him. She showed no residual signs of whatever had hit her last night.

After checking a Mason jar full of fuel oil she had Rob drain from the supply line, she declared it to be visually free of suspended 'crud,' as she called it. Reassembling the unit took only minutes, and when she turned on the furnace power supply, the burner fired up as it should.

"Now I reek of diesel fuel," she said, sniffing her hands with a wrinkled nose. "It's as bad as the jet fuel in the turbos. I'm going to stink like this all day."

"Good thing you have your handy-dandy city slicker Flyboy here then. After years of helping Dad in his shop, I've got the cure for that," he replied. He was relieved that he could provide some useful advice on at least one aspect of the job.

—

They went back to bed after Sam got cleaned up. And as the house began to warm, they tried to get even warmer with some passionate lovemaking. Only, Rob couldn't perform. A cloud was still hanging over them. He knew he had to broach the subject that had worried him all night.

"Sam, what happened last night? I was worried sick about you."

"I'm sorry Robbie. I didn't know what it was at first either, but then I realized it stemmed from when I was a little girl." And she told him about her mother's anguish every time her dad would work a night shift. "And last night, I thought about you and that horrible Morgan guy and I just collapsed, I guess."

"Okay, so this is an even harder question … and it has serious implications for our future together. Is this going to be a problem every time I head out the door to work? I mean, I couldn't live with it … with you breaking down every time I put on my uniform Sam. It would tear us apart, sweetie."

"No, I'm okay Robbie." Judging from catch in his voice and the rigid tension she felt running through him, she knew that he was nearly paralyzed by the idea that they might not last together.

"I'm stronger than my mom. She's always told me that. Last night was just a convergence of everything that's been going on over the last three weeks.

"Yes, I'll worry if I know you're headed out to nail that particular son-of-a-bitch. But he's a special case, isn't he? I mean, *everyone's* got knots in their guts over that guy, don't they? Don't *you*?"

"Yeah, when it comes to Morgan, it's okay if you worry. And yes, I worry too. I can't hide that from you." She snuggled closer as he spoke.

"You know Rob, on a day-to-day basis I head off on a flying job that puts me at greater risk than the average working person. I'd like to think that we're more or less equal in terms of the hazards that our jobs present. And I'd like to think that each of us is strong enough that neither one will resent the departure of the other when we head out that door each day."

He thought about it for a moment before replying. "Yeah, you're right. I never even thought about yours as being a dangerous job, at least not until you got shot down. And that was no doubt, a once in a lifetime event. Anyhow,

I'm just glad you're okay Sam. I love you more every day and I couldn't stand for something like that to come between us."

"Are *you* okay now Robbie?" she asked, reaching down to check. He responded immediately, and after what she called a 'nooner, only sooner,' they rolled out of bed to get their day started.

They had a late breakfast, dawdling over a third cup of coffee, and Sam asked Rob if he would like to go for a long walk with her.

"On the way back, I've got to stop at Archie and Jeanie's to apologize for last night — and to thank them for taking care of me. I feel so embarrassed about the whole thing Robbie. Archie must be wondering if I'm even fit to fly anymore."

"Maybe we should go there first, and then do our walk afterward. That way, seeing as how it's just after eleven now, we'll have an excuse to keep it to a brief visit, and get out of their hair before lunch time." That idea appealed to Sam, and it was almost 11:30 when they knocked on Foultons' front door.

—

"Ach, you dinna have to knock when you come here. We're all family," Archie greeted as he opened the door. "Jeanie, set out two more bowls my love, Rab and Samantha have just arrived," he called over his shoulder.

"Archie, no, we're only staying a minute. I just wanted to apologize to you and Jeanie for ruining your wonderful party last night," Sam started, but within seconds the young couple had been herded into the dining room where James and Maggie Bird were already seated in front of steaming bowls of homemade 'd'over' soup as Archie called it — a combination of leftovers from last night's dinner.

"I really feel awful about last night," Sam began, holding up a hand to stifle the protests she could see coming. "No, please let me explain before you think I've lost my marbles and I'm no longer fit to fly." Holding back another stream of objections she quickly told them the story of her mother's concern that gradually grew to abject terror every time her father left for a night shift.

"I never understood Mom's reaction until last night. I know she did her best to hide it, but I guess we still picked up on it. So when I added that sudden realization to the highs and lows of the last three weeks — missing my best friend's wedding, meeting a great new guy, being torn between two lovers, shot down by Morgan, rescued by my lover-to-be, acing my firearm's exam — and then on top of it all, drinking my normal *weekly* quota of booze in just over an hour, seeing the love of my life go out the door to face a very dangerous man and finally, dancing up a sweat in a hot room full of people ... well I guess I just threw a circuit breaker," she finished before taking a breath.

The four older adults all broke out laughing at Sam's analogy. Smiling, Rob quietly watched the proceedings from behind his bowl of soup. He was relieved that Sam had been able to lay it all out and did not avoid voicing any of the contributing factors. He was relieved too, that the senior generation obviously felt that the circuit was now safely restored.

The six of them sat around as they ate, talking about local events, world events, past history and future aspirations for some time. It was a long lunch in comfortable company and it was about three that afternoon before Sam and Rob set out on their abbreviated long walk. They were at peace with their world, and their supervisors were satisfied that the 'kids' would be just fine.

They wandered arm-in-arm around the town until after dark, then headed back home. For a change, Sam cooked a light supper — grilled cheese sandwiches and dill pickles.

CHAPTER 57

Tuesday, February 21 — Timmins

At 1:45 a.m. under the cover of darkness, Gerald Morgan walked up the driveway at 1812 Cedar Street North in Timmins and accepted the generous loan of licence plates from Pierre Boudreau's Chevy pickup.

Since it was snowing at the time, he took a moment to use Boudreau's snow shovel to pile a little of the fresh stuff on top of the snowbank, covering the truck's front bumper. Out of sight, out of mind, the bank manager wouldn't need to be worried about his misplaced plates for at least a few days. The man who had formerly called himself Eagle Feather did have an eye for detail.

An hour later the stolen plates were proudly displayed on the poacher's truck in the quiet privacy of his rented garage.

—

Rob McNabb and James Bird had flown to Timmins the afternoon before and checked in at the Bon Air Motel in the east end of the city. After breakfast they caught a cab to the regional office where the bi-monthly meeting of regional enforcement supervisors would take place.

McNabb was the only field CO there. He had been invited to present an update on the status of the Morgan case and James was not the sort of boss to take credit for the work of his officer.

Nervous when he first arrived, Rob learned that the supervisors were just a bunch of older COs, most of whom seemed to regret, at least in part, having left the field and joined the desk jockey club. And they put him at ease with some informal queries before the meeting started. No longer nervous, he walked to the head of the table.

"I'm one of the six people assigned to the joint task force set up between MNR and the police. Our mission is to track down and nail Gerald 'Eagle Feather' Morgan. Our group is made up of four police members plus James, and me, the rookie."

"Don't sell yourself short Robbie," James Bird interrupted and looked down the table at his fellow supervisors.

"This young officer has demonstrated amazing resourcefulness ever since things started to heat up on this case. For someone who came from the south with a completely different set of cultural values and outdoor experience, he has shown that he can plan and implement a major investigation and at the same time go head to head with Murphy's Law and come out on top. He ranks right up there with the best of us."

Everyone in the room had already heard of his Otter solo flight to save Clark, and the hypothermia incident with Sam Williams.

"In an era when the outfit seems to attract so much negative media attention, he has given us some much needed positive coverage. Sorry to interrupt Robbie, please continue."

"That's okay, thanks James. So the guy has vanished again, even though he drives, or did drive, a late 1990s Chevy pickup. If he still has it, it should be pretty hard to miss.

"Some folks think he'll have gotten rid of it by now, but I kind of like the theory that James and our local staff sergeant have. Morgan's expecting us to assume that the truck's gone, so he'll keep it and find new plates for it. The police are keeping an eye on missing and stolen plate reports, but nothing helpful has shown up yet."

While McNabb continued with his report, James handed out copies of the information package they'd put together.

"We still don't have an up-to-date picture of him. Boyd's pilot gave us a description, saying that his hair is shoulder length and black, but his military records indicate dirty blond. So it could be any length, any colour, or he could be shaved bald now for all we know. For what it's worth, I've included in your package, the twenty-year-old picture from his military days plus a duplicate, photo-shopped to resemble Smith's description of him.

"He's a crack shot with a rifle, and we've got a bunch of seized bear hides that can attest to his accuracy … only one bullet hole per hide. But the scariest part to me is that anyone who can lead a plane by the right amount to take out the engine while it manoeuvred a thousand feet up is either damned lucky, or he really knows what he's doing.

"And after seeing the video footage that the Military Police major showed us in Petawawa, it wouldn't surprise me at all if Morgan hit the plane in just one shot." McNabb briefly filled them in on the images he'd seen there, and his skin raised goosebumps at the memory of that horror.

"We believe he's still got at least eight more bear skins stashed somewhere near Onakawana. If he does, he'll have to go back there to get them. And we haven't released to the media that we have five more that we seized at Sutton Lake, so there's additional bait to lure him back north.

"In the meantime, you really need to impress on your COs that if they see a Chevy truck that looks like his, or any other vehicle that doesn't seem to belong in their area, call for police backup before attempting to make a stop and they are to treat all stops as high-risk situations.

"This guy really worries me. Spending that night with Sam in the downed Beaver, it sure creeped me out, knowing that he could be somewhere nearby. Until we are done with him, I don't think he'll be done with us.

"That's all of the information we have to share at this time. Thanks for inviting me here today."

During the lunch break, McNabb's cell phone rang. It was Sam.

"Hey Robbie, I'm going to be finished the Kirkland Lake moose survey by mid-afternoon and I'll be back in Timmins in time for supper."

"Hi Sam, glad you called. The meeting's going well and I should be out of here shortly. I'll head over to your apartment after I get some shopping done. I'm really looking forward to seeing you tonight."

"Don't expect to sleep in comfort, Flyboy. There's not much left in there. Almost everything I own is in Moose now. We'll be campers more than apartment dwellers tonight. It ain't the bridal suite in the Chelsea Hotel, but it'll have to do.

"Oh, and my car's at the garage, ready to be picked up when I get in. I'll catch a ride over there with someone at the hangar. All that's left in the apartment is just a couple of boxes I've got to load before you head out in the morning."

They had decided a week earlier that he was going to drive her Sunfire up to Moosonee. Then they would bring his quad-cab truck out to Timmins before the winter road closed. It would be more comfortable for long distance travel any time they came south on personal time.

"I'm booked for a check flight in the morning, Rob, so I can't fly out until after lunch. You'll probably get there first. Anyhow, my moose counters are back from lunch, so I've gotta fly."

"Okay Sam. Don't keep them waiting."

"Love ya Robbie McNabb."

"I love you too, sweetie. See you tonight."

Back in the supervisors' meeting, he spent another twenty minutes answering questions, then he left and the supervisors moved on to the next agenda item.

He caught a taxi out to the Timmins Square Shopping Centre to pick up some things they couldn't get in Moosonee, and then he set out for the half-hour walk to Sam's apartment.

CHAPTER 58

Timmins to Fraserdale

Gerald Morgan backed his Chevy truck out of the rented garage just as the Timmins afternoon rush hour was reaching its brief peak. By 5:00 p.m. he was headed up Highway 655.

Keeping to the pace set by the pack, he managed to pass unnoticed by the law almost to Fraserdale. There he was stopped by a lone police constable. The officer was filling a one-hour gap in the coverage that was supposed to be a two-unit, twenty-four-seven road check that had been set up for the sole purpose of watching for Gerald Morgan.

Constable Wilkins knew what kind of vehicle Morgan had been driving last but he was skeptical that a wanted criminal who had evaded capture for so many years, would keep the same truck after it was shown on the national news. What caught his attention about this particular truck though, was that the front plate had an expired validation sticker on it. So despite the fact he soon had to drain his bladder, he flagged the driver down. He'd done a lot of these stops over the years. It was a pretty routine event and he was nearing the end of a boring twelve-hour shift.

After running the licence plates through the system

and learning the truck wasn't reported stolen, Wilkins approached the driver. The guy behind the wheel was by all appearances a clean-cut man who was also very polite. He was disarming in fact. He was able to produce his ID, a driver's licence which the constable didn't realize belonged to one of the less fortunate souls from Morgan's boarding house — a man presently impounded in the district jail. Coincidentally, there was an amazing resemblance between the photo ID and Morgan's new look. It was close enough at least, for a cop who was in a hurry to take a leak.

"Is this your vehicle Mr. … Poisson?" He did a bit of a double take. 'Damn, the name doesn't match the vehicle registration.'

"No sir. Mine is in the shop with transmission troubles and my friend, Pierre Boudreau, kindly let me borrow his truck to go and visit my sister. She's teaching in Moosonee, you know."

'Okay, that explains why Poisson is driving Boudreau's truck, but there's still the expired plate … awe shit, a warning will get me to my piss break soonest.'

"Did you know that Mr. Boudreau hasn't renewed his vehicle registration yet for this year?"

"Oh, no!" Morgan exclaimed, feigning surprise. "You would think that the manager of a bank would stay up on things like that wouldn't you? And you know, I never even thought to ask him to leave me the ownership or insurance slips. He just left the keys in his mailbox and said she was good to go. I guess I'm in a lot of trouble then, eh? "

"Well, it's his problem more than yours sir," the constable said, hurrying to finish with the guy. He really had to drain his bladder, soon.

"But you should have made sure everything was in order before starting out today. How long are you staying in

Moosonee?"

"Just a couple of nights officer. I'll be going back home on Thursday."

"Okay, so I'm issuing you with a production order to give to the owner," he said, hitting the 'Print' command on his handheld printer. "It requires him to take the validated registration renewal and his proof of insurance to the Timmins detachment before the end of business on Friday. If he fails to do that, then for him there *will* be trouble. For you sir, it's just a warning today." Now the constable's mind was fully occupied by the need to pee.

"Well thank you officer. I sure do apologize for not even thinking of it. I was just so busy getting ready to go, it completely slipped my mind."

"Drive carefully now," Wilkins finished, quickly handing Morgan the notice before hurrying behind his cruiser to relieve himself.

Gerald Morgan breathed a sigh of relief. As cool as he was at sweet talking his way out of tight spots, it could have been a near thing. But he'd displayed all the right non-threatening body language and said all the correct, respectful things. And as so often happens, the constable missed some useful clues — the most obvious being that there was no overnight bag visible in the truck. That should have gotten the policeman's internal radar going, but Morgan appeared just too honest to be doing anything other than what he claimed to be doing and Constable Wilkins was too preoccupied.

With the excitement over, he left the big pistol hidden under his jacket on the seat beside him.

—

Timmins

Sam had been living in a basement apartment on the west side of the city. Using her spare key, McNabb let himself into the house, and went downstairs.

As she had warned him, the room was bare. Sam had donated her bed frame, box spring and mattress to Value Village at the end of her last stay in town. In its place was a pair of air mattresses the landlady had loaned her for the night.

He scavenged a straight backed chair from the laundry room and picked up a novel Sam had been reading. The striking cover just begged to be opened.

Rob was nicely into the third chapter of TOXIC WATERS when Sam arrived.

"Oh, I see you found something to read. Great story. Where are you now?" she asked, looking over his shoulder as she hugged him from behind. "Oh, I almost cried at the part where his wife died in...."

"*Sam!* Don't spoil it. This is turning out to be a good read, so let me find out when I get there." He dog-eared the page, closed the book and opened a beer she handed him.

After catching up on the highlights of each other's last two days, Sam drove them across town to Mike's Restaurant, next to the Bon Air. There, they lingered over a great Italian dinner.

With little to do in the nearly empty apartment, an early bedtime was the order of the evening. McNabb wanted to get an early start on the six-hour drive to Moosonee, and he had to drive Sam to the airport before leaving her without the car.

Near Onakawana

Morgan's final challenge in planning his return trip had been figuring out where to park his truck. It would be a dead giveaway to use the winter road works yard again, but a bit of online sleuthing had provided him with a solution.

The railroad, a provincially owned entity, was being forced into downsizing its overhead and had several unused sheds at the Onakawana siding going up for auction in April. Public viewing of the buildings was set for two days early in the spring but until then there was to be no public access to them. He had seen them on his previous visit to the site and knew from the online notice that one of them was easily large enough to accommodate his truck.

Fortunately, the access road into the railway property had been plowed following the big storm so Morgan was able to drive right up to the place when he arrived at 10:15 that night. A whiz at picking locks, he placed a crowbar through the shackle of the railroad company's padlock and twisted. The lock deformed until it fell apart, dropping into the snow below.

The windowless building was empty and he moved his truck inside right after unloading his Polaris. A 'new' railroad lock, one for which he had the only key, replaced the original, and all that remained was a quick dusting of fresh snow he sprinkled over the tire tracks leading into the shed.

He returned inside and locked himself in. Satisfied with his accomplishments for the day, he stretched out across the Chevy's front seat and dropped off to sleep.

CHAPTER 59

Wednesday, February 22 — Timmins

When Rob dropped Sam at the Timmins airport at 7:40 a.m., the temperature was hovering around -18°C and there wasn't a breath of wind. It was a perfect winter morning to his way of thinking. The back seat of her little blue car was full to the roof. The 'couple of boxes' she'd mentioned the previous afternoon had doubled the instant the landlady reminded her of the childhood treasures her mother had brought up during one visit. And then there were odds and ends of household supplies, a bag of summer clothes and her mountain bike. Rob removed the wheels to get it in the car while she packed.

Standing in front of the ministry hangar, they stole a few hugs and several passionate kisses before breaking off.

"Drive carefully Flyboy. Don't you dare put a scratch in my precious Sunfire." The little Pontiac was eight years old, and had seen better days.

"Fly safely Butterfly. Keep that thrift store Beaver out of the trees." She turned and stuck out her tongue at him. He watched her walk to the hangar entrance, then got back into the car and headed north.

—

Onakawana

It was 7:50 and a fine, clear winter morning up north too. Morgan started his Polaris and headed out to reclaim the remainder of his Onakawana treasure cache. Following the railroad access lane out to the winter road he turned south. He stayed on the main road for several kilometres until he came to where a diamond drill crew had pulled their equipment out of the bush a few weeks earlier. Their crude bulldozed bush trail was snowed in but it wasn't nearly the waist-deep snow that covered the rest of the landscape. This was the trail he had come out on when he finished relocating his fur hoard after shooting down the Turbo Beaver.

A kilometre after leaving the winter road, he came to a small blaze he'd cut into the bark of a spruce tree that night. This was his exit. He turned right, leaving the drill rig's trail behind. The sledding got tough, but because he'd already bulled a trail through there on his way out, there was a firm base and the snowmobile reluctantly snarled its way back through the deep snow. It would get easier with each pass he made. Without a sleigh it would take him three trips with fur bags piled high on the machine's carrier rack. It wasn't just the bears he had to bring out, but his arctic fox and wolf pelts this time as well.

After going another half-kilometre into the bush, Gerald Morgan arrived at his white tent. Though partially buried under snow it was as he had left it. His remaining booty was still intact. He'd certainly been granted a dose of good luck with the arrival of the big snowfall the night he left for Timmins. If not for the snow, there would have been no covering his tracks. He would have had to risk moving all of his stock to his shipping containers in one trip. And as it turned out, he would have lost everything to the law the following morning. He was still cursing the storage guy for his clandestine security cameras. His profits would fall way short of his original estimates.

Morgan's first run out to the railway shed went smoothly. The first three white commercial fur bags — each containing one bear hide — were now securely locked in the truck, which remained hidden in the locked shed.

On his second return to the Onakawana siding however, he had to stop short of his destination. A work train was parked with the locomotive idling right in front of the shed, and all work appeared to have ceased. Even though the garage door he had used was facing away from the train, it wouldn't do to just start carrying bags of fur into a building that still belonged to the railroad.

There was nothing for it but to head down a side trail he found. He stopped at a place where he could watch the railway siding and wait for the train to leave. That required a great deal of patience — railway maintenance trains always seem to operate on their own time.

—

The Moosonee winter road

School bus No. 73 was southbound on the winter road. Its driver, Jim Wylie was in a hurry. Departure from the Moosonee high school had been delayed by circumstances not of his making. He was carrying the twelve-member school basketball team and Mr. Dawson, its coach, plus two chaperone parents and another dozen students who had won the privilege of accompanying the team to the mid-winter tournament in Timmins. But because of their delayed departure, making it in time for their first game was going to be touch and go. Wylie was doing his best to make it happen.

Coach Dawson was a nervous passenger. Wylie hated transporting people like that. Half the time he was urging Wylie to hurry up and then moments later, he'd be slamming his foot down on an imaginary brake pedal on the floor in front of him — just inside the driver's peripheral vision. Fortunately, traffic on the winter road was rarely an issue, so he could make good time on the straight and level stretches and he did his best to ignore the coach's annoying habit. At 12:55 he blew by the Onakawana access road.

—

Onakawana

The work train eventually left the siding allowing Morgan to get going. After depositing his second load in the truck he headed back into the bush to retrieve his remaining furs. He briefly contemplated abandoning the Polaris at Onakawana, but caution overruled such a rash decision. One never knew when an alternate form of transport might be needed. Keeping his options open had always been a key to staying at least one move ahead of the law.

Despite the delays, he had his truck loaded and was ready to roll out of there by 1:10 that afternoon. Minutes later he was southbound on the winter road. With any decent luck he'd be down to Highway 11 in several hours, and from there, Vancouver bound. Out there, he had enough contacts in low places that he knew he'd easily be able to pull off what hadn't worked out in northern Ontario.

CHAPTER 60

The Moosonee winter road

For Rob McNabb, the drive north from Timmins to Otter Rapids went without incident. Traffic was light and maintenance contractors had the overnight snowfall cleared from the highways.

He made a stop to grab a takeout lunch at Smoothy's Restaurant in Smooth Rock Falls before heading north on 634. He stopped at the roadblock and chatted with the police for a few minutes before continuing north. The secondary highway was narrower than Highway 11 so he rolled along at eighty km/h or less.

Traffic on the winter road, when he got there, was very light other than some pickups, a few delivery trucks and farther north, one southbound school bus that seemed to be in a hurry. He was pleased that the road surface between the stream crossings was hard packed and smooth and kept wide by constant maintenance. As a result, Sam's little Sunfire rolled along those stretches easily at just under ninety km/h.

After rounding a curve not far south of the ONR's Onakawana siding, he headed down a creek bank ramp where he met an oncoming pickup. The driver of the truck was slowly easing the vehicle over some rolling moguls as it crept up the south slope of the bank.

McNabb was paying more attention to guiding the little Pontiac over the moguls than he was to the oncoming truck. But he suddenly realized that he was looking at a light brown Chevy from the late 1990s.

He didn't initially recognize the man behind the wheel, but it wasn't the old fellow they'd stopped a few nights earlier. The tops of several white commercial fur bags in the pickup's bed were flapping listlessly in the light breeze caused by the truck's slow progress up the bank. That got his internal radar going. And when the vehicle drew closer he was able to mentally transpose the face he saw, to the face in the twenty-year-old picture of Gerald Morgan.

"That's him!" He checked the impulse to immediately stop the car. Any sudden reaction might clue the man in to the fact he'd been discovered. McNabb continued to ease the car down the bank as the southbound truck rolled past and then disappeared from his rear-view mirror. Only when it was out of sight did he initiate a quick U-turn down on the ice of the frozen stream.

He fumbled awkwardly with his satellite phone while steering the Sunfire back up the bank he'd just descended. Getting the device turned on and dialling 911 while dodging the moguls required dexterity.

When he crested the stream bank, the brown pickup was already half a kilometre ahead of him and pulling away fast. To minimize the chance of getting into a wreck, he satisfied himself with cruising at less than eighty km/h while he tried to conduct an emergency call on the phone.

—

At the same moment that McNabb started Sam's car down the riverbank, Gerald Morgan was just heading up in four-wheel drive. He'd felt the suspension bottoming out against the frame when he hit one of the moguls a little too quickly coming down the other side. The big snowmobile was weighing down the rear suspension and he didn't want to wreck his ride — not out here in the middle of nowhere.

Caution would be the byword during all remaining stream crossings. The problem with that plan was that the warning signs at some locations were buried under the snow. Several unmarked crossings lay ahead of him.

As his truck began its climb, the blue car got closer. Just before they passed he saw a look of surprise on the driver's face. And at the same instant, he recognized the face — it was the local hero game warden whose smug mug had been on the TV news for almost a week.

"Aw shit, I've been made," he cursed, feeding a little more gas to the truck, willing it to get up to the level road just a little faster.

—

Connecting to the right police dispatch centre took time. After several precious minutes passed, McNabb was finally talking to the dispatcher for his area. And after providing his full identification he finally got down to the meat of his call.

"Yes, I'm positive that this is our wanted man … Yes, I'm following him right now, southbound on the winter road, just south of Onakawana … No, I'm not *chasing* him, but if I don't hang up and start following faster, he's going to be in Smooth Rock before I get to Otter Rapids!"

There were no police available on that part of the road, he was told. The nearest help was forty kilometres behind him. All the units south of him had been pulled from the road check in Fraserdale to rush to a domestic hostage taking standoff in Smooth Rock Falls. There were currently no other units available to set up a roadblock between Otter Rapids and Highway 11.

McNabb was at a loss for what to do other than try to catch up to the brown truck and somehow keep it in sight until the police organized a roadblock somewhere. He was fully uniformed and wearing his pistol, but stopping a big 4X4 from the platform of a subcompact car was just not on. And knowing who he was dealing with, he was definitely waiting for police backup before attempting to bring the man down.

But it was essential that Morgan be kept in view until he was nailed. The guy had a real knack for disappearing just when everyone thought he was in the bag. Out of desperation, McNabb hit the speed dial for Sam's sat-phone.

If she was already in the air she'd probably have it turned off. He didn't want her to get anywhere near the man. The bastard had already shot her down once, and he couldn't bear the thought of any harm coming to her again, but this might be their only chance to grab him. So he still needed her help.

The satellite system advised him that the number he was calling was not available at this time.

He hit the speed dial for the district office and was relieved to hear Marion pick up. After explaining the situation, he asked her to radio Sam by VHF and have her call him on his sat-phone. The receptionist, multi-tasking as usual, got the local police detachment up on another land line just as Sam was responding to the radio call. McNabb could hear all of that going on in the background before he ended the call. In less than a minute his sat-phone began to deedle.

"Hi Robbie, what's up?"

"Where are you now Sam?"

"Coming up on Otter Rapids in a few minutes, why?"

"Gerald Morgan just went by me less than ten minutes ago. I've turned around and I'm trying to follow, but he's going like a streak of lightening, southbound in the brown pickup we've been looking for. There's no police help anywhere ahead of us — they had to leave the roadblock for another emergency. So I need to keep an eye on him until they can get something set up south of here. I don't know the road well enough to keep up his pace without launching your car into the trees at one of these creek crossings. Do you think you could go high and tail him with the Turbo until we get some help?"

"I'm climbing now. I'll watch for him, and when I see the S.O.B. I'll stick to him like shit on a blanket. Where are you?"

"I was just at the first creek south of Onakawana when I turned around. If you see him, stay high and just watch him, *please!* I don't want you getting shot at again Sam. Call me back when you've found him. Love you."

They broke the connection and McNabb picked up his pace in the little car. A hundred and ten km/h on the level was all he felt confident doing. Even though Sam had winter tires on all four wheels, the car felt really twitchy on some of the undulations in the terrain. Several times it felt close to going airborne.

—

School bus No. 73 was making good time on a straight section of the winter road, ten kilometres north of Otter

Rapids. The basketball team was getting wound up, displaying a healthy dose of teenaged rambunctious spirit. The coach wasn't doing anything to settle them down — he needed them pumped for their first game — and Wylie, the driver, was able to ignore the commotion, having built up an immunity to noisy kids.

What did annoy him though was Coach Dawson continually slamming on his imaginary brake. Wylie had just finished casting an irritated glance at the coach and was looking forward once more when the road seemed to disappear from under the front of the bus. He was suddenly looking down at another of the river crossings — one of the steep ones. The warning sign was buried under the recently accumulated snowfall.

Wylie gasped.

"Oh fuck!" came from the coach.

The bus was momentarily airborne. When it came down, it slammed hard onto the frozen road surface, compressing the front suspension to the max. The front end of the bus dug into the sloped riverbank before the back end landed. Student and adult passengers were thrown forward, colliding with each other and with the solid fixtures in the bus.

Desperate to bring the vehicle under control, Wylie slammed on the brakes — there were rolling moguls right ahead. His action was ill-timed however, and the rear wheels, still not bearing weight, began to slide to the left. Suddenly the bus was sliding sideways down the hill.

The moguls halfway down the slope caused both back and front tires to dig in at once, flipping the big yellow beast on its side. The wild ride didn't end until the bus was almost down to the river ice.

After the briefest of hushed silences, screams broke

out amongst the panicked and injured passengers. Wylie was the only occupant with a seat belt. He was the first to react and his training kicked in. Some of the boys near the back had been cushioned, landing on the victims ahead of them and appeared to be suffering only minor injuries. He yelled out over the commotion, instructing them to get the emergency door open and start helping any mobile students out.

Fortunately, several grade twelve students and one of the chaperone parents had recently taken first aid training, and despite their own injuries, showed the presence of mind to take care of less fortunate passengers near them.

Meanwhile, Wylie began triaging victims at the front. The situation there was not good. Several students were in a really bad way. The coach, whose face was a bloody mess, actually rallied and proved helpful too. It wasn't long before the walking wounded were evacuated and the more serious injuries sorted and their treatment prioritized.

—

McNabb slowed the instant his sat-phone deedled again. A quickly stolen glance at the display showed Williams.

"Yeah Sam?"

"Rob, the police just radioed me and they advise that Mother Jones is north of Kapuskasing in the Twin Otter with a whole complement of eager uniforms. ETA in our area twenty minutes, give or take … Oh shit!"

"Oh shit what, Sam?"

"There's a school bus on its side down in the first river crossing north of Otter Rapids. Oh God, there are kids getting out of it and milling around. It looks like it's just happened. Rob, it looks really bad. I've got to radio for medical help. I'll call you right back."

Six minutes later he answered his phone again.

"Air ambulance is being dispatched from Timmins and land ambulances are starting out from Cochrane and Smooth Rock. I can't do anything else from up here, so I'll keep heading your way."

McNabb speeded back up to over a hundred km/h. Another ten minutes passed and there was still no sign of the pickup ahead of him. 'That guy must really be flying,' he thought, as he picked up Sam's next call.

"Rob, I've got him. He's about twenty kilometres north of the bus and he's motoring hard. That bus is in one of those river beds that you don't see until you are right on it. This could turn really ugly if the guy forgets the crossing is there and goes flying over the lip of the bank. He'll never get stopped in time! I've got to stop him."

"No Sam. You stay away from him. Can you see me behind him?"

"Uh … Yeah, you look to be about two klicks back. You'll never catch him Rob. I've got to do something."

"Hey Sam, don't do anything dangerous. Maybe land south of the rollover and taxi up to the lip of the river bank and get everyone out of there … shit, if … they can even be moved...." his voice, along with the validity of that idea, trailed off.

"Sam, can you fire flares in front of this guy, get his attention without getting too close? Or even just fire flares onto the roadway a kilometre out front of him."

"Let me work on it. Call you back." She broke the connection again. She needed to concentrate without distractions.

CHAPTER 61

Above, and on the winter road

Banking the Turbo Beaver in a tight turn high above the winter road, Sam lined up behind the speeding pickup. As she began a steep descent she opened her side window and steadied the flare gun, angling it down toward where she figured the road would be when she was in position. Diving on Morgan's truck, she was above the visual range of his rear-view mirrors. She had the shabby looking Beaver doing easily fifteen knots over its hundred and fifty-knot rated maximum cruising speed.

In metric speed, she tripled Morgan's hundred and fifteen km/h at the instant she fired her flare. It hit the road a hundred metres ahead of the truck. It had the desired effect of getting his attention.

—

"*Fuck*!" Morgan just about lost control of the pickup when he was startled by the sudden roar of the Turbo Beaver overtaking him just yards overhead. At the same instant, a dazzling red flare bounced along the roadway right in front of him. With the heavy snowmobile weighing down the back end, it took some careful steering corrections to bring the fishtailing 4x4 back into line. Though his pistol was sitting on the seat beside him, there was no way he would have had a chance to open fire on a plane moving away from him at that speed — not even if he'd been ready for it. And his rifle was on the back seat under bags of fur.

His carefully planned financial windfall was being threatened once again. These government people were really beginning to piss him off … s*everely*. And the game warden's car wasn't far behind. He'd caught glimpses of its headlights in the mirror several times just before he got buzzed.

His mind kicked into overdrive and he pushed the truck to go even faster. He began to work out a strategy for dealing with this new challenge. Obviously, in order to get these immediate threats off his back, there would have to be a showdown somewhere — really soon. But police involvement was sure to follow, so as well as eliminating the eyes that were on him now, an immediate change in vehicles was essential right after that. All he needed was a convenient location to make a stand. He thought he remembered just the place.

Yes that would work. He would stop and set up an ambush around the big bend in the road just before Otter Rapids. It was the perfect spot to take out the game warden and then knock down another bush plane when it came near to check on the warden. Then he'd make a dash to Otter Rapids and grab another pickup. He only had a few more kilometres to go.

—

'He's not going to stop,' Sam was convinced. There were not

enough flares in the whole provincial air service to persuade this guy to stop or even slow down. Her only remaining option was to land near the bus and try to help clear the scene before the inevitable crash happened.

When she was back over top of the pandemonium in the river valley, she realized that the winter road south of there was a twisty hilly stretch, with not even the shortest flat spot to land her plane. She hadn't really paid attention to it on her first pass; her main concern then had been the bus roll-over itself.

The only clear level stretch of road near the crossing was the three-kilometre straight stretch immediately north of it — between the bus and Morgan's speeding pickup. She would have to land there. She wished Rob was in the plane with her, but there wasn't enough time to go back and pick him up. Morgan would arrive at the crossing well before she could get back in place with her man aboard.

Sam was nearly in tears. Her first plane wreck, caused entirely by Morgan's hand, was largely forgiven by the air service. But now she was about to set up a million dollar roadblock at her own discretion. She could foresee a rapid end coming to her hard-earned career. But there was no way she was going to allow that murderous dirt-bag to plow into a busload of injured school kids. Not if she could help it.

With skis up, flaps down, propeller speed and power set for landing she swept down along the road, approaching from the north. Straining to pick out the nearside lip of the river bank she held the plane aloft until she was within the last three hundred metres of that spot.

Touching down on the hard packed winter road, she squeezed down on the brakes and applied maximum reverse thrust to the propeller. Snow flew up wildly in front of the plane until the braking action was no longer needed, and she came to a stop, just metres from the edge of the bank. Before the turbine had even finished spooling down, Samantha Williams leapt from the plane and ran hard the hundred metres downhill to the overturned bus. The coach told her that two students were still inside. One was unconscious, and both were in a bad way. The remainder were walking wounded, but some of those in pretty rough shape too.

As briefly as she could, Sam outlined the impending emergency and urged the man to shepherd all who could be moved, up the road to the south side of the creek. Leaving him to organize the exodus, she sprinted back to the plane.

CHAPTER 62

Opening the back door of the Beaver, Sam reached in for the rifle that Rob had secured in the rear storage compartment. Looking down the straight section of road to the north, she was relieved that the brown pickup hadn't yet come into view. She grabbed her sat-phone and called McNabb again.

"Rob, I've got most of the kids heading away from the bus, but they've got two in there that can't be moved. And Morgan really hit the gas when I laid the flare in his path, so unless he's taken to the bush, I'm going to have to stop him here. I love you."

"Sam...." her message sounded so final; he didn't know what to say next. 'Be careful' just didn't cut it. "Sam? You've done everything you can. Get out of there now. Please!"

"Are you anywhere near to catching up with him?"

"I've caught brief glimpses in the last couple of klicks, but nothing right now. The car starts dancing all over the road at anything approaching one-twenty."

Well, at least she knew that he'd be out of her effective range of fire when she opened up on Morgan. Another look behind her revealed the bulk of the kids moving farther away from the overturned bus although some screaming from inside the vehicle suggested that someone didn't want to leave a friend there to an uncertain fate.

A VHF call from Mother Jones gave an ETA of less than ten minutes. 'Not soon enough, Mom,' Sam said to herself as the distant glimmer of daytime running lights announced the approach of the brown pickup. It had just come around the last curve at the far end of the three-kilometre straight stretch. The swirl of snow stirred up behind it suggested tremendous speed.

With a pilot's memory geared to details and checklists and the new confidence that she'd gained after passing her firearms exam, she mentally went through the pre-firing steps for the .30-06. With the rifle loaded, cocked and the safety off, she looked through the scope, sighting on the approaching pickup.

Magnified three times, the image was still awfully tiny, so she adjusted the scope to its full nine power setting. The effect was somewhat disorienting until she steadied her aim by leaning on the Turbo Beaver's wing strut. Now she had a much more stable view.

Taking a couple of deep breaths, she waited. 'This can't be any more difficult than when I made my first night landing,' she told herself. She was scared and nervous then too.

Ready now, she tried to mentally calculate how near the truck needed to be when she fired. She wanted to immobilize its engine so that its momentum wouldn't carry it any nearer to the bus wreck than her present position. And knowing what she did about the dangerous man behind the wheel, she would prefer that it stopped at least a hundred metres up the road from her. At an approach speed of nearly one hundred and twenty km/h, it would entail some really long distance shooting. But she had read of hunters on the open prairies shooting big game at well over four hundred metres so she knew that the rifle was capable of such a shot.

She also knew that she had no time to make elevation adjustments to the rifle's scope, so as the charging vehicle kept closing the distance, she decided to simply aim above the intended target spot and see what happened. 'I'll fire one for effect,' she thought. It was an expression she'd heard used in war movies.

Sam Williams peeked up and over the scope to better judge the distance to the pickup. Even without the scope it seemed god-awful close now — it felt as if the thing was moving toward her at mach speed. Quickly back to the scope, she sighted halfway up the windshield in the middle of the truck. She was not planning to shoot the man — that was not in her DNA — she simply needed to disable his truck. Her first shot rang out.

—

"Fuck!" A big hazy star of shattered glass spread across the windshield just below the rear-view mirror. Morgan was sprayed by pellets of glass. Some cut his hands and face but missed his eyes and didn't incapacitate him.

But now his blood was up. He was furious. His first instinct on seeing the plane parked in the middle of the road was to stop and stage his shootout here and then steal the yellow bird. But having never flown a gas turbine engine, he knew he wouldn't even know how to start it.

However, the Beaver didn't occupy the full roadway, so he could easily pass on one side of it, under the wing. He would slow down at the last second and pump a few .45 calibre rounds into the engine compartment as he drove by. Then in less than ten minutes, he could be 'car shopping' in

Otter Rapids, and on his way to freedom. In the meantime, he kept his foot pressed to the floor.

—

Sam saw her shot was too high. And since the truck was now within her originally intended distance, she aimed straight for the weak point she'd chosen. As regular as a piano teacher's metronome she squeezed off the four remaining rounds in the magazine.

Steam immediately erupted from under the hood of the truck, and she heard the engine go silent. The timing chain case was destroyed and the chain itself broken as it snatched up chunks of the metal housing. However the pickup was still coasting ever closer to her, and not losing speed nearly as quickly as she had hoped. But suddenly, less than two hundred metres away the man behind the wheel disappeared behind the deployed airbag.

—

Inside the truck, the impacting rounds from the high-powered rifle made loud cracking noises as they hit the front of the engine block. Some hideous metallic screeching immediately followed, and then came the sound of silence as the engine abruptly quit.

A blade broke off the spinning radiator fan and slammed into the airbag sensor behind one of the headlights. The sensor, dulled by old age and corrosion, took a couple of milliseconds — precious lost time — to pass the message to the body module computer. But the airbag did deploy and the last thing Morgan saw before catching it with his face was a red-headed gunner standing braced against the

Beaver's wing strut.

Stomping hard on the brakes and cursing the red-headed bitch pilot, Morgan lost control of the truck. It swerved and bounced off the passenger side snowbank, then crossed the road and lodged firmly into the bank on the other side. It stopped no more than eighty metres from the government plane.

—

Sam waited. She was shaking like a leaf and relieved that she had succeeded. However, it was a short-lived intermission.

The man in the pickup flung open the driver's side door — now on the side of the truck farthest from Sam. Holding a bloody nose with one hand, he gripped a big ugly pistol with the other. Standing unsteadily by his truck, the man rested his gun hand on the pickup's hood and took aim at her.

She started to dash down the hill toward the protection of the school bus, but then realized that she would be bringing danger down to the immobilized victims inside. Worse, in leaving her place at the side of the aircraft, she had left the box of ammunition abandoned on one of the landing strut footrests. Exposed and vulnerable, she felt like a deer caught in the headlights of an oncoming car, not knowing which way to turn. So it was with great relief that she saw her little Sunfire racing the last kilometre toward the action.

Gerald Morgan, who had not taken a shot from his first position, had moved around the back of the truck and was walking in a shooting stance, down the middle of the road directly toward her. He was steady on his feet now and moving fast, and even at that distance, his bloodied face couldn't begin to hide his rage.

Sam ducked around the nose of the Beaver trying to put some cover between herself and the outlaw. He changed course and quickly had her in full view again. Ducking back to the first side of the plane, she grabbed the spare shells as she passed, but loading even just one round into the open breech of the rifle while on the run was impossible for the terrified pilot. She was shaking so badly that she fumbled the box and all the remaining shells fell to the ground scattering out of sight under the snow.

Now in a blind panic, all she could do was dive over the snowbank at the edge of the road and try to crawl away through the deep snow. With all other options exhausted, she knew that the deep powder wasn't going to give her any protection from the large calibre rounds in Morgan's pistol. Unless Robbie intervened soon, she knew her luck would run out.

CHAPTER 63

Rob McNabb came racing the last few hundred metres toward the poacher's truck just in time to see Sam dive off the road beside her plane. He too, was close to panic, seeing how near Morgan had gotten to her. And the poacher was obviously ready to shoot. If he drove her little car right up to the action, Rob knew he was going to be too late to intervene, and at the same time he'd have no real cover from which to shoot.

Slamming his foot down on the brake pedal, the antilock system brought the car to a stop within inches of the side of Morgan's pickup. McNabb jumped out without taking time to put the transmission in park; the Sunfire rolled ahead the last few inches, stopping when it nudged the truck's rear wheel.

McNabb was already leaning on the truck hood and braced to shoot. His disciplined training took hold and he yelled at the top of his lungs, "*Police – freeze*!"

—

At that same instant, Morgan approached the spot where he'd seen the woman go over the snowbank. Raising his pistol, he was about to pull the trigger when a shout came from back at his truck. A quick glance showed the hero game warden steadying his arms on the truck's hood and pointing a pistol in his direction.

—

Sam's heart leapt. Rob's shouted challenge meant he had arrived to deal with Morgan. She was safe now. Exhausted by her efforts, she stopped and turned to watch her pursuer's reaction.

—

Morgan doubted that anyone other than he himself could shoot a pistol accurately from eighty metres away and without pause he turned back to his immediate prey.

"If *I* can't have you, you pretty little bitch, then that cocksuckin' game warden ain't goin' to have you either!" he bellowed. He knew that his first round hit home the way the target pitched backward into the snow after his shot rang out.

—

Sam's elation over the arrival of her man evaporated as quickly as it had arisen. Morgan's final taunting words rang clear. But as terrified as she was about this being her last moment alive, her free-flowing tears were for Robbie. She knew how much he loved her and she knew he'd be totally crushed by her violent end. And that was her final thought as the first heavy bullet slammed into her chest. Her man's name was on her lips as she went down.

—

McNabb did not have to wait for more than a heartbeat after his shouted challenge to know that Morgan was now fixated on Samantha rather than defending himself. A man-to-man gunfight was what he had hoped to provoke to draw the evil bastard's attention away from Sam, but he instantly knew that wasn't going to happen. Without further warning, the CO fired his first shot at exactly the same time the poacher had fired his first round.

—

Just as Morgan began to spray the downed pilot with more lead, a series of impacts began hammering into his left side.

Weakened by the blows, his aim quickly wavered and he collapsed to the ground. He didn't get a chance to turn his gun on the fast-approaching game warden because his eight-round magazine was empty and he couldn't move his left arm to access his spare mag.

—

After emptying the fourteen rounds in his pistol at Morgan, McNabb went for the downed murderer on a dead run. He covered the eighty metres in Olympic time despite his encumbering winter clothes. In a blind rage he slapped a fresh magazine into his pistol butt as he ran.

With hate seared in his brain, he arrived to stand over the man, severely tempted to empty the second mag into Morgan at point-blank range. It took all of his training and self-control to refrain. Instead, he stomped hard on the empty pistol still clasped in Morgan's right hand. An enraged kick to the same hand sent the useless weapon bouncing a third of the way down the hill toward the overturned bus.

Just then, Detective Inspector Jones taxied her Twin Otter around Morgan's truck and brought it to a stop right behind the Turbo Beaver. A procession of uniforms rapidly emerged from every exit. It was a miracle that no one ran into either of its still spinning propellers.

About to kick Morgan in the head for good measure — that would have felt *really* good — McNabb regained enough control of his rage to settle for dropping hard with his knees on the poacher's injured side as he prepared to secure the man's wrists with handcuffs. The cuffs were standard procedure even with an apparently dead or badly injured perpetrator. History had shown that bad guys, presumed to be dead, sometimes came up shooting.

The first cuff went easily onto the injured poacher's left wrist, but as McNabb tried to secure his right, the big man struggled desperately, the fight not all out of him yet. He was still wrestling with Morgan when Ranjit Singh came to help. McNabb was too upset by what he'd seen happen to Sam to give him any more than a brief thank you. The instant the second cuff went on he turned around and jumped over the snowbank, plunging forward toward where she had gone down.

Grief-stricken, he stopped. Her motionless body was lying in the snow on the far side of the ditch. Blood was splattered across her chest and one thigh was oozing red into the snow around it. He'd been through this once before when he'd found her half frozen at the Beaver crash scene just ten days ago, but that time she had survived.

This time however, even from his shooting position back at the poacher's pickup he'd seen her body thrown backward as Morgan's bullets had slammed into her.

Uniforms had already gathered around her, but through his tears he couldn't focus on who they were. And when he heard them agreeing not to send her out in the air ambulance, he knew that was it. A broken man, his dreams were shattered — his future an empty black pit.

"Oh God, why did I ever involve her in this?" he sobbed as he dropped to his knees in the deep snow. He wasn't a religious man; the question was an indictment of his own actions, not an appeal to a higher being. He knew that he'd had no business risking her life in something that wasn't even her job. And he knew that while it was Morgan who had pulled the trigger again, he had only himself to blame. "How could I be so *stupid*?"

His grief was inconsolable, and he barely registered the gentle hands on his shoulders until a familiar voice finally got through to him. He looked up into the face of Inspector Jones.

"April, she saved the busload of kids from him, but I couldn't save *her*," he cried, burying his face in her parka. "I loved her so much, but I failed her. I got her killed."

"Robbie McNabb, you give up too easily," Jones began in a reassuring tone. "You did save her. You took him down quickly — we all saw it. Sam will be just fine once they get a couple of leaks plugged. She'll be okay, honest."

He pulled back and focussed more clearly on the inspector and then, confused, looked over to where two paramedics were working on Sam. "When did they get here?"

"We were doing a joint disaster training session in Hearst with a big group of paramedics. Five of them flew in with us yesterday morning. We were airborne and partway back home when the first call came in. And when Sam radioed about the bus rollover, I put the pedal to the metal.

These guys say she's just got a couple of flesh wounds. The blood spatter across her chest is from a nasty gouge on her upper arm. Makes it look worse than it really is. But we are all puzzled as to why she is wearing body armour."

"The vest? She put it on? She said it was a silly idea and she'd never wear it." Tucking it in beside the rifle had apparently paid off. His spirits began to soar once more.

"She would have died instantly from the round that hit her in the chest and the abdominal shot would have been just as deadly. But because of the vest, she's just badly winded. For the next while she *is* going to have some awful looking bruises and probably some cracked or broken ribs, but she'll be okay."

"Thanks for hurrying, April," he said. He looked away, embarrassed as he tried to wipe his eyes dry.

"Rob, you'd be one cold fish if an experience as traumatic as this hadn't brought you to tears. I was ready to cry myself when I saw her go down." She gave him an extended motherly hug and nodded toward Samantha.

"You both did a great job here under desperate circumstances. Now, you go and see to your woman. I've got to go and scrape some shit off the road." She struggled up over the snowbank to where Gerald 'Eagle Feather' Morgan lay moaning.

The poacher had also been wearing body armour, but twelve of McNabb's rounds had hit him. Four of those found a way through the narrow gap at the side of his Kevlar vest to incapacitate the man in permanently damaging places. He would spend the remainder of his life breathing with one lung and walking with a pronounced limp.

McNabb waded through the last few metres of snow toward Sam and he knelt by her head. Trying to stay out of the way of the paramedics, he looked down at her sweet face. It was partly obscured by an oxygen mask. Her eyes were screwed shut with the pain. He bent down and kissed her forehead. She opened her eyes.

"Robbie …" she was gasping heavily, still struggling to breathe but she pulled off the oxygen mask anyhow. "I hurt all over … but they said … I'll be okay. Thanks for … saving my life. You're my hero … again." She smiled briefly, then grimaced. "I'd have never … worn the vest … if you hadn't told me … about those videos."

"Sam, you're the hero today. You saved all those kids. I just wish I'd shot sooner."

"You went … with your training." The pain was getting worse and one of the paramedics was about to give her a jab of morphine. She waved him off, so she could finish. "Ya done good Flyboy … Thanks."

The needle went in, the mask went back on and Sam drifted into a welcome state of semi-consciousness.

Epilogue

Rob McNabb accompanied Sam Williams to the hospital in Timmins aboard the Twin Otter. Over the next forty-eight hours he never left her bedside for more than a couple of minutes at a time.

It took another four weeks at home before Sam recovered fully from her injuries. But with Rob overwhelming her with love and attention she was climbing the walls and just about ready to get back to work in three. Fortunately, her doctor sided with Rob and withheld her flight medical for the remaining week.

The least badly injured of the two students remaining in the bus was strapped to a backboard and flown out with them. The student in the worst condition was evacuated in the air ambulance. Six more injured students, along with the poacher, departed by land ambulance. All of the victims of the school bus wreck survived, though several would take months to recover.

—

Months later, Gerald Morgan was led limping into District

Court in Cochrane. Following a long and widely publicized trial he was found guilty on all counts of the many criminal charges laid against him. His conviction for the brutal rape, savage beating and eventual death of the young teenage girl in Petawawa, and the premeditated murder of Billy Joe Boyd earned him two consecutive life sentences. In the judge's summation, the two attempts to kill Samantha Williams were all that she required to upgrade the remorseless criminal's sentence from life imprisonment, to that of 'dangerous offender' status. There would be no chance of parole. He would never leave a Canadian prison — ever. At least, not until 'in death did he part.'

In a separate trial for his wildlife offences he was convicted on a series of counts of illegal hunting, trapping and selling of the various animals whose remains or even just a DNA sample, McNabb could tie to the man's ruthless wildlife crime spree. All assets and equipment seized from him during the investigation were forfeited to the crown and sold at auction. The proceeds were added to the seized cash and used to help finance a new polar bear population study to be conducted by the James Bay Cree in conjunction with MNR biologists.

—

Cyril Smith was returned to the United States where he was charged under the Lacey Act, a delightful piece of U.S. legislation which allows prosecution of its citizens involved in wildlife offences in other jurisdictions. Pleading guilty to his role in the illegal purchase, sale and export of polar bear parts out of Canada into the US, he was fined $90,000.

On the plus side of the ledger, he was finally vindicated in the airliner crash that had precipitated his slide over to the dark side. An identical aircraft, also nearly new, had an identical landing gear failure. The problem was finally determined to be an onboard computer error.

Smith was given a generous settlement to compensate for his wrongful dismissal. It paid off his fines and left him enough to help with his son's college tuition, but he was not rehired by the airline. A criminal record for smuggling did not fit the profile of a commercial airline pilot.

However, he did manage to land a job piloting the business jet owned by his favourite country singer.

Afterword

As I finished writing this story, the global market for luxury furs had sagged considerably from the highs of 2013 – 14. As a result, an inventory of lawfully harvested polar bear hides remains unsold at the fur auction houses, and bear prices have dropped from the record high sale prices set in 2013. There is still an occasional top grade bear bringing over $13,000 US at auction, but such returns are rare now.

Activity on the black market, however, may be an entirely different story. Each time governments place a prohibition on any product — think alcohol, ivory or 'recreational' drugs — underworld profiteers find creative ways to do a booming business.

The title and subtitle I quoted (on page xi) for the article written by Leslie Anthony in Canadian Geographic magazine sure grabbed my attention. Along with his convincing article, Anthony included the following sobering sidebar which I have reprinted with his permission:

PROCEEDS OF CRIME

The street value of an illegal live gyrfalcon? An estimated $360,000. The value of a kilo of heroin, the most expensive narcotic by weight? About $135,050. The following chart compares the prices (in Canadian dollars) of select illegal wildlife and drugs based on a recent report from the wildlife enforcement branch of Environment Canada – more proof that wildlife crime is big business.

SPECIES/DRUG	**EST. PRICE**
Gyrfalcon	$360,000 alive
Bear bile	$200,430 per kilo
Heroin, brown	$135,050 per kilo
Methamphetamine	$109,165 per kilo
Cocaine, salts	$79,805 per kilo
Wild ginseng	$46,110 per whole root
Opium	$30,695 per kilo
Polar bear pelt	$17,000
Hashish	$14,735 per kilo
Ecstasy	$8,045 per 1,000 tablets
Marijuana	$7,365 per kilo
Narwhal tusk	$3,935 per metre

Also by David G. Ferguson:

TOXIC WATERS

AVAILABLE ON AMAZON

Erin Franklin, an environmental crusader, goes up against Mid-Con, a waste management company that has been playing fast and loose with the law. Found hiding on Mid-Con's property, she doesn't know what she is getting herself into.

Judge Franklin has his own bone to pick with Mid-Con. They are up on new charges and back in his courtroom again.

Willard Reiger, owner of Mid-Con, built his company from nothing and is not about to let anyone take it away from him. He will do what it takes to keep it.

Conservation Officer Rick Webb still doesn't understand why Judge Franklin dismissed the case against Mid-Con. The evidence was ironclad; it was a slam-dunk, but something went wrong. Now Webb is looking forward to a vacation on his classic sailing yawl — his pride and joy. But his vacation is cut short when he is unwittingly drawn into a fight for his life. And when he realizes that the fates of two innocent people are at stake, he uses all his knowhow and his guts to set things right.

Non-stop action, tight pacing and believable characters make this an excellent read for anyone wanting to escape into a nautical adventure sprinkled with romance.

To sample the adventure, read on.... Sam and Robbie sure enjoyed it.

July 18, 0700

Erin Franklin breathed a sigh of relief as the forklift shut down and the yard crew finished securing the load in the back of the covered stake truck. She lay in a space between the eight remaining pallets of drums. When the crew moved to another part of the yard, she tried phoning for help, but Mid-Con had some sort of signal-blocking device running — Reiger found it a useful tool for stopping his employees wasting time texting and making personal phone calls. Her cell phone was useless here.

It looked as though she was just going to have to wait it out — lie there all day until darkness fell. Then she would steal away with the samples she had gathered and get the ball rolling with the ministry people.

Her attention was suddenly drawn to the two guard dogs, now fully awake after their tranquilized nap. The big dogs began to approach her position, but not maliciously. They were likely looking for more treats. They located her with no difficulty, and no amount of hushed 'shooing' would send them away. Eventually she was able to convince them to lie down. Perhaps the workers wouldn't notice.

"Between a rock and a hard place, eh?" A big voice, coming from behind her, startled Erin. Before she could even begin to react, she was grabbed by the ankles and roughly dragged over the gravel, out from her hiding place and into the open daylight. Looking up, she saw the largest giant of a man she had ever seen, staring down at her.

Forty-one-year-old John Gant was the chief of security for Mid-Con Waste Management. He was six feet seven inches tall and possessed a bodybuilder's physique. With his black hair cropped in a severe crew cut and his face wearing a permanent five o'clock shadow, Gant was not an attractive man.

Ever since childhood, his sheer size had predestined him for roles as an enforcer. He had protected the bullies in the schoolyard, played aggressive defensive positions in hockey and football, and worked as a bouncer in local bars even before he had reached legal drinking age. He was ideally suited to the role of encouraging people to toe his employer's line. While he could follow the boss's instructions to the letter, he did not possess the imaginative mind of a leader.

"Who are you and what are you doin' here?" he demanded, picking up Erin's backpack and rifling through its contents. He raised his eyebrows at the sight of the sample bottles, the barrel wrench and the protective gear in the bag. She was too shocked to reply, or even to move.

"I think it's time to go and see the boss," he said seriously as he reached down and grasped Erin's upper arm with a hand the size of a baseball glove. Without as much as a grunt, the big man 'helped' her to her feet. Wincing, she knew she'd have an ugly bruise on that arm later.

July 18, 0815

Willard Reiger was reviewing a waste oil disposal contract for a major U.S. trucking firm when he was interrupted by a commotion outside the warehouse door. He was about to shout through the closed door for some peace and quiet, when John Gant entered.

"Look what the dogs dragged in boss." Gant grinned as he directed Erin Franklin into the office and shoved her into a straight-backed chair in front of Reiger's desk. "She was snoopin' 'round the shipment for the barge," he added as he dumped her backpack casually on Reiger's desk. The glass sample bottles she'd filled so carefully, clinked loudly together. Fortunately none of them broke.

"What, your dogs lost their teeth?" Reiger asked. "I thought you got them because of the damage they could do to intruders. There isn't a scratch on this woman!"

"I don't understand that either. Seems they took a likin' to her …." Gant's voice trailed off sheepishly.

"Well, Christ!" said Reiger, turning to fix his gaze on Erin. "Miss Franklin here has caused me a lot of trouble in the past couple of years. And tomorrow the saga continues … in your father's court, where I have to defend myself against the frivolous charges they laid after the last time you broke in here. I should have you charged with trespass, and get a court order to keep you away from me."

"I had nothing to do with the last time you were caught," Erin stated bluntly. "The COs learned how to do it all by themselves once I pointed you out to them. And my father would have disqualified himself from hearing your case tomorrow if I'd been the one to turn you in. You should know that." Leaning forward over Reiger's desk, she went on the offensive. "All of that information will be in the brief the prosecutor disclosed to your lawyer. Can't he read?"

But Reiger hadn't known — he had just assumed she was the one, based on her performance the first time he'd been caught. She had been the original informant and he'd pointed that out to his lawyer.

He sat silent, perplexed, for several minutes; to Erin it felt like hours. Obviously the lawyer hadn't read the brief, Reiger thought, beginning to do a slow burn. This was bad news. They had been planning on claiming a conflict of interest — anticipating the likely prospect of Franklin being disqualified from presiding over the trial because of his relationship to the informant. That would have bought more time and given them a chance at being tried by a more lenient judge, and just about any other judge would be more lenient than James Franklin.

If Reiger was convicted again, he was certain that all of his licences would be revoked and he would be hit with some stiff fines. The CO's were tougher than the people at Environment had ever been. That would be the end of his company. They could even send him to jail. That's how strict things had become. Damn that stupid bastard lawyer, he thought, fuming. He's supposed to anticipate these problems. What am I paying him for anyway?

Now Reiger desperately needed a new plan. Staring right through Erin, he began to speak slowly, while allowing the seeds of an idea to germinate in his mind.

"I told you the last time we met, to stay off my property for good. But, maybe . . ." Reiger paused, his thoughts expanding quickly now on the concept of his new plan.

He turned to Gant. "Miss Franklin is going to be staying with us for a while. Make her comfortable in the basement storeroom, and for Christ sake, don't let her get away. And don't breathe a word to the women in the office." He didn't dare let them get even the slightest hint of this situation; they'd turn him in for sure.

Reiger turned dismissively back to the work on his desk signalling an end to the conversation. As soon as Erin had been led unceremoniously back out the warehouse door, he began to formulate a plan to use her as leverage in tomorrow's court battle.

About the Author

David Ferguson's career as a conservation officer (CO) in the Ontario Ministry of Natural Resources (MNR) spans almost thirty years and began in eastern Ontario as a deputy CO when he was a fish hatchery technician in 1970. He became a full-fledged CO in the MNR's former Moosonee District in 1975 where he enjoyed what he says were three of the greatest years of his career.

Outboard powered freighter canoes and runabouts were the mode of transportation used for local summertime travel, and several times he was required to navigate out of sight of land for hours at a time on James Bay — before the days of GPS.

Snowmobiles and aircraft were the only way to get around in the winter.

Ministry air travel was done in government and chartered bush planes and helicopters, as well as on regional airlines. In the 1970s, World War II vintage DC-3s were the aircraft most commonly used by the local carrier, Austin Airways.

During his time in Moosonee, Dave took part in wildlife management projects such as goose banding, managing waterfowl hunter check stations and as an observer on aerial polar bear surveys. His law enforcement role there, and in more southerly districts later on, required him to deal with resource users caught breaking the law — often in remote locations — often working on his own without any backup.

And like all conservation officers, he also investigated offences at 'crime scenes' where there were no obvious suspects to nab on the spot. These investigations required the evidence gathering skills of a CSI team and the analytical mind of a detective — all wrapped into one body.

During his career, he came into contact with thousands of people. By far, the greatest percentage, were law abiding folks. Of those he encountered breaking the law many would politely accept their fate, causing no problems for the officer. But there were also some of the kind of people you didn't turn your back on — men of the sort frequently known to the police.

In 1999 Dave retired with his mental warehouse full of memories that could be woven into the fabric of his stories. His believable characters are composites of the many people he has met over a lifetime. The places he has lived, worked and travelled provide the realistic settings for his fictional stories. This is his second such book.

Dave lives with his wife Pat in northern Ontario. When they are not on the road touring the continent, Dave can be found working in the yard or out on the lake in the summer, and shovelling snow or feeding the wood stove in the cooler seasons, all the while, conjuring up his next story.

62855006R00217

Made in the USA
Columbia, SC
05 July 2019